WILD CHILD

ALISHA NURSE

Sylvie Press

Also by Alisha Nurse

The Return of the Key

Living the best life with fibromyalgia

The Invisible F (blog)

Praise for The Return of the Key

"Filled with lush detail, inventive creatures, scenarios, and schemes. This book is great for young fantasy readers. Themes of identity, self-confidence, and loyalty will resonate with readers. A great fantasy adventure novel for teens grades five and up'

— Erin Cataldi, Blogger, Barbarianlibrarian

'...a thrilling plunge into a fantasy world filled with magic and adventure, yet it's uncannily real. An incredible voyage of an unassuming girl has the 'Alice at the other side of the mirror effect', in which the quirky and surreal realm is the reflection of the earthly trials and tribulations'

— Elena Krovvidi, Former Journalist, Russia Beyond The Headlines

'You will take a way a deeper understanding of the courage it takes for someone to rise above the prejudices of those around them to become whole, strong and awe-inspiring people!'

— J.P Wilder, Author

'An imaginative and engaging story of mystical places and heroic characters'

— Lynda Anning, Author, Dreams of Death

Developmental Editor: Jhaye-Q Baptiste | Editor: Samantha Gordon

Cover illustrated by Vicky Scott

Cover layout by Streetlight Graphics

ISBN 978-0-9931451-9-3

A catalogue record of this book is available on request from the British Library

For Dad

Note to the readers

This book contains themes around trauma, loss, violence, sexual violence, abuse and slavery.

Home

Like you, I am born into a world of falsities
And I must trudge through life with an anchor
        affixed to my feet
I must play the game where material rules, vanity
        favoured and prestige rewarded
When all I want is to go home

Take me home to the seas that beckon my soul
Lay me back and let the calm waters carry me away
My burdens be lifted as I float from the trappings of
        this life
If only I could go home

Home to a love like no other,
shared in exchanged glances of affection
Home to embraces that drown out my sorrows,
Home to warmth that fills us up, bringing laughter
        that rings into the night sky

At home you are safe from the lurking darkness

Worry not about the ubiquitous dangers of this
      world
At home nothing can harm you love
You are sheltered by my arms

The wind brings me the song of the sea
Tempting, torturing, taunting a broken soul
An empty soul that wants nothing more
Than to sail home into your arms

Prologue

My lips moved in a rhythm as I sang a mantra. I wasn't aware of which one I was mouthing. I couldn't hear myself. I couldn't hear *anything* around me for that matter.

The morning twilight had brought a stillness. I could feel it in the air, as a magical red glow spread across the skies. The sun seemed to not want to break the horizon.

From on my knees, I briefly contemplated my bow and arrows fallen in the dirt beside me. I had stored them for emergencies beneath one of my favourite sequoia trees in the woods. So much for that.

I was gaping into the barrel of a gun. I had never seen one so close. The soldier pointing it at me was shouting something. I could tell he was shouting from the way that vein in his neck bulged, while spit flew from his widening mouth.

I should pay attention … but my thoughts were scattered. Everything … so scattered.

I stabbed my sight towards where smoke billowed from some of the huts. Could I talk the shouting gunman down; ask him, "What is happening?" Did I really want to know? None of it might matter. In a few seconds I would probably be dead. Like my friend lying beside me. She had been breathing just a moment ago.

Maie was still gripping onto her pocket knife. A weapon? Hardly. She used it to peel mangoes at her father's fruit stall. On a different day I might have seen her gap-toothed smile once more, as I passed through the square. She might have traded me a mango if I'd come back with something she fancied.

But Maie was gone.

How could this happen?

Oh, Goddess!

The pain of heartbreak didn't get a chance to fully register. My thoughts were pulled to one of the enemy's jeeps jolting by loaded with women of my tribe.

At the very back, I spotted a face even more familiar to me than my own. My mother looked her usual cold, vacant self. I stared. Her dark skin always glowed like she had oiled it, and her bright almond eyes and crown of thick, jet black hair made you want to stare at her all day. She was beautiful. Even when she was being cold and vacant she was beautiful.

She saw me looking at her, but even then her expression didn't change to maybe say *goodbye*, or *I love you, I've always loved you*. Instead, she reached her bound hands into her bosom and pulled out a vial. I wanted to shake my head to tell her to stop, but I couldn't move. I could only look on as my mother flicked the stopper off the vial, and with an abrupt twist of the wrist flung its contents onto her tongue. Hardly any time passed. In all the surrounding commotion, no one noticed her head slump sideways; her eyes seeming to gape in my direction even in death.

It fully hit me then …

It's all over.

As if in agreement, my own poison-filled vial poked

under my bosom, digging into my ribs. It beckoned me to some unknown fate.

"We cannot know what will come," tremored Mother every morning, while imagining aloud what hostile possibilities might befall us — if this or that happened. "And you'll be glad to have a choice, then!"

I'd gotten so used to the routine of attaching these vials, like an extra braid or ribbon, on each dress I donned, I'd sometimes forget it was even there.

After those very short yet endless seconds watching my mother "have a choice," I remembered to look back in front of me. The gun was waiting.

ONE

War

Some time in the distant future, near the old Amazon rainforest

I am getting ahead of myself.

I ask, *How could this happen?* In truth, I know very well. Today's consequences are the offspring of yesterday's decisions and actions. Or inaction, I should say.

Sometimes our stories unravel to expose places we don't expect.

My name is Idzorah-Ulka. To my mind, I am just an ordinary girl: a child of the earth. I am named after some rare shooting star that apparently is very special, or so Papa used to tell me (repeatedly). Perhaps he had been trying to convince me of some higher purpose to my creation. This exercise was as ineffective as sowing pineapple seeds then expecting to harvest potatoes.

I am one in a fairly large tribe inhabiting the west of the Grand Baiuchi Forest, near what used to be known as the Amazon in the *Old World*.

The *Old World* is what our world used to be before everything turned to shit. Well, ash really.

We humans had caused the end of the world. Sure, the world was always ending, except it never quite did; though it was like living in a never-ending nightmare, scavenging for a mere existence. Humans had actually had time to turn things around, to make a change. But no one listened to those of us who cared for the Earth, or to the scientists or people fearful and protesting for the future. No one even listened to Mother Earth herself.

My people were lucky to have left when we did. After the *Old World* turned to chaos, nature answered back with magnificent earthquakes that turned everything topsy-turvy, creating new borders and redefining countries; more wars broke out; thunderstorms and floods drowned entire societies; droughts and scorching heat ignited and carried wildfires across leagues with a vengeance. Deaths followed deaths.

Still, humanity carried on in its old ways, forging a post-apocalyptic world built on greed and power. People were either filthy rich or dirt poor. Fun fact: In our history lessons we were taught that there used to be a term called "middle-class," to refer to people in-between, who had a decent-ish standard of living and weren't rich or poor. The *Old World* sounds inconceivable.

But what do I know? I was born right here in the Baiuchi Forest, thanks to my people moving here years and years ago to make a better future for us. Everything I know of the Old World is what Papa and our elders teach us, or what we read in books so old the pages feel like they might collapse like a butterfly's wings if not handled with care.

We are a simple and reclusive people, by choice. We were once part of a large movement concerned with peaceful, communal living centred on protecting and saving our Earth. But deep fissures developed among the ranks when confronted with some choices to be made around embracing or rejecting modernity.

Those who renounced "civilisation," opting instead to live in the wild, had felt that ultimately the price of progress would be the death of us. They (my Papa included) could see it: the great advancements in technology, though making things easier for our way of life, would come at a heavy heavy price. The cars, trucks and planes made it easier to transport people and things across vast distances; but we inhaled their fumes that slowly poisoned our air and killed us. We wasted our Earth's resources; when we weren't fighting over them. The wars … so many wars.

Entire species had been wiped out, never to return. We bulldozed trees, many magnificent trees, older than our great, great grandfathers. Trees that would have remained even after we became dust and returned to earth.

We saw advancements shred away our gratitude to Nature, and all it freely gifted to us. The more we gained, the more we wanted. So we took more and more … more trees, more plants, more animals, and never gave anything back. It was a world where people no longer valued life.

My people used to be teachers, explorers, adventurers, inventors, even. But the rate at which humanity was advancing meant that we looked less to our Goddess, our Earth and each other. Technology was the new god of the era. It birthed a kind of materialism and envy not seen before. The more we took, the more our humanity was whittled away. Somewhere along the line, Papa and other wise elders saw that we would cut away ourselves, too. So we moved from mainstream society and let modernity, for the most part, pass us by, looking to it only when necessary.

Our leaders felt it important to find balance by depending on ourselves and our world, in a mutual, respectful relationship. If the Earth was turned to ashes, then so would we be.

So when my forefathers broke from their original group for the sake of self-preservation, they retreated further into the belly of the Baiuchi Forest and never left.

We weren't the only ones who departed the *Old World*. Our tribesfolk have encountered other nomadic peoples traveling by.

We also know of civilisations and advanced peoples much greater distances away, too; where they depended heavily on electronic devices that allowed them to live in a digital world; where people interacted primarily through devices and not in person: trading their goods, learning their skills and even meeting their life partners in a fake world simulated after the real thing.

These people, Papa said, had turned the *Old World* into a concrete jungle, and did not stop until everything green had been paved. They claimed to have left the old life behind, but brought some of their viruses, including greed, into one of the last green sanctuaries on the planet.

These are the things my ancestors left behind, for a simpler way of life. This is why we mostly kept to ourselves, save for trading in the early days. We dwelled mostly alone in these wild parts for a century.

Then *They* came.

They came with their strange and powerful technology offering *more*. *They* came promising the truth, *salvation*, or whatever through their way of life. Digital technology that allowed them to be two places at once; weapons that gave people too much power over the will of others, and abilities that made them seem like gods. Like gods is what they sounded like to me, when Papa said they had the power to create diseases that could kill multitudes.

They came in friendship, keen to engage in discourse. They brought gifts: beautiful garments, jewellery, alcohol, medicines and many other things they perceived would win us over. Really, it was just to freely flaunt all their god had done for them and would do for us, if we but turned to their way of worship.

It was, tempting; particularly for younger ones like me born into our uncultivated way of life. The lure of an easier existence filled with luxuries and beautiful material things was powerful.

But Papa said I should not be tricked; that he had seen it all and knew the price we would pay. We would risk becoming like people in those long left behind societies who had lost touch with their humanity — living fake lives in a simulated world, fixated on material things and hollow aesthetics, destroying our earth more each day.

These outlanders doled out shiny possessions that, combined with their unusually attractive gestures and charming manner, succeeded in converting a small number of my people, who left in the visitors' vehicles for a new, easier life somewhere obviously far beyond our beloved forest.

But for those of us left at home, dialogue with our visitors became strained, as their real motives grew ever-increasingly more evident. They had not come here to offer us anything; especially not to enlighten and improve us with their peculiar faith. They had come to conquer. And when they grew in the realisation that we would not relent and turn from our deeply ingrained spiritual practices and beliefs, conflict grew as well.

Five years of tense anticipation declined into lazy disbelief that we were under any true threat of danger. What could those odd others do to us anyway? My people were strong, filled with faith, sure of ourselves.

War might have never come for me, to grab me up in its abominable clutches. I might have been somewhere far away from all of the mayhem that lunged at my tribe and

5

ravelled us up in foul-scented folds of death. *If only I had followed the path others had laid out for me ...*

But no. That little devil inside me always dared to defy commands that threatened to bring order to my existence. The people who appreciated ordered lives no doubt wondered what spurred me to appear to prefer seeing my mother's eyes bulge in embarrassment; to prefer the subsequent ten lashes in the village square with my own belt over, say, just taking her not always bad advice once in a while.

Everyone always said this lack of behaviour would land me in trouble. For some reason, I carried on with defiance, as if expecting some other, very different result from all the times before. Hopeful, maybe ... or just plain daft.

Even as a babe, my rebellious nature had been made manifest to all.

On the day of my naming ceremony, only ten days alive in the realm of mankind, as the village Oracle spoke on my future life, my little leg kicked the sacrificial cup from her hands in protest.

"A fair name; intended for a fair heart and destiny," the Oracle had been proclaiming. "But Idzorah-Ulka's defying nature will bring about her demise. She will be no more when she cradles a babe in her womb ..."

From Papa's account, there was a collective gasp, and people's eyes popped wider in shock. Before the Oracle could say anything more, my little leg knocked the cup from her hand, spilling the water, and causing a delay in my ceremony. My leg had committed an offence, to say the least.

That, and the stain of the prophecy, had followed me since. My family, too. And I got it. I mean, who would want to associate with the tribe rebel? Or let their children play with a girl who didn't follow the rules, and had some terrible looming downfall? I think people thought it would somehow rub off on them. Maybe they thought I would bring trouble home. Why tempt fate?

I understood, many of the older ones had witnessed the collapse of the Old World. There was an underlying fear at a blood level that no one spoke of. They had built this new world for us from nothing, and they treated it like a delicate thing whose immunity relied on order and rules, lest it be infected by the smallest misbehaviour.

I understood. I wasn't trying to be difficult. I was just being me. I understood, too, why it must have been hard for my mother who, from that earliest mishap, spoke little to me my whole life.

You see, my people revered the woman, and were led by matriarchs. We worshiped a female deity: The Mother who lives and breathes in the land and rivers and trees and skies. She gifts our women with many blessings, including wisdom, insight, and healthy bodies to bear more who might serve Her purpose. Priestesses, oracles, channellers, mothers ... this was our worth. This was our power.

My mother had never been allowed to expect goddess gifts to come in the form of grandchildren from me, given that I was destined to die before giving birth. Beyond that, in her eyes, I showed little inclination to offer anything else.

If only she could see me now in the throes of this losing battle, waiting for no man to protect me; fighting down to the last to protect our own, and about to die with a bullet through my skull. Then she would have known that even oracles could be wrong. I was worth more than someone else's words about me. I had worth as a human being. And I was about to die, fighting with all I had to the bitter end.

++
++

SLAPPP! A heavy hand brought me back to the present, leaving a hot stain of burning across my cheek. The same weighty hand tumbled me face-first to the roiled up dirt. The soldier with the gun was still at it, shouting something at me, spit hitting the musty air. My mouth was clogged with dust, but past my coughing I was still reciting unvoiced mantras. I was trying to focus, but my mind, mouth, and heart were disconnected from each other and the rest of me.

A heavy boot against my chest forced me onto my back. The soldier kneeled beside me and nudged my face roughly with the gun barrel, snarling now. Somehow his lowered voice was worse.

I could feel his other hand grasping at me under my skirt, pinching places no man had ever even gently touched. I slowly began trying to prop myself up, glaring deep into his green eyes: a beautiful shade of green, too pure to belong to such as him. He stopped growling as I inched closer, and his expression twisted deeper. His gun's barrel shifted off my cheek, paused coldly against my moving lips, lower … lower. He shoved it under my skirt, where his other hand was still groping. My body quaked, like a reed under a storm, like my soul was trying to dive out of my skin to escape to anywhere but here. *Somewhere safe,* my trembling limbs begged. But no escape. I was being invaded, on stage.

Other soldiers, comrades to the animal dragging hands over me, grinned this way from a jeep nearby. I still couldn't hear a thing, but their guns were lifted in the air, their faces leering masks of overdone anticipation. In the distance, from somewhere beyond the jeep, an individual soldier approached at a measured pace.

I struggled to keep bringing my legs back together as

he kept trying to force them apart. Frustrated, he tried to ram the gun inside me. I grimaced, but never took my eyes off his. My heart pounded heavily, threatening to beat out of my chest. The hairs on my arms stood, and it was like an out of body experience. Like my spirit went somewhere else to shield itself, while my body handled mortal affairs. *Please*, I silently howled in prayer. *Please*.

Miraculously, my right hand scraped across something on the trampled earth. A grounded piece of heaven the Mother had placed there just for me. I smiled at the soldier as invitingly as I could. He pulled the gun from beneath my skirt and smiled greedily at the expression I faked on my features. I moved my parted lips closer to his gaping mouth, as he climbed over me. He never saw the small boulder in my hand, until it was too late to stop it from furiously bashing into his skull. He fell sideways.

I paused and looked him over, my shaking hand still fused to the rock. I, too, felt stone cold and sharp. *What's happening to me*. Abruptly my thoughts were shattered like broken shards of clay. I let them be and obeyed the surging intensity that dashed through my body to fuel my righteous rage. I flung myself with all that power upon the man.

The soldier had stopped squirming and writhing in the dirt he'd made me taste. He lay unmoving, but I would not stop now! I lifted my hand high. I kept pounding the glorious gift-stone down, down, down; into his head until he was completely bludgeoned. I looked at him, lying splayed on the ground, his leaking life-juice turning the earth to a pretty shade of mud. I looked at my hands, covered in crimson as beautiful as the blood-topaz hummingbirds that would feed on our hibiscus plants each morning. Such a hue … so, so beautiful. But I had done a dirty thing. My own hands had done this thing.

A small part of me cried out to feel anything instead of the immense numbness now blanketing my ire. My body no longer felt like my own. I faced a stranger in myself. I looked to Maie, still lying beside me, motionless.

Today, so many of us had done dirty things.

‡‡
‡‡

I STOOD myself up straight as soldiers stalked toward me, guns aimed at my face, hungry to send me to meet their murdered comrade in death. But one hand went up, and all the guns went down.

In the created stillness, my hearing chose to return to me. The first thing I heard was a shadowy breath whispering, "Easy." The voice was that of the man who had raised his hand. The hand was lowered now, slowly reaching as he stooped to gently coax the blood-slicked boulder from my shaking slackening fist. He let it fall to the ground. This was the calmly walking soldier; his shirt collar and breast pockets adorned with insignia.

His face was pale beneath dark hair. Also dark, and stark against his skin, were thick bushy eyebrows that couldn't be forgotten. We both regarded the dropped makeshift implement of death. Then he looked into my eyes.

"You killed one of my men," he said coolly, but like we were friends. "They," he nodded at the pack of soldiers gathered near, "will want your head."

I stared at him intensely, before suddenly bursting into an uncontrolled guffaw. I'm not sure what it was that made me laugh. Maybe I was perplexed that they would kill me over a man they had done nothing to save. Maybe I secretly provoked them to come kill me. Just, I cackled so hard I couldn't stop for some time.

He let me laugh. It's like maybe he understood that a fair dose of insanity was descending upon me, in the aftermath of the various traumas I had endured in one horrific morning. The soldiers stared at me curiously; then at their superior, as if trying to discern how to react.

He was calm when he sighed heavily.

"Bring her to my vehicle," he said.

And so it was done.

TWO

Life's End

B y sunset, the line of enemy jeeps and trucks was riding out of my ruined village with my people in bonds. The ones that were left anyway. As I watched from the back of the jeep I crouched in, I considered how unusual the circumstances were. For all the wealth these outlanders had, they clearly weren't satisfied. What could we give them that they didn't already have? Only ourselves, apparently.

Those of my people who did not want to go resisted. "We will not go," many of us had said in previous, more peaceful dialogue with the outlanders. On this bitter day, some tried to flee, some were prodded by threats of hostility to go quietly, and some died when they objected via aggression.

Some, like my mother, gave up altogether. I think I understand why. Seeing your whole life unravelled before you, being wantonly pulled apart, thread by thread, is destabilising. Would it matter at all if you stayed or left? Either way, things would be lost, that you couldn't recover. And even if you could stitch back fragments of your life, nothing would ever be the same again. The pieces you're left with never quite fit in the same good way.

The faces at the back of the vehicles that passed me were a mix of emotions. Some vacant, some carried heavy anger, fear, panic. I saw tears. I saw torsos bent over double so wailing could spill freely from bellies. It's like I could see their songs of hopelessness float into the winds.

Near me, Maie's brother Dill (the one with a half-shaven eyebrow, who whistled sweet tunes in the early mornings with the wood thrushes and wrens, while setting up their fruit stall) was trembling in fury. Ma Moonie, the midwife, had furrowed brows and pursed lips, but stretched her bound yet reassuring hands to Dill's thigh.

I say my village was ruined; but really it looked empty. Save for a few signs of struggle in places — blood, strewn weapons, barrels or whole stalls overturned, smoke rising from a few huts — it looked empty.

Homes that were usually alive with children's laughter and play; men and women hustling about their productive days, had disappeared. The well where people chattered while drawing water; the stalls where handymen, hunters and fisherpeople plied their trade; the heartland of it, where people would sit in circles by evening fires, singing under the stars, sometimes praying to the Mother for rain, or sun ... all were empty. There was nothing. No one.

An ominous silence hung over the place like a gloomy cloud waiting to burst and pelt rain. My village was unrecognisable. War had made nothing of us.

As we rode through, slowly, bumping over detritus and uneven ground, I tried hard to collect my senses, to bring them into focus past the tide of confusion that kept scattering them to far, far corners of my mind.

The commanding soldier, seated at the front, seemed to have some kind of unfounded faith in me, because he had permitted my hands to be left unbound. He did not know me, this man. He did not know the tricks these hands had played, or the mind that enabled them. I was, however, guarded by two armed soldiers, one sitting opposite me, another beside me, in the back of the vehicle.

For the most part my people were passive and unlikely to attempt escape. They were my people, and I knew them well. Though I had never been like them. Ever. The prophetic stains on my life marked me like a vile odour, thus, while I had lived in the same community, it was on the periphery, watching everyone else live out their days together.

I hadn't seen my father or my twin sisters since the raid began. I thought of the path my mother had chosen, and wondered if they might have done the same. So when we neared my family hut, I furtively made my eyes watch long and hard, hope and unease in every sinew. My body made an anxious twitch when I saw a shadow duck past one window. It was fleeting — vanished no sooner than it appeared. My thoughts leaped.

I had been lost in the moment, and was dismayed to focus and find the two soldiers peering at me. Their cold stares turned from my alarmed eyes to my family hut. My heart flipped. My mouth tried to murmur "No," but my tongue had gone as heavy as the stone with which I'd earlier killed a man.

One of the soldiers said something in their mother tongue to the commander. There came a barked command that knifed at my heart. *No, no, no!* But nothing left my lips as the jeep broke the line of vehicles, made an abrupt turn and halted. One of the soldiers guarding me, and another at the front, jumped out of the jeep and ran toward my family's hut.

Rage, anxiety, dread drenched my heart and coursed into my bloodstream. Rational thought deserted me. I sprang from the jeep. I was running! My heels were on fire.

There was a chance the commander or his soldier would shoot me in the back. Let them try! I was fast. Faster. A sharp heat stung my face as blood rushed to it. My long, plaits dragged behind me, pulled by the wind as I sped forward. My forest-strengthened limbs pumped, pushing me unerringly forward. I sucked breath in to fuel me. *I'm coming!*

The soldiers were intent on shouting at the front door, feet planted, guns trained on it. I soundlessly raced near. *Don't let them turn! Must get to the shadow before the soldiers. Close enough.* Now! I propelled my body upwards and flung myself through an open window. I hit the ground lithely and rolled. I popped up to find a gun pointing at me. Powerful emotions roiled to sudden life in me, and I cried out.

"Papa!"

"Idzorah-Ulka!" He had already lowered the gun, "You never —"

"Run!" I screamed.

The door splintered inward. Soldiers charged in. Papa and I turned as one to face them. We both roared: his sounding like a challenge; mine, the word I'd uttered already, "Run!"

I blinked. My world changed again.

Loud drumming battered my hearing a split second after my father shoved me. I landed heavily, and hit my head. All was silence here. It took a few disoriented seconds to shake the ringing out of my ears and the blurriness out my eyes. I raised myself up. I saw. Oh … please, no. Papa was lying on his back, life oozing profusely from his chest. That crimson flow was the only thing moving on him.

I crawled to my dear Papa. I trembled head to foot, but I crawled to him. My hand reached delicately out to hover over the wet spot. Blessedly, his eyes were open. He was alive. Alive? Papa was staring at the thatched roof, an unusual, soft expression on his face. I followed his gaze. There was nothing there.

"Papa," the word came out softer than intended … a whisper that almost wasn't spoken. I paused, searching for more words, but could not find any for what I was feeling.

He had heard me. His eyes fell to look into mine. My father's fine eye-corner wrinkles deepened as he smiled for me.

"Papa! Don't leave me. Please. It's nothing … I'll get the — the herbs. I'll help …"

Even in such a moment, urgency taut on my every trailing word, my Papa was smiling at me. "I will never leave you, my baby."

"Papa …"

"Shhh"

"Papa, if you leave —"

"Nothing can separate you from my love, my beautiful girl. Nothing …" he whispered, choking over words he wished to speak.

"Nothing in this life or the next," I finished it for him. Our words. Our words often shared. Our words shared one last time.

Then it was as if the words got caught somewhere in my chest, too, and Papa and I each drew a shuddering breath that sounded exactly the same.

"Fight, Idzorah-Ulka," his speech slurred. "Live."

I watched on in horror as Papa exhaled his last breath. I waited to see if he would blink, move his lips, or perhaps his chest might rise and fall again. I waited for a sign but none came. When I realised, I sucked a short breath of air in and held it. My soul was being sucked into a vacuum.

There was a pain under both my arms as I was lifted away from him, bawling every emotion and feeling I could not name; furiously kicking and throwing every possible part of my body violently about.

Then all the lights went out …

‡‡
‡‡

PAPA HAD GIVEN his life for mine. He was one of only a few people I knew who had believed my life was worth something: worth defending, worth loving … worth saving. Even in his last moments he had been giving me orders that demonstrated this. *"Fight." "Live."*

Live? How could I live when I'd just lost everything I loved. Papa was gone. Home was gone. My papa was home.

The subconscious is a funny thing. I didn't know where I was. I couldn't remember what had happened to put me wherever I was. But in the enveloping darkness my senses swam through I was aware that all wasn't well. Dominant was the sensation of being stuck in a life-like dream, while dogged by a niggling feeling that something was awry.

I don't know how much time passed by. My mind wandered far away.

‡‡
‡‡

THE PROPHECY that stained my life meant my mother would never have had a chance to be the envy of other mothers, adoring the beautiful bride I might have made. However superficial that may seem, you have to understand that sustaining and carrying on our way of life was important. So our people had attached value on the ability to bear children who would become part of our fold.

My beauty was to be discounted. My illustrious dark tresses, that I sometimes glimpsed girls in the village secretly admiring, was never publicly pointed out (like my mother's). When elders openly commented on the good-looking children among us, pinching cheeks and cupping faces in hands, I rarely was on the receiving end. But Papa always complimented the rich earthy tone of my skin, my muscular physique and my animated eyebrows which looked down over a playful smile.

"The rarest beauty of them all," Papa would say, winking at me, whenever he noticed my sulk.

To some of the elders, I was only trouble, bad luck. I felt like no one really wanted me to be there, actively involved in anything. Hunting, fishing trips, excursions, birthing ceremonies, marriage ceremonies, you name it, I remained uninvited.

Once, little freckle-faced Gaia got afflicted with swollen cheek glands. They said it was because I drank from her water pouch. Never mind that we'd both been dabbing the milky secretions from a mildly toxic plant's leaves all over each other in play; or that I had swollen glands, too. *She brings bad fortune*, they buzzed.

Some folk insisted my parents would be lucky if they managed to secure me a good husband at all. Mother turned her focus to the two girls she bore after me. And I revelled in my freedom.

While girls my age celebrated their femininity, adorning each other's bodies with ink during temple exercises, I snuck away into the thick bushes to go hunting with Papa and the wolves in the dark of the night.

We did not own the wolves. We were not bonded to them. But they allowed us to share their hunts and embraced us as wild things for the duration. Well — at least in Papa's case it was for the hunting time. I was a wild child through and through. What the wolves accepted in me was the very same thing that made my village spurn me.

Bless him, my papa. He, at least, tried his best and always stood by me.

On the last of our secret hunting trips, I realised my life would never be the same. It was not anything he said. It was more all Papa did not choose to say.

The night had still been young when I'd heard Papa's light whistle outside my window. My heart skipped with gladness that manifested into a grin. I rushed to scramble through the window and drop onto the still sun-warmed earth below.

"Where the wolves, Papa?" I asked, looking around for our regular hunting companions. That's when the suspicion struck me that all was not right.

Papa looked away. I followed his gaze, and noticed the wagon in the distance, bearing a familiar but not regularly used container in the back. I gulped.

"For dinner later today," Papa said, as if reading my thoughts. "Your mother wishes something special. We hunt with the black toad."

Something was amiss. Dining on meat from the waters tended to be synonymous with special occasions.

Papa, had walked to the wagon and lifted the front bars to pull it forward and open. The mud-coloured amphibious creature inside the container flexed its six legs uneasily.

I shuddered visibly. Papa saw, I knew, but did not react.

"Let us hurry. It will be over quickly."

Papa tried to quell my disquiet, but no reassurances had ever been able to allay my uneasiness about this strange creature. You'd think it was so called because it was as black as the night. But that part of its name came from the creature's association with death. The black toad was useful, yes. Its poison, though, was lethal — far more potent than a pit viper's, and one single gram of the black toad's venom could kill about a hundred people.

Apparently in times past, these creatures used to be a lot more wild. But evolution worked in our favour. Now those of us who knew how to handle them could work with these ugly-looking things.

Ok, maybe I was a tad unkind in my assessment. But picture big rounded black eyes on a 13-inch, 10 pound, mud coloured body, striated by cream and black. Doesn't sound so bad? Well wait for the bony spikes that thrust from its skull to pierce through its head. That's how it delivers poison into the bloodstream of its prey. And oh, wait to see it flex and twist its head (Ughhh!). That's how it makes sure to fend off its predators.

Great Grandpapa Apow taught Papa how to work with these toads, using a pin. Stick them right, and their spikes don't get you.

Down by the river bed, cool ochre-coloured mud squelched between my toes. The pure, earthy smell of the river glided through my being, and the tall, tall bamboo shoots whistled serene songs in the breeze. Normally, these liberating forays with my father out in the wide, wild world would have made me feel elation. Like I could sing with my earthen brothers and dance with my flowing sister, whose waters shimmered spellbindingly under the light of the early moon. *But!* There was a but.

The toad was killing the ambiance.

"Papa, why'd we have to bring this stinkin' toad?" I asked in earnest.

He laughed. The kind of deep laugh that made his belly jiggle slightly. He sat to attend to the amphibian.

"Sometimes we have to do what we have to do. Duty," he said. "Duty to all before desire to self."

What duty had to do with the stinkin' toad, I didn't know. I sat propping my chin on my knees in frustration, awaiting answers, though none seemed forthcoming.

Papa let me be upset. He did not ask for my assistance for some time. Papa had fed the toad a bucket of worms. Eventually, quietly, he took a flat metal holder from his pocket and pulled out a spindly steel pin, no thicker than a strand of my own hair. He deftly gripped the toad by its throat sac, and stuck the pin gently into the back of its skull.

"Take it out of the container now," Papa coolly ordered.

"What?" I must have misheard.

"Take out the toad, Idzorah-Ulka," Papa affirmed, in a voice that made him sound unfamiliar.

I obliged reluctantly. I pushed my shaky hands in the container and lifted the heavy toad out. Its skin was slimy and damp. Its folding legs creeped the hell out of me. I led it to the water, and watched it leap in. Despite washing my hands in the night chilly liquid, it's like I could still feel the weight and shape of the eerie creature on my flesh. That feeling remained even after I returned to sit and wait impatiently next to Papa, for the toad to return with the river's offerings.

I had decided to protest by giving Papa the silent treatment. But when the toad hurled the first catch of fish for the evening at our feet, something began to gnaw at my conscience.

That toad I thought of as ugly and unwanted, born and bred in our backyard pond, was still doing our bidding even when we set him loose in the deep, open river. Even when he swam to places we could not hope to catch him.

"The toad doesn't leave while free in the river, Papa. It comes back, every time. Why?" I asked.

"He doesn't like the pin in his head, so he will come back. We have a working relationship, Idz —"

"No we don't!" I interrupted. "You stick him with a pin to force your rule over him."

Papa sighed, "This is just how it is, Idzorah. The toad helps us find the food at the bottom of the river where we can't go. It is nature. Its kind keeps the waters from getting crowded. It provides us with some of its catch, and in return, the toad knows it is free to live and eat and just be a toad."

"But Papa," I said plainly, "our toad is not free to live if he has no choice. He doesn't know what it is to be free?"

Under the light of the moon Papa's forehead crumpled up like banana leaves when I had folded them wrong.

"You don't have to do it, yuh know."

"Do what, Papa?"

I don't know if he genuinely expected me to know. Maybe I was naive.

He seemed to shift inward, away from me. For a long time he only stared out at the surface of the water. The black toad brought another fish, and another, before my Papa came back to me.

"Only few things in this life worth fighting for, Idzorah. We fight to follow our own path." He stopped to nod his head.

"We fight for love," Papa continued, then nodded again, as if agreeing with himself.

The man who always had comprehensive answers to give me, even when I probed and prodded, said no more that night by the river. The absence of words confirmed my suspicions. Dinner tonight was to be no ordinary event.

And, indeed, it turned out a significant occasion had been planned … for me. That in itself was special. Nobody ever did anything for me! But I still didn't like it one damn bit. So I burned with fury and turned away into the open arms of death.

⁺⁺
⁺⁺

SOMEONE WAS SHOUTING near my face. Had been for a while now, I think. Briefly, I came to. The shouting got a little less loud. This was nobody I knew. But there was something dreadfully important I had to remember. It was in my mind. I tried to reach it. I tried so hard I felt myself drifting back inside me. The shouting got louder again, but it couldn't keep me from my mind. It could not keep me from going back to the moment when someone else was shrieking at me to "Wake up! Open your eyes! Face the truth!" Someone? My mother.

"Ungrateful!" she had reached a crescendo, before throwing herself to the ground, prostrate in mourning or protest or whatever that was. It was later in the evening following my hunting trip with Papa and the toad.

I wanted to run far away and dive into the river to cool my burning cheeks; but instead I stayed and looked to our table of dinner guests. I had just declared I would not marry my childhood friend, Yanu. I understood it was a profound insult. I think all involved had expected it to have been an easy match to make. We did look good together: that savage, muscular beast of a friend complemented my strong, angular features and thick, intimidating black plaits. We got on well and I loved him. Like a brother. That, however, was not the core reason I could not love my friend differently. It wasn't just me. Everyone gathered

23

there had all known something no one wanted to affirm. So yet again I had to be the desperado.

"I can't join my heart to Yanu's because he can't love a woman!" I erupted, fed up of people's expectations making fools of us all.

A piece of fish shot from Yanu's father's nostril and dropped into his wife's half-empty water glass, as if trying to get back home. I had a giddy moment of enjoying that thought; then I looked up directly into Yanu's eyes. My friend stared at me in shock and betrayal.

"He would prefer a man," I tried to clarify with good intentions. It pacified nothing. Turns out they didn't want clarification. Yanu stormed out of the room, his mother hot on his heels.

Had I agreed to marry my friend, my story would have taken a different turn. Not long after our wedding would have seen us travel high in the west's hidden hills *en route* to the Skylands, our new village, new home, new life. There, many of Yanu's other relatives lived out their lives alongside kin of mine and others in our tribe.

But no. I had to say no.

We could not find Yanu in the hours or days after that.

When I gave up on searching with everyone else, I realised I had done a terrible thing to someone I loved. He would not have treated me so. Which made it worse to realise that, if I had a chance to do it all over again, I would still say no. It was all too much. I had really done it now.

So I had run and retreated up into the trees' canopy, where I stayed for some days, picking leaves apart; inspecting, or hiding things I found in the copious crevices of the tall, thick trunks, and carving idle markings into the yielding wood with my knife.

Papa came, (he alone, I might add) and tried to get me to come down. My middle name was "Stubborn," so he left me alone, but bestowed little baskets of berries and bread. That only made it possible for me to stay isolated and up high for longer than if I'd been allowed to get hungry.

By sundown of the fourth day, I heard my village warning horns sound.

THREE

Irony

T climbed back to wakefulness through a blotchy haze … my cheeks throbbing and my head set to explode.

"I told you not so hard!"

The room spinning … sounds sluggish and echoing … my tongue a thick, heavy presence stuck to the roof of my mouth … a darkness before my eyes, thankfully fading. Was I shaking my head to try to clear my thoughts? I didn't know … anything.

But I made out that voice: the commanding officer, the one with all the insignia. It sounded like he spoke harshly through gritted teeth to the shadowy man bending over me.

Colours and shapes kept blurring unsteadily; then slowly … slowly coming together as my vision focused. This time they had made sure to bind my hands. And my feet.

We were in a tent, and the clamour coming from outside told me that camp was being set up.

How were they holding my people? Was father safe? And mother? Then memory pierced me at my core: *They're both gone!*

That realisation turned my thoughts to my younger sisters. Were they protected? … Was any of us? I swept narrowed eyes over the men here: the commander; the brute leaning in like he couldn't get enough of hitting me; another armed soldier in one corner of the tent, digging his boots into the dirt, and yet another standing at the entrance of the tent, watchful of both inside and outside, ready to bar entrance or block exit.

I returned my look to the commanding soldier, giving him the full glare of my fury and suspicion. He was quick to respond. With a clipped flick of the head he made the nearest, threatening soldier step away.

"I won't hurt you," he said, briefly lifting both hands as in defense against any ill thought I held of him.

His light skin had a glow from the sun's exposure. It made him look alluring — like a hanging mango in a perfect state of ripeness, fragrant-smelling, blushed in areas, and firm-skinned — in that exact moment. Dark, disheveled hair flopped over his forehead when he moved. He used four fingers to comb it backwards in one swift motion.

He raised a cup of water and lifted his busy eyebrows, as if to ask if I wanted some. I felt my own brows curve downwards, and grimaced by way of dissent. Was that disappointment on his face?

He turned to pick up a bowl and spoon from a fold-out table. I figured he was going to eat, so was stunned when he came and sat next to me. *What game is this?*

He stirred the contents of the bowl, perhaps so the scent of food would make me pliant; then brought the spoon, with a piece of stewed game, still steaming a bit, toward my mouth. *He must think me a fool.*

I jerked my head away, hungry as I was. I don't know how long I had been blacked out. My body lacked strength, that food would surely fuel. I couldn't think

27

straight. Food could fix that, too. Even though eating would hurt, with my jaw still tender and my throat raw, the best thing I could do for me was to eat. But I was myself.

"You have to eat something. You don't know, but it's a long journey back to Pontem. That's where we are going," he said.

I turned farther away and set my full lips hard. He huffed, squinted a while at me, finally moved to put the bowl down. I watched him drive his hand through his long hair.

"That man, he was your father? I am sorry. He had a gun. My men thought … we didn't want violence. We did say to come quietly and all would be okay. The only people who were hurt were those who resisted —"

"What!" I spat out. "We'd have been blessed to become your slaves?" I mocked, angry tears escaping my eyes. I stifled the rest back.

He shut his eyes and turned his head away. "No, not slaves. Our … people," he pounded his fist to his chest where someone else might have had a heart. "You'll see: it will be a better life there."

I laughed scornfully, "Better life? You have no idea."

I had to look at him fully. I had to let him see the over-flow of emotion on my face, the storm in my eyes. It was the first time I properly looked at him. He had striking hazel eyes.

Those eyes gazed back at me, and for a moment, briefly, I saw something in them that … *What?* He didn't seem a soldier.

"You murdered my Papa!" I bellowed, to remember why I hated this man. "Papa took my place! Now I am here, in this world without him. Better that I had died! But I have small sisters — I have not even seen them!"

"I will find them and bring them to you tomorrow,

your sisters. What are their names? What do they look like?"

I narrowed my eyes at him. I was baffled. *It must be tricks!*

Except, I wanted to see my little sisters. I needed to know they were alive still. I needed to tell them about Papa and Mother. I told him their names and described their likeness. I felt the only thing worse than learning they were dead was not knowing what was happening to them. This must have been clear on my expression, because the commander tried to reassure me.

"Look, you say they are only seven. No one would have hurt them."

I clenched my teeth and stared at him. My sisters might be alive. But the reality was they might also be dead, from soldiers' bullets or violence; even from poison, if they had copied our mother's desperate example.

"Why did you do it?" I cried out.

His eyes popped. "Eh?"

"Why did you do this to us? We have nothing to give that you don't already have."

"Listen, my name is —"

"I don't want to know your name! I will never speak it. Just tell me why this was done to us."

I never truly expected honesty. Why would he tell the truth? But what he revealed was so — so shocking, what else could it be but true. In hindsight, I might have preferred a lie.

"My family has expectations of me. I have duties," he started. "My grandfather, Prince Ion, was one of the five sons of King Amargh. A long time ago, our Kingdom Pontem came under siege from Eastern forces wanting our strategic position in this part of the continent. It was a great battle, and against all odds my grandfather and great uncles prevailed.

"My grandfather felt it would be unfair to give the throne to the eldest when all his sons had fought bravely, so he ordained that there should be a royal contest to see which child would win the throne. The rules were simple. Royal heirs set out to achieve immense, impossible tasks of their choosing. Upon return, the king would weigh the success of each mission and decide who was victorious. That winner would be named Lionne of Pontem."

A long pause followed. He opened his mouth to say more, but nothing came out.

"What!" I spat through my teeth. I could feel a boiling heat rise through me.

"I'll kill you! You piece of SHIT!" I was screaming so fiercely my throat felt scalded.

My home. My family. My people. Our whole way of life. Ripped apart from us for some ego-building shit contest.

A hotness fit to set the very air on fire rushed to my face. Blood-red throbbed across my sight, becoming more intense with each ragged breath I forced into me. Were these the games civilisations played when they owned wealth and an insatiable hunger for power?

I must have looked fit to murder, even bound as I was. The soldier tried to keep looking at me, but my revulsion prevailed, and he awkwardly cleared his throat, shifted his stance and moved a few paces away from me.

My next words were snarled, "What was so impossible about winning a confrontation against my small, simple village?"

"It wasn't the winning. It's bringing home that many new people into our fold at once. We needed more people to build our Kingdom, to strengthen it. I thought it would please father," he said, unabashed.

Shock seemed to blessedly block my ears for a while as his lips moved. I was pulled inside my own head.

Once we were in Pontem that would be it.

There was no chance I would be able to persuade my people on my own to fight or leave. Our numbers were much smaller now in captivity, and we were not soldiers. We were nature-loving people with a dream, and had been fortunate to survive as long as we had without interference from outside forces. Maybe it was over for us the minute some of our villagers decided to take the outlanders up on their offer.

I, though, had never said Yes to these monsters.

First time in my life my defiance focused on more than just breaking rules to vent my temper. I had a vision that entangled my life with this man's beyond current place and time. He would be delivered to me. Or I would use brutality and deception to turn our tides, till he was the one drowning in my currents. This mission of revenge gave me a reason to carry on. I could die only *after* that. Then, it wouldn't matter.

I could not hold myself back from exposing a hint of my twisted thoughts: "When — *if* you win your title and you are crowned king, every time you go to sleep, you will feel the weight of the price you paid for all of it. I will even help you remember, by haunting your meaningless ass. Every time you shut your privileged eyelids, I will be there. Every waking hour. Every breath you take."

"Look," he shifted uneasily, "I am sorry you and your village got caught up in this, *but this is just life*. You have to take what you want. It will not be given to you freely," he rasped.

"Say whatever you must to deceive yourself. You have done wrong."

A resonance to my tone made him jerk around. Our eyes met. His lips parted, but no words escaped. I felt my voice was not my own; the knowledge I imparted older than I would ever live to be: "My people and I were pawns in your game of crowns. Because you control that game you think you are in control of everything, even life itself. One day, you will see that life is no man's game. It will play out how it chooses. It will bring to you what you brought to others. In a time to come, life may choose to place you on the losing side."

I convulsed suddenly, then stopped and drew a laboured breath. The world seemed soundless, motionless and waiting.

The soldier said nothing. It was a while before either of us moved. The other men in the tent were not looking at us now. But I sensed they had listened keenly to our exchange.

After that the evening wore on slowly. As he moved, going in and out the tent, the soldier entered and sat down in a corner. "I — look … when you're ready to eat something let me know. Uh … What do they call you?"

I looked up at him briefly, then moved my eyes to the opposite side of the tent.

"Idzorah. Izdorah-Ulka."

"Idzorah-Ulka" I heard him whisper, then he got back up and walked outside the tent.

In my tribe, when you ask a person's name, it is under the expectation that you will tell them yours in return. It was dishonourable to do otherwise. But what could one expect of a brute like that soldier.

Hmm. That soldier? *Soldier.* That is what he is, all he is or ever may be. Not a hunter, who provides for those he loves. Not a warrior who fights to protect his family from harm. Not a man with his own will to know right from wrong … like my Papa. *Soldier.*

‡

IT HAD TURNED ALMOST quiet out there as the night wore on, except for the snatches of manly laughter and banter I caught. I was low on energy, and while dozing in and out I wondered how far the convoy had managed to travel while I had been out, and where had it camped for the night.

Soldier returned to the tent, some time in between my sleepy musings. When he sat to have his dinner, I saw him look up at me. He had asked me a couple times in the evening if I wanted food or drink, and each time I had said no. Now, he came forward and planted his despicable backside next to me and lifted a spoonful of potato in front my face.

I watched him as hard as I could. Down. Up. I would spit in his face … if my mouth wasn't so dry. He looked into my eyes, then at the spoon, and then he was staring at my lips, until I turned to look the other way. He moved away. I thought he would stop and eat, but he came back to sit near me again. I shifted, and found a cup of water held near my parched lips. The food I probably could have turned down a few times more. Water? My lips parted without my bidding, and I drank. And drank. So enthusiastically water spilled past my chin, down my throat and ultimately between my breasts.

"Shit," he muttered, reaching into a pocket of his trousers. It bemused me to see him draw out an embroidered handkerchief. It was a fine thing. It was a woman's thing.

After patting around my mouth dry, he touched it against the trail on my neck. He stopped. I saw him look from the cloth he clutched to the water pooled in my cleavage. When he realised my manifest horror, he put the cloth back into his pocket, mindfully, and cleared his throat with an uneasy sound. This time when he tried to feed me — a meat I wasn't familiar with — I accepted.

My plot to wreak unforgiving havoc on his life meant I had to live; I had to stay tough … mind will, body. I needed to start regaining my strength.

After a few chews, I stared suspiciously at his bowl, then at the second spoonful of food he brought to my mouth. I held back, not chewing any more.

He let out a boyish chuckle, revealing a deep dimple at the right-hand corner of his mouth. He shoved the spoonful of food in his mouth to show me it was safe to eat.

"See. It's all right. It's roasted crocodile."

I spat it out so fast. That uncomplicated chuckle in response drew my stare from his dimple to his mouth. When he caught me, and I caught myself, I let myself return hastily to anger. He seemed to think it was over the kind of meat he'd made me eat. No, it was the other thing.

"My sister hates it too, crocodile. But it's not bad. A big delicacy where we come from, you'll see." He smiled at me.

I fidgeted and moved my eyes to the backside of the guard standing at the entrance.

Soldier bent closer, reaching to unbind the ropes around my feet. I thrust my tied hands forward eagerly and raised my brow. He shook his head and grinned in a way that seemed to say, *Good try, but hell no!*

"I've seen so much of your people in my village before; but I never seen a soldier with a handkerchief," I held my voice flat as I concentrated on fanning flaming passion for payback inside me.

"Ha. Well, I'm not really. A soldier, I mean." He looked at me with jovial eyes. "But don't tell my men, or they'll overthrow me," he joked, like we were old friends.

He could afford to laugh. It irked me he thought I could, too.

"The kerchief is my mother's. A keepsake she made me

34

promise to bring safely back to her. Which means I have to return safely to keep that promise. That's really why she gave it to me."

Sweet. The thought of me returning the blood-soaked kerchief to his weeping mother warmed my heart in a way I didn't think it could.

Later, the land succumbed to deep night, lying in the darkness with sleep eluding me, I wondered where my Papa was. My mother, too, despite our edgy relationship in life.

"Where did you go Papa?" I whispered. Tears skulked soundlessly down my cheeks. I dashed at them with ruthless fists, hating myself a moment.

I curled into a foetal position on the mat, and let my thoughts drift.

I needed to stay focused. I needed to not see this Soldier as a man with a mother and father and brothers and sisters. He was the killer of my father, even if he hadn't pulled the trigger himself.

My Papa was gone.

"Sweet, sweet Papa," I whispered under my breath, before I drifted off.

✝
✝

WHAT MADE my senses shamble out of dog-tired sleep? Half awake, I was smacked by a most foul scent. Instead of coming fully awake, I induced myself to drift off again, into even deeper reaches, to a place where I could be with Papa.

That didn't last.

I was dragged out of sleep by horrific screaming and

shouting. My eyes burned! I could hardly see through the pain. So much smoke! It did not smell like from wood-fire. Coughing prevented me from immediately shouting. Then a sudden, one word idea: *Escape!*

I leaped up, forgetting my hands were tied together. When I overbalanced, I could not use them to stabilise me. I toppled sideways, sensing I would thump my head hard a mere second before I crashed to earth and did exactly that. All went back to night-blackness and silence.

Not ungentle hands, and sweet sunshine on my cheeks, brought me back this time. My eyes tried to focus from ground level. I could see I was no longer inside the tent. Smoke was just clearing around us.

I lifted my head a bit and was able to just about make out tents standing askew or mostly torn down with their contents strewn all around. When I tried to sit up, everything bucked violently. I swayed, and collapsed; unable to break my fall back because my hands were still bound.

"Shhh. Gently, Idzorah-Ulka," *Soldier* cooed.

My heart almost stopped. He was sitting alongside me, legs plaited, arms bound in chains. *I must be dreaming.* Had justice come so soon?

I tried to shake off the vertigo, slowing my breath, staying very still, as I took another look around. Through my blurry vision and burning eyes, I saw terror. Blood and bodies. Coughing, lots of coughing. Confusion swamped me, and my eyes darted all around in an effort to assess the situation.

In between the clearing smoke, I realised my people were still bound, yes … and so were *Soldier's* men.

The camp had been hijacked. It must have been something in the air — the smoke …like in one of those books Papa had brought for me from the Old World.

Soldier had hunched nearer. I realised he was hissing under his breath for me to hear: "They used some sort of aerial sedative to knock us all out for a few hours. We get exposed to it as part of our training, so we can identify the toxin by its effects on —"

He was silenced by a blow to the back of the head with a hatchet.

That moment taught me one of the foremost lessons of conflict. *The tables can turn any time.*

My captors were now captive, too.

FOUR

New Captors

It wasn't like déjà vu. Conflict had beset my people only two days before, but this … this was sheer nightmare.

Haunting screams escaped the mouths of mothers whose babies were dragged from their frantic, reaching arms to be carried away, dangled by one foot; elders had their legs kicked out from under them, and were left to struggle to rise on their own, if they could manage, any possible helpers brutally shoved to the ground themselves and warned, "Only pick yourself up!" Skirts were ripped down and bodices torn off, baring breasts and other body parts, that women tried to cover with the scraps of their clothes picked up from the mud. Fingers, hands, entire forearms were lopped off with cruelly casual swings of machetes. And if the blade was less than sharp, the victim was left with the appendage swinging by thin or thick sinew … to figure out the rest.

Soldier's men were not exempt. They, if anything, were handled with more aggression. Anything other than outright capitulation was met with brutal force. One soldier, hands up in compliance, opened his mouth to say

Goddess knows what. He was slashed across the chest with a big knife — swift and to the point. Then dragged to the side and left groaning, bleeding out in the dirt.

Uncountable brutal, rugged men, wielding cutlasses and other sharp, nasty implements, committed these vile acts. It wasn't enough to capture us. They had to demean, to torment, to dehumanise, as they made their way through my people and Soldier's.

I couldn't continue to look.

I'd always been more hardy than most girls in my village. I am a wild child; I have always been; But even I couldn't stomach what I was witnessing. I thought I'd felt rage before. What churned in me now was like a beast within trying to break through. I held my stomach and bent over; thinking I might vomit.

"What's going on?" I asked, when the nausea subsided. There was no answer. Behind me, Soldier was flat in the dirt, wincing and moaning muffled words.

The scarred-face militants had many more men than Pontem's soldiers, who had captured my village. As they had done to us a little over a day ago, they were rounded up alongside my people, now as weaponless as we had been.

A piercing whistle echoed in the wind. A muscular, mature-aged militant, with a single plait atop his otherwise clean-shaven head, held up his blood-bathed machete, and silenced the madness. Was this the leader at the heart of this slaughter? I fixed my glare on his face. He bore tattoos in the shape of a dagger under each eye, their pointy tips kissing his cheeks. Scars rode up and down his fitness, adding a terrifying artwork of their own. How many battles had he survived? How much war had he waged?

He moved with animal grace, barely considering the living, indifferently crossing over the chopped bodies of Pontem's soldiers and my tribesfolk.

"From now on, you are the property of Master Carovor, Lord of the great Veridhakth Lands. You will from this moment call him Master, and you will live to please him even when you are not in his sight. Any opposition will be trodden," the big warrior declared, extended arm sweeping across dead, dismembered bodies around us.

"I am the Master's servant, Oktar. Until you are near our lord, I will be his proclaimer, thus, you will do as I command."

He grinned. Pitilessness was etched on the face of this monster.

I had heard stories of the secretive movement based in the Veridhakth Lands, far, far away from my home in the Baiuchi Forest. These stories were of the mysterious kind: evoking fear and dread, but laced with enough superstition to make one believe they were merely inventive tales.

Now, the myth had been made manifest, and I wondered what was truth from stories. What would happen to us? Would we be tortured? Experimented on? Brainwashed? Would we be turned into shells of our former selves? *Goddess* …

They were separating us by sex, then making us queue for rigorous inspection. I struggled to stand steady on my wobbly legs, others having the same difficulty, clearly all rendered dizzy by the after-effects of the vertiginous gas.

A wailing rose suddenly up and snagged my attention. Past milling bodies, I saw a girl, barely older than me, fighting to keep hold of a baby. It was an ugly tug-of-war between parent and cold-hearted militant. I twisted toward it.

Soldier grabbed my arm from behind.

"Be still," he whispered with urgency.

I tried to tug my arm away, but he would not let go.

The mother's howls intensified. The sound plunged into me and wrenched me forward. Standing bodies clustered together, maybe backing away from the commotion. *Soldier* lost his grip on my arm. I had to force my way over there. When I was clear, and could see plain, I knew I had to act. The babe was dangling by his foot in the militant's hand.

"Give the baby back," I commanded, staring into the militant's chill eyes. He smirked, and let his flat gaze move off me to inspect the young child squealing in his hold.

"P-p-please …" pleaded the mother with outstretched arms. "She's just a few months old. Just a baby."

My insides churned. I really might vomit this time. What did I think I could do? Tied hands and spinning head. People always said I was too hasty. *Wild child, that one.* Damn their judgment! I was willing to try anything.

"What's this?" Oktar approached, flanked by several huge, dangerous men.

"Give the baby back," passed my lips a second time.

They glowered at me.

"Please!" I managed with great difficulty, but I was sincere. Or trying to be.

Oktar inclined his head, the better to scrutinise me. His eyes shifted to look behind me, at *Soldier*, who had followed. Neither of us seemed to impress him. He turned his back and nodded to his colleague; who took the baby away, off through trees where our eyes could not follow. The young mother collapsed.

Rage roiled inside my gut, and the wild beast in me wanted to come out — be unleashed. The feeling intensified, my heart threatening to shatter my chest, when Oktar suddenly faced me and swiftly invaded my personal space. My face did not seem to interest him now. His vision flared as he pressed a leering look down over my high breasts and long limbs. He was close enough that his breath filled my eyes and entered my nostrils. He smelled like death. A rancid, stale kind of

41

death, like he hadn't washed off his sins from previous wars.

"You, come with me," he said bluntly.

"No!" *Solider* exclaimed. He stepped in front of me. Oktar's fist flew right into his face, knocking him to the ground.

I watched *Soldier,* who had fallen flat, struggling to get up. Oktar dragged me along with him to the front of the crowd, where a dirt road met the forest clearing.

Here, it looked like an organised mess, as the militants arranged groups of prisoners into ranks.

Where were the children? My head spun around, neck straining, sight searching, desperately.

Oktar's touch stopped me cold, brought me back. He was close again. His hand traced a line up my cheek, over my brow, then over my thick plaits, right down to their ends, at the tail of my spine. I stiffened when his palm spread against my bottom. My mouth opened to protest; but without warning, he grabbed my shoulders and force-fully swung me around. I would have reacted, except he seized my dress at the nape and ripped violently, tearing it almost all the way down. At the same time he barked out a name. He released me so abruptly, I almost fell to my knees. I fought to regain my footing past the erratic thumping of my heart reverberating through my whole body. Before I managed to stand upright something struck across my back and pelted me fully to my knees.

"Mother Guhh—" I groaned.

My flesh burned so badly I thought I would die. Sound vanished. There was left in its place a knife-sharp, high ringing that seemed to also blur my vision.

Sound returned with a snapping noise … the cracking of the whip again. Another lash, more scalding than the first, that dropped my elbows to the ground as well. I could tell it cut through my skin. I gritted my teeth and dug my nails into the earth. The third lash left me flattened, writhing in the dirt and leaves. My back felt set afire. Yet, there was a wetness trailing to my sides, causing parts of my split dress to cling to my hot skin. A warm wetness poured between my legs. I rocked on the ground, prostrate. I turned my head. The earth was warm, rough, but kind, too, against my cheek. I couldn't tell if there were tears. From down here there were no heartless faces to look into. Instead … feet; legs. The legs of the captives blurred into the shapes of swaying bamboo stalks at the riverbanks Papa and I would frequent. Papa? He appeared. He was here … with an outstretched hand, reaching, taking hold, pulling me upwards.

Get up, Idzorah-Ulka.

Yes, Papa.

And just like that, I was on my feet again; shaking, agonised, still in a stupor. But standing. Faces gawked at me, horrified.

I imagined that they pitied me. Maybe I wanted it … the little girl in me who had never felt enough sympathy. I looked deeper. What I saw in their faces was fear … broiling terror in their eyes. It's like they were looking at a thing unfolding on itself, like a monster, blossoming slowly, while they waited painfully to see what it would turn into.

I swayed where I stood, all eyes on me. I looked behind me. A barebacked, muscular man with smooth skin the colour of copper, held a firm grip onto a whip now bedecked by my blood. His gaze was fixed on me, blank and unreadable.

"I am the Chief Whip," He hissed, flexing his wrist to undulate the whip he held, underlining his title.

"This underling girl has just helped me show you what happens when you do not obey orders. You are sheep. You follow orders. Our orders are those of the Master himself. Oktar is the Master's voice out here. Oktar says eat, then you eat. He says you drink your piss, then you drink your piss!"

The copper-skinned whip-wielder looked older than Oktar. I imagined the terrible things they had done in the past, to people like me. His words cut like a rough knife-blade being dragged through flesh. Still, there was something about him that was different from Oktar. I couldn't fathom what it could be … not here and not like this.

The soldiers herded us like cattle into large open carriages. The sounds of sickening wails were hard to stomach. We passed a smaller cage with our village's children. They were crammed in, like the day's catch. Something broke inside me.

I wished I could do something. We had to do something. But my people, they were too resigned. No, not resigned. They didn't have that thing — the kind of fire in their bellies that we needed now.

Papa said in the *Old World* they had peacefully resisted, protested, and stood their ground. They'd always been unprepared to take up arms. An admirable quality, perhaps? I was never sure about that. When it became clear their peaceful resistance wouldn't be enough, they left for a new world, in the Baiuchi Forest. You see? They were not made in a way that could cause a reckoning.

A peaceful resistance would not help us now. It had not helped us then. Yet, they would *never* listen to me, even in these circumstances. Such were the limitations of their mindsets.

My body started spasming. I didn't think it was the result of terror or shock. My muscles were jumping eagerly, as if telling me things via my own flesh. *Reminding me of something.*

I rolled my disillusioned sight across the woebegone faces of my tribesfolk. Whatever they were, I was a wild child. I belonged to the Earth, and it belonged to me.

Earth had always spoken to me, and I would always comprehend the language.

As if in affirmation, the wind sighed a mournful yet majestic tune, hallowed and sweet. It brushed against my face in a sweep, before climbing to linger and whistle through the encompassing trees, rustling their leaves in an unsettling, profoundly stirring manner. I seemed to be the only person affected by all of this natural magic around us.

Yes, the Earth was talking to me alone. I was its child, after all. It was mine to roam through. I could never be caged. I had to escape, somehow. I had to make things right again. Even if alone and wretched, I would do it.

The Earth silently echoed all my Papa's recent words. It's like it spoke in his voice: *Get up, Idzorah-Ulka. Live. Fight.*

Yes, Papa.

FIVE

It Can Always Get Worse

T he journey to the Veridhakth Lands took us through rough territory which made it a bumpy ride in the open-back trucks. Paths had been carved into the side of the lush, perilous mountains, which we went up, and then down, and then up and over again. Winding paths turned dangerous corners, sometimes tapering to narrow edges.

I sat silently, making fist, among 20 or so people — a mix of my villagers, and Pontem's soldiers, with two of our eagle-eyed captors armed with machetes at the end. The tension in the atmosphere was ripe, and the stifling heat added to an already ominous feeling that there was some ugly, unseen thing ready to erupt.

I offered a sympathetic look to the village butcher's elder brother, Melon, a pudgy, usually jovial character with wispy hair and golden skin. Now, he looked ghoulish, with beads of sweat dripping down his face, hand gripping his other arm, which was wrapped with a piece of blood-dripping cloth. He was sat opposite me, and his eyes had looked at mine, or rather, through mine. I don't think I actually saw me. He was somewhere else.

Earlier, Maiee's cousin, Choco, had ripped the hem of her skirt and wrapped Melon's gashed arm. But when the guards felt she was being too careful about it, one barked, "Hurry up!" before signalling her to shift back to her seat and not move again. My shoulders had gone rigid, when the guard shouted; and the elderly Flo twin sisters furtively slid their hands across the small gap between them so their fingertips could meet.

It's ok, it's ok, I imagined their hands signalled to one another.

I was flanked by two Pontemi soldiers. The one to my left was a lanky lad who didn't look much older than me, while the battered looking one to my right must have been around Soldier's age. Neither of them made any eye contact with the rest of us, while we stole stealthy glances every so often.

When I tired of looking around, my eyes stayed on the green outside: at this unknown land nonetheless full of raw beauty. I had never travelled this far from my village, so it amazed me that this forest felt … familiar. The tip tops of trees, that I knew in my bones were older than all of us, stirred my heart like the recognisable trees back home. The waters splashing down the earthy mountainsides trilled to my soul in the same way the river running between its accustomed banks used to do as I fished with Papa. And the birds! The free birds sailing on the wind, calling out to each other, made me feel I was in the same place as them … but so far away. I could almost touch their freedom. It was a primal calling, echoing my name every time the wind howled, or an insect buzzed through the bushes. I wanted to be where they were. The distance between there and here tasted sour, like curdling milk.

Eventually, we left the cool air of the forested mountainsides behind, and we journeyed through a dirt road off the forest trail, every breeze wafted us with thick pungent scents of vegetation, dead leaves and soil. Beyond the dirt path we travelled, the sounds of nature's symphony echoed on the wings of the wind: buzzing, thrumming, howling, humming. I let it in. I let it fill me up. I drowned myself in it. I let it overtake me for long moments that were something like … escape.

We captives were progressively overtaken by exhaustion. I had been counting the days, but the sweltering heat of this new terrain gave weight to the fatigue. I could hardly fight past a relentless, dizzying brain-fog, let alone keep track of time.

En route to the home of our captors, some of the trucks following behind us broke off in another direction. Something twisted in my stomach. More separation?

They didn't feed us, just a taste of stale water sun up and sun down. We drifted. It was like a fever-dream. Melon was in and out of it, like the rest of us; until we noticed he never closed his eyes.

'Till we meet again,' Choco whispered, holding back tears as she risked the militant's wrath to reach and lower Melon's eyelids. We took pause, us Baiuchi villagers. Then one by one whispered the same.

"Till we meet again …"

Deep down, while I was saddened, beneath that hid a little envy that it wasn't me instead. I shook the feeling away. When the captors ordered two of the Pontemi soldiers to toss Melon's body out the moving truck, there was a low, collective, indistinguishable sound of pain. Bowed heads, in respect to the life that was.

Mother Goddess.

I closed my eyes and tried to shift my thoughts. I was sad for Melon, but he was now gone. And we were still left here. We had to think about us now. Insensitive or logical thinking? I'm not sure.

I think exhaustion, real exhaustion, does that to you.

The kind that slowly causes the unraveling of all the pieces of you that make you whole. You know it's there when you're too tired to feel. You know instinctively that the emotion, sadness or whatever, is floating around somewhere on the inside of you, making your stomach twist, or your fingers twitch, but your body is too drained to function as it should. Your brain never properly receives those messages from your body saying, *'Aye, you're fucked! Shake from terror; cower in fear. Cry, because you've lost someone.'*

I didn't know what lay ahead, but recent trials told me to expect the worst.

By the time we reached our destination, most of us couldn't stand. The heat, hunger and thirst were tormenting. Dehydration made my mouth so dry, my limbs wobble and my thoughts thick and slow. Water was life and over the past days I'd felt my life-force ebb slowly out of my body. I was a withering tree that had almost used up my reserves. Something had to give, or we would all meet Melon again … soon.

‡

THIS PLACE WAS the grandest monument to man I had ever seen. If I didn't know better I'd have said I was suffering delirium. All around, towering buildings shot up towards the blue skies, their facades engraved with ornate patterns, which appeared bronze and regal under the light of the sun. The structures were exquisite, but seemed incongruous, smack in the middle of a rainforest. Beyond these nearer buildings, something golden sparkled incredibly.

Somewhere in the distance I could hear the steady,

49

rhythmic flow of water. My left eyebrow jumped. And again. Then I was trying to process the flicker of something inside me. My tummy trembled in an accustomed way. Hope, is what I thought it to be, that thing that often seems unrecognisable to us, yet when it hits we know it is what it is.

I inspected my surroundings. I had never been anywhere near this end of the world before, but I could feel a vast expanse of woodland within range. Some forests are more dangerous than others; but I would survive if I could escape to there. The wild was my territory.

And how like hope to be so fleeting. *How can I escape when my body is unspeakably weak, and packs of soldiers keep watch like wolves over injured deer?* I had to regain strength. I had to plan.

When they commanded us out of the carriages, we were led through to an enclosed grassy area just inside the grand entrance to these lands. We were met by masses of women and men clad in pristine white apparel, organised in straight lines and extending water and food to us, while wearing unbelievably plastic smiles.

I took a morsel of bread and small bowl of water from a tray and forced myself to eat and drink slowly while carefully inspecting the surroundings. Around me, many of the captives were not as controlled in feeding as I was being. They would make themselves sick, and bring back up everything they had gulped down. I was momentarily angry at their lack of restraint; but then I remembered all this was being forced on them. I turned my incensed feelings on those who had brought us to this.

These strangers bore skin in every possible shade one could think of. I had thought my own village to be ethnically diverse: we had started as families from different ethnic groups sharing similar values and beliefs, before we became one miscegenated people over time. Here, there was more variety, and shades in between shades of skin tones I'd ever before seen — porcelain, ivory, milk, all shades of brown from coffee to butternut, coppery reds, golden hues and everything mixing in between.

Some of these people bore tribal markings, others none. They all wore white clothing in different designs. But they all mostly carried themselves in the same uniformed manner: broad cool smiles, upright posture, poised, graceful movements … stark contrast to their armed men. They were like a different species altogether.

"Welcome to our family," the white-clad servers kept saying, with each bit of longed-for nourishment passed to and accepted by trembling hands.

They did not make us stop feeding when they ultimately herded us into some semblance of order and started leading us to a sizeable open area ringed by the sky-reaching structures. It was like our village square, only thirty times bigger.

I gasped, and others around me expelled sounds of surprise, too. A magnificent giant, golden idol of a man stood before us, at the centre of all things. The small cup slipped from my grasp and was forgotten in the face of this towering object. As tall as forest trees, this was the thing I could see sparkling even from inside the carriage. It commanded awe from all seeing it.

The statue carried a muscular frame that spoke power, and rounded face with human-like eyes that looked down on all of us. Even when I looked away, I felt its eyes following me.

An elderly woman with a mane of shining black hair that clearly wasn't hers stepped up on the idol's platform and demurely clasped her hands at waist level. She had a gritty soft voice, but projected it with ease, sternness encrusting her every word.

Briefly, my mind flitted to Soldier. Was he here? What

would happen to him? Would he negotiate for his freedom? What was going through his mind now? I stole a few glances about me, before the voice in front brought me back to the present.

"You will soon become our brothers and sisters. Your past will be left behind. Your new life will begin here with us. Our secrets will be yours; our successes will be yours, and you will be free to live as we do, because we will be one," said the woman, looking intently into different people's eyes.

In between her words, I filtered through the odd mix of sounds around us.

My heart thumped in my ears…

Around me, people murmured in confusion, whispered instructions to *sit here, move there, I will help you* …

The rumbling of the odd vehicle coming or going …

A distant hubbub …

Overhead, an afternoon sun shone down bright. I looked above me as a flock of starlings glided on the wind.

Shak-kak-kak-ka-kak, a magpie protested. I turned to look towards the trees bordering the entrance, or perhaps it was coming from one of the paved paths leading farther into the compound.

The woman had stopped talking. I hadn't noticed. Eyes back at the podium: She was staring right at me, pursed lips, an eyebrow up.

"Hmmm," she cleared her throat.

"But before you step into the heart of our sacred home, you must be inducted." She offered a coy half-smile, her wrinkles shifting just enough. "All you need do is step up, bow to this likeness of Carovor, our ruler, our king, our Master … your new god. You will wash your hands in this bowl of water, to signify that you are leaving behind every-thing from your previous life."

Delivering these instructions seemed to fill the woman with great pride; her smile widened marginally as she fell silent once more, a waiting air about her. Were we being given time to think?

My fellow prisoners wordlessly looked around at each other, the woman, the statue. Pretty young girls from this strange land approached and began leading us up to their statue. I watched as members of my village and Pontemi soldiers gave their allegiance, their life to this new unknown.

A ceaseless stream of tears began to make their way down my cheeks. It all felt unreal. I tried to steady myself. A heavy tide of emotions flooded through me, to every nook and cranny of my body; its waves crashed back, then without warning, forwards, rocking me violently, and I felt I would tip over an edge, into a vast sea of nothingness.

An older man from my village approached the altar, and paused in front of the four steps leading upward to the golden likeness of the oppressor. On the smooth concrete marbled floor rested the bronze basin of water. Its position must have been intentional, for no one could reach their hands into it without bending over or kneeling on the stairs.

The man approached cautiously, wringing his large, trembling hands. I recognised him. Mr. San. He could repair just about anything that needed fixing and usually liked his payment in fish, accepting with a twinkle in his eyes. To see those capable hands look so destabilised, the smiling eyes so undone, struck a hard, bitter blow. I swayed.

"I will do as you ask; if I will be reunited with my family. My wife and sons? Please?" he entreated.

The elder, ebon-haired woman pushed her nose upwards. She stepped down off the platform, to come pace

53

back and forth before the lines of prisoners, her brows furrowed and lips severely pursed. After some moments, she spoke as if to dim, errant children.

"When you wash your hands, your old wife is no longer your own. If you have a child, that old child is no longer your own. You are made new. You can have all these things here … anew. We will give them to you if you obey. You will have new wives, new children. Whatever you desire! But you cannot have a new life without discarding the old. How else will you integrate into our clean society?" She lifted widened eyes and swung them to look back at the nervous man.

He turned and stared into the crowd. I followed his eyes, past lamenting men and women, their pain manifested in all shapes, and sizes. A weeping woman with two mid-length braids was staring back at him; then she was gasping, trying to force a sound, a word, that refused to take form, out of her mouth. It caught in her throat, then she pushed again, barely audible, before breaking into a wail. But I made the word out. It was his name. She was trying to speak her husband's name. He burst into tears.

I felt for him. For all of us. How could this be deemed a choice? Did we really have one? Who would force us all this way then offer choice? Was death or imprisonment a better outcome, when he would still have to leave his wife and children behind? Or was the answer to turn from all that he loved, if by accepting a new life it meant he would survive another day. There could be some hope of a future reunion. I concluded the latter was another kind of death, perhaps worse than the former.

Mr. San's reluctance was profound and patent. Nevertheless, he shuffled to the idol and bowed, immersed his hands into the bowl of water, let his head fall in shame, droplets falling from his fingertips. He was led away by a white-clad woman. He never looked back to see his wife crumple to her knees, weeping inconsolably.

The new converts were being taken away, and I watched them walk deeper into the compound until my eyes could no longer follow.

I longed to go numb to the pain, become a vast space of emptiness, so I could feel nothing while watching my people take vows that could have no meaning but bitter betrayal. I might have stood there rocking in my tired body until I was called to bow before the bowl; but an urgent voice inside reminded me: Do something!

Yes! Make a start somehow. My eyes began searching for my sisters in the remaining crowd. Even when it was my turn, I scanned the crowd one more time.

A young women egged me on, her arm extended towards the altar. One, two, three, four ... I counted my steps to the platform, as to the edge of a cliff. When I stood before the lofty idol, the ripe pain inside me began to throb harder, and harder ... lapped over on itself, expanding, and filled every space inside me. I felt hot, on fire, on the edge of something frightening, but knowing I had to step over. When the thing inside me burst open, it was sudden and complete. I thought I felt it shake my frame. Very calmly I turned to the regal woman and said, "No."

Stunned, the lead woman looked away to the militants skulking nearby. As if to say *Did you hear that?*

Cue the theatrics.

She jerked her sight back to me.

"I am not certain I understand. Did-you-say-*No*?" She emphasised the word *No* in a rising tone.

I stared back. I gazed out at the remaining crowd of prisoners. I could see the despair and misery in my people's faces. There was anticipation throbbing from King Carovor's fighters, watching for my next move.

I ascended the stairs and looked at the bowl on the floor. But instead of bowing down, or reaching my hands into the water, I kicked it as hard as I could, pushing it over and spilling its contents.

A chorus of loud gasps and murmurs sprang out.

The lead woman hissed and snatched the back of her hand to her lips. Amid her gathered folk, there were similar soundings and stirrings. Widened eyes, shaking heads, some curled lips … None looked kindly upon me now.

The woman's eyes were bulging. Her face was stretched into such a mask of shock her wrinkles seemed wiped away. Her gaping mouth moved but nothing came out. I, though, could speak for all to hear.

"If I could, I would knock over your idol too. I am Idzorah-Ulka. My life is my own."

"Take her!" I heard behind me. The voice of Oktar, the scar-faced militant.

I made to spin about, but suddenly there were militants laying dominating hands on me. Fists clenched, I pushed every inch of me back and forth, threw my weight every direction I possibly could. It didn't take them long to over-power me and drag me roughly by the arms past the altar, and across a vast garden with the crowd's murmuring fading the farther I was taken.

‡

THE GRASS eventually turned to paved streets that split in a number of directions like the legs on a spider. In the distance, a blur of beautiful green hills stood out, houses speckled on them. *Focus*. They eventually let me up to my feet but I was so worn out, that often my feet would hit the ground hard and I'd lose my balance and topple over.

We had taken one of the paths, and the militants grabbed onto my arms and slowed down. We ended up in a circular area scattered with the odd tree and buildings— some rounded with pointed rooftops, others rectangular two-story, with little circular balconies at their fore.

I tried to take in as much as I could, marking the surroundings, looking for anything that would aid in my escape; because that's what Papa would do. He would say *"Observe. See what works for you and use it. Map it out in your mind."* But it was hard to focus. My heart thumped fast and heavy.

Rat ta tat tat…

Rat tat tat tat … just like the woodpecker who frequented one of the trees near our village hut, as the sun came up. The throbbing vibrated in my ears.

Focus, focus!

I blinked hard, squinted, then opened my eyes wide, as if it would help me see more clearly.

Groups of people walking together stopped to observe. The Chief Whip was among them, staring intensely, whip coiled but still in hand. I couldn't read his expression, his face a blank sheet that could have been masking anything behind it.

Rat ta tat tat … my heart announced, again. Fear curled like a snake in my belly, made me look to the whip, then back to the copper-skinned man's eyes. I waited for something bad to come. But the moment my eyes caught his, he turned away.

We stopped and I was abruptly released. I fell painfully to my knees, but not for long. The big, hard hands tugged me up, around, forward. I was thrust against something unyielding, and that hurt, too. My bone-weary body was bruised, battered, scraped, probably bloody in parts. My arms were wrenched around the solid thing — a wide pole of some kind — and my hands were bound. This forced embrace made it impossible for me to slide down. For the first time since Soldier's attack on my village I felt utterly trapped. I might never know freedom again.

I was gasping for air now, anticipation of the worst was building up. It mounted fast, a boulder picking up momentum as a hill steepened.

Breathe Idzorah, breathe….

I sucked in air through my teeth in a rhythm, hoping to slow down the bolder. Closing my eyes, I tried to centre myself; bring myself back to calm, to me, the core of the true me.

I lapped it up for a moment before opening my eyes again. Oktar's merciless face filled my vision. *What does he look for in my eyes?*

"Leave her there until Master decides her fate," Oktar turned his back to me and strode away, calling over his shoulder, "Enjoy."

My heart skipped briefly in relief. I was still here, alive. The relief was fleeting. Alive for now. Mother Goddess, what were they planning for me?

Rat ta tat tat …

Some of the new converts were being shepherded past me by chaperones. I kept watch for my sisters but never saw them. No one said a thing, but the way the white-clad women looked to me as they led the people, it was like an unspoken pointer: *Take note, this is what happens to troublemakers.*

By nightfall I had been dancing with delirium so much that I no longer had control. Bouts of unconsciousness washed over me, when I wasn't shaking uncontrollably. My bladder emptied itself without warning. I barely noticed.

The sounds of passing people and nature receded completely as the night deepened. Artificial lights shone bright from the tall buildings and street lamps, but the night ruled. I wished that none of these lights could encroach on the sky's nightly veil. I wished to see that I was blanketed overhead by dots of twinkles in the black distance. But I could not see the sky past these man-made lights.

Echoes of unconsciousness whispered songs through my ears, calling me to a distant place. But I forced myself to lift my head up, however briefly. To see the stars, sitting in the sky, untouched. There was no such sight. I was wretchedly alone. Then I felt Papa's sweet presence. I couldn't see him amid the ubiquitous blackness before my vision, but I heard his calming voice.

Take shelter, Idzorah-Ulka. Whatever trials come, you will be made strong. This Earth is your home.

And out of the blackness, a magnificent eagle appeared over me. I cried out in wonder as its enormous wings spread wide then, strong and gentle as peaceful sleep, folded me in.

‡
‡

A DASH of cold water against my face woke me back to the nightmare I was now living. The day was new. Papa was not here. Had he ever been here? But his words had been so deep and real that even now I felt them resonating in me. I was so very tired and hungry. I was in such pain. All alone. *What could I ever do, Papa?*

Then the order was given, and I was cut loose. I collapsed away from the post and cracked into the ground. Everything spun around so quickly, I shut my eyes tight and retched. When the revolving decreased I reopened my eyes and tried to steady myself, tried to see. I tilted my head.

Oktar was standing over me with two of his men in tow. A small crowd of onlookers were gathered around. These people seemed eerily ordered, white-clad, impassive and vacant. Others, some bearing baskets in hand, seemed to be going about their business as though there was nothing out of the ordinary happening.

Are they dead inside?

Well if real death awaited me, I welcomed it over this so-called living I saw before me. I would rather be with my Papa. He gave his life for mine because he so wanted me to live. But that did not seem possible. How could it be? Papa had been taken away from me. My tribe had been taken away from me. My freedom had been taken away. I didn't see any others strung up like I had been, so I deduced my tribesfolk had all taken the oath for the sake of survival.

Must I have my very will taken away as well? It was a life I didn't want, because it was no life at all if I was not free to make my own choices.

Weakness and weariness had worn through my resistance. So when Oktar grabbed my arms from the back, and shoved me along ahead of him, I went like a sackcloth doll. He shook and yanked me like such a doll. I stumbled and heaved along before him, moaning or mewling. Because I could only breathe through my nose, I was forced to smell the sickening death-stale odor he wore in his flesh. I was relieved that I had not eaten enough to vomit.

Oktar jostled me into a large building, guarded by militants and riddled with smaller versions of the Master idol I had refused to bow down before.

Inside, it was quiet, pristine, dimly lit. Oktar led me down long corridors with cold, smooth floors and walls.

The scent of a strong substance burned my nose and made my head abruptly ache.

We passed tiny rooms with thick metal bars in place of doors. There was no security, but occasionally, the odd armed guard would pass by on patrol. This was a prison.

"This is our special place for people like you," said Oktar. "People who refuse to bow. We rarely have need for it."

Probably the place where I would meet death at last.

I would soon find out that these people viewed death as an easy penalty; which was a thing they were unwilling to give to me after what I had done.

I tripped and landed on my face as we went down a flight of stairs, compounding the pains I was already dealing with. Oktar hauled me up and took me to the gate of one of these small cells. He opened it, thrust me toward a confining space, and sneered, "Take in your new home."

It was a cruel cubicle, tiny, murky, emanating coldness from every surface. A lot smaller than the other cells I had passed. I would be able to stand and sit in there, but I would not be able to lie down or stretch out my legs. A square window rested high up in one corner of the confines, offering little light from outside.

"Do you like it?" he asked with a grim smirk.

No chance to figure out if he really wanted an answer. Instead of closing me in the cell, Oktar rammed me against the gate bars and ruptured what was left of my dress. He pressed himself against my naked shivering body; the icy, unforgiving bars marking the flesh on my back and keeping me prisoner against him.

"Please —" I tried to implore, but even my voice had been eaten away by hunger, thirst and despair.

He shoved his hand against me, forced it hardheartedly into my soft place. It was like a wound that tore my breath away. It wasn't like he was made of flesh, but wood, stone, sharp metal.

The pain ripped through every part of me, like he was tearing me with his hand. I tried to let out a scream, shriek, wail. Nothing had ever hurt like this. Goddess, help me! Please, please … *Let it stop!*

Everything went black.

SIX

A Caged Bird

I'm not sure how long I had been unconscious, but a twittering drew me out of my stupor: the sound like a miracle amid the horrible voices that had filled my fitful dreams, telling me I was nothing but a curse in the mouth.

I was cramped in the hell-hole that had witnessed the dreadfulness committed upon me, before I had blessedly blacked out from pain and shock. I cocked my head, to hear the birdsong, but nothing came, now. Perhaps it had been as much a dream as the vicious voices.

My knees were aching, but I couldn't stretch them for lack of room. I shivered from the coldness, coughing profusely for a long time. I tried not to focus on the walls that felt like they might close in even tighter on me.

I reached for the bowl of water beside me and tried to bring it to my mouth; but my trembling hands couldn't manage to lift it without tipping.

A raw, fiery pain stretched along my insides, stinging my once untouched flesh. I didn't want to think on it, no! Thinking about it made it more real; almost made the sting harsher.

My eyes traced the white grimy walls caging me in, floor to ceiling. In one corner an oblivious little spider weaved a web at intervals. Did it know where it was? Where it was building its home? Was this spider free? Freer than me? The long metal bars stood guard together at the front, still, uniformed, and in line. Between them the spaces sat in a seductive form; a window — a tantalising lure to the unconfined spaces outside.

Mother Goddess, my insides! Spirals of pain snaked up from between my legs, settling below my abdomen, clawing at my flesh.

My fingers caressed the soft fabric of my dress. Torn but still delicate, like the petals of fragrant roses Mother used to simmer in water, or the tail of Maie's favourite ribbon, intertwined in her plait.

I clutched my own long plaits, drew them against my cheeks and smelled them. I buried my face in them, and held them there. They still smelled like home, felt like home. I caressed my face with their comforting familiarity and closed my eyes.

A sudden loud clank jolted me. My plaits skated off my shoulders as I scrambled, taking all comfort away.

Light footsteps approached.

The Chief Whip towered there. Instinct pushed me against the wall, and I turned to grip its solidity as if it could protect me, when in truth, all it did was entrap me. The elder man reached toward me. I shrank back, but there was no possible escape. Was he here to have his way, like Oktar, too?

His powerful grip clamped on my upper arm. I struggled feebly, trying to pry myself away. *Goddess, I was so weak.* With little effort, my captor pulled me out of the cell. I was too weakened and battered to stand. I cringed as the Chief Whip pulled me to sit upright, propped against the bars and stretched my long legs out in front of me. My legs, I

64

say, but they weren't my own. Not today. I couldn't feel them. They were useless.

Despair wailed soundlessly through all my tired, hard-taxed limbs. I, who had been so fleet and strong, what had they made of me?

He produced a small jar. When he uncapped it, the smell of certain healing herbs and spices swept memories of my village healer through my senses. He stretched the jar in an open hand before me. When I didn't take it from his hand he calmly rested it on the floor beside me.

The Chief Whip went to the sole nearby sink, with shelves along one wall, and returned with a bowl of water, a few knobs of cheese and pieces of bread on a tray. He sat opposite me, doing that staring thing again, like he was looking, searching for something past the windows of my soul. I looked at the food.

"Eat," he indicated.

With trembling hands I brought the water to my mouth, and after a few sips I started gulping, streams of water running down my face. He cautioned me to stop. I had sense enough to obey. After, I ate bits of cheese and bread, then placed the rest in a flapping pocket of the dress.

I didn't understand what was happening.

"Why are you helping me?" I asked, squinting at him.

He glowered and after some moments rejoined, "What are you trying to prove, child? You will get yourself killed if you do not obey. If you want to live, you have to listen."

I took a proper look at him then: this older, bald-headed man always with a whip. Up close, I could see markers of his years around his eyes, on his copper skin. I should have stayed quiet. Maybe.

"I think I know why you help me. Because you're like me."

The Chief Whip stood and drew back in one fluid

move. He scowled down at me. "I am nothing like you," he spat, his forehead creasing.

"You were a slave too. Now you're doing their bidding," I rasped.

He didn't like that. He lifted his head higher, like he was retrieving his pride from on high, before rumbling "I will not do this again. Keep the ointment hidden. Try to make that food last."

He walked back to the shelves near the sink and produced a neatly folded white fabric. He flung it at me. "Put that on when I leave." It turned out to be a dress.

After, he maneuvered me back into the tight prison.

He swung the gate closed and twisted the key to once more lock me in. The Chief Whip walked away without looking back. Tears started sliding down my cheeks as I watched his receding back. Tears to what purpose?

Tears of dread, that no one might ever come back to find me; of relief, that he hadn't whipped me again; of revulsion at the horrors that this place had already inflicted on me, and the ones that might be in wait, that no ointment could soothe away. It made the teardrops slice my soul like cutting rain. For a while, it was all I could do … weep and pity myself.

After, I was so emotionally drained it was almost like a calm. I felt the enormity of my problems. I didn't know how I could escape this wretched little cell, let alone the vast prison. Where would I run?

My home was gone; there was no one left in it. My people were scattered like fish when a big stone was slung into shallow river waters: some here, pushed to renounce the Mother Goddess; others taken to who knows where, borne away in the carriages that had separated from the main convoy on the journey to this place.

Even if I could escape, what would be the purpose of it? I might never find my little sisters out there in this huge society, or much, much farther away. Where could I start to seek them? If I did manage to find them, what then? How would I escape with small girls? Where would I take them to be safe? The questions dashed around my mind, like leaves in a blustering wind.

Why proved the heaviest question. Why would I live? Why live with everything I loved gone? Why would I cling to free will, when it only made me a target for abuse and degradation? Why was I still alive at all?

Part of me instinctively wanted to fight. That was me. Still, something was missing.

Before, in my village, anyone looking at me might have thought my life did not seem like much, living the way I had to all along. But it was my life. While my people had not seemed my own, with my Papa, the place we called home was mine. It was my life especially out in the wild: the soft earth, the lakes, the streams, the creatures and hollow trees; the peaks and coves and flowered fields. I had felt so alive!

Now ... there were so many questions. Until I could answer those questions within my innermost being, I would find no meaning in anything ever again.

I didn't even know if I could live with myself. I hated that beast, Oktar for violating my body, my shrine. But he had violated my mind too. I felt strong disgust at myself. At my now sullied body, which could never be made clean or whole again, no matter how much I might wash it with water. And shame. Above all else, I felt great shame.

My thoughts were racing and became too much. Unconsciously I covered my ears, as if I could hear these thoughts aloud and doing this would quiet them.

I was shut inside close walls with no way out. Worse than that, inside this cell, I was locked into an even tighter prison: the walls of my own haggard mind.

My resolve was sorely tested.

Days wore on along with the thoughts in my head. My fighting spirit wavered. I was constantly having to encourage myself to fight. Fight! I was in a tug of war with different parts of myself — the part that wanted to live and the part that didn't.

It was leaving me, the will to continue. It was dissipating like night mist under strong sun. I wanted to die. I felt with the deepest conviction that this world was no longer my home; that I had no place on all the Earth.

Papa was disappointed with me. That's why he didn't appear to me again. I was sure. Then I doubted whether I had ever really heard him. *I must be going mad.* Now, in my mind's eye, I saw only his lifeless body in our hut.

I played the moment of his death over and over in my head, detail by detail, as if it was happening new each time. I'd smash through the window, but always too late. No matter how fast I ran, I was always too late. In my dreams I failed Papa again and again. Each time I awoke to my own screams, the pain fresh like it had just been inflicted.

I had let my Papa die; now he would let me die. He had left me for good. I was all alone in the world, and it was my fault.

Save for the guards who came twice to replace the chamber pot in the cell and toss in a morsel of food, no one came to me.

By the sixth day I was dragging my dirty fingernails across my arms. They were brittle from poor nourishment, but longer and jagged. My blood was deep-crusted under and around the edges of them. Speckles and spots of blood stained the dress I wore almost artfully, like an intentional pattern. I was at it again when several armed guards appeared, escorting a woman, who stopped and clasped her hands behind her back.

She was full-bodied, with a freckled face, and auburn

hair pinned up in an elaborate style. Her pursed lips turned downwards before she lifted her head and spoke.

"The Master is all-merciful, so he will give you a chance to repent at the altar."

They drew me out of the cell. I could neither help them nor resist them as two of the men bore me away, holding under both arms. They had to almost drag me along … right back to the Master's golden idol. I thought idiotically, *I've been here before.*

They let go and left me on my knees as if I had already yielded. Then they waited patiently, perhaps hopeful, not prodding me or anything, as I gazed up towards the thing. But, I wasn't actually looking at it. I was looking past it, to the blue skies and pale fluffy clouds, wondering what was up there. Was the Mother there, looking down on me still? Would She keep her promise not to forget me, the way any nurturing mother would never forget her young? If Papa was with her, would he fight to make her not forget me?

Maybe they had both forsaken me.

My captors waited, without speaking. At high noon, Carovor's people took me back to my cell.

But they returned every day. Every time, they took me to the gold figure of their master and waited for my repentance. But I had never been good at asking acceptance. I wasn't going to start now.

This ritual went on for three days. On one occasion, after I'd been flung into the cage, and the guards stepped away, the woman stood gaping at me. She clung to the cold bars with the hands she always held behind her back; only now they were shaking fists. Her expression had many layers: confusion, doubt, irritation, disgust … and other things I could not identify.

She shook her head and spoke, but as though for her own hearing only, "She doesn't deserve it! I don't care, she doesn't deserve it!" Then it's like she came back to the present, and my staring, astonished eyes set her spinning on her heels and walking briskly away, the armed men following in her wake. They vanished like ghosts. But the only ghostly creature here was me, fading, fading, fading.

I had an instant of realisation, and my lips moved over it: "Tomorrow, I will break."

And then the bird began to sing.

At first I just listened. Then I tiptoed and peeped through the narrow window, a small hole in the wall leading to another world. A green bird with a yellow head swung spritely on a perch, inside a small cage hanging from a nearby tree.

My heart filled up and frothed over. The feeling washed through me with serenity, evoking nostalgia for things lost. A dampness rolled down my right cheek.

I found myself tuning in to the small creature's undulating melodies, felt their harmony drowning out the pervasive undoing thoughts.

Who had put this little bundle of brightness and song there? The Goddess bless them. I felt my mind transported back to sweet days spent in my forest, sheltered in high tree branches, birds winging in and out, alighting near my unmoving form, singing their hearts out. Free. We'd all been free alike.

Then I realised that this bird and I were also not so different. We were both in cages against our will and, given the chance, we would both choose freedom. Yet … it was singing. That bird in captivity was singing.

That same plaguing question again: *Why?* From where it mustered the will to sing, and with such delightfulness, was beyond me to know. But I could be taught by it here and now. I had to survive. I accepted the lesson from this bird. I had to learn to sing in my cage while waiting for the door to open.

WHEN NEXT MY cell was opened, it was Oktar who held the key. Like the woman, he was flanked by four armed militants. Two of those, as usual, had the task of extracting me from the restricted confines. Between them, they held me up in front of the leader. I was so wasted away one of them could have managed the job easily.

I still wore the blood bespattered dress. It was far from white now and made my skin itch. Oktar's granite gaze took stock of my filthiness. Shame burned itself into my cheeks, so I turned my face to the floor. But then, it's like my own voice uttered in my ear, *There is more than one way to sing, Idzorah-Ulka.* Like birds, yes; and like rain, like thunder, like flood. I lifted my head and committed the only act of force left to me: I spat in Oktar's face. I didn't have the satisfaction of enjoying his reaction because the punch to my face knocked me out cold.

✝
✝

MY UNCONSCIOUSNESS EBBED, and slowly rolled back like foamy waters pulling from shore. A buzzing sound in my ears reverberated with a pain that exploded in my head. My body sore, weak … not my own; my mind latched on to the thinning threads still connecting it to my body.

Come together. Stay together.

Am I being carried now? Everything swirled in dazzling colours, streaks of greens, yellow, blues … unruly patterns intertwined and merged, then came apart. A sickening feeling settled in my stomach. I blinked again. And again, trying to lift my head. We were inside a grand building, with smooth, cold glossy floors. Thick, tall columns propped up the high ceiling one minute, the next they morphed into coconut palms, dancing in a rainstorm.

Focus, damn it.

I blinked again.

Winged otherworldly creatures peered down on me from the ceiling. They were made of flowing locks, naked bodies, some bearing golden glows around their forms. A lion had an eagle's head and wings, like in the mythical stories and books Papa had shared with me. All the parts went hazy, then streamed into one, a dazzling globe of confusion, just turning and twisting.

Eventually, my vision started coming into focus.

Along the long hall, there was a panoply of exotic wild animals on display — a menagerie of creatures from my world. Slithering snakes, monkeys on trees, and multi-coloured birds, caged as ornaments amongst plants and statues of men and women. An orange-billed toucan peered at me from between foliage in one of the glass exhibits, its blue-rimmed black eyes following me as I passed. It croaked on and on, like a frog by the river on early mornings.

Beyond this bizarre passage, we eventually got to a far more brightly-lit place. The sudden gleam hurt, made me shut my eyes tight. We stopped, and I heard Oktar call out in a controlled, commanding tone. After a moment, we moved on again. Next I knew I'd been unceremoniously spilled to land in a pile on the floor. I lay there, eyes still closed, not minding the coolness and smoothness of what-ever the ground was made of against my grubby, scratchy skin. Too soon, I was hauled to my knees and left to sway there like a stunted sapling in an unsheltered clearing.

Somewhere in the distant corners of my mind, the bird's song echoed and played on.

The Chief Whip gripped my neck and forced my head down, as he himself, and the attending militants bowed low and chorused, "Master!" They straightened, and I was allowed to look up. The Chief Whip strode forward, stopped by a figure standing in shadow, and folded his arms. He looked in my general direction, though our eyes never met. The form stepped out from the shadows into the light falling in from the window.

That was the first time I saw him in the flesh, after having grown completely familiar with his giant shining likeness: Carovor, the professed god-king, who held my life in his polluted hands. The statue inspired awe. This heavy lump of a man, looking out a window, propping himself on a stick, did not.

He remained standing in the natural light and turned to face us. I took in his milky, half-shut right eye with a gash running across it from brow to cheek. He had a bulbous nose, a long brown beard and a revolting belly that protruded and folded over the waist of his pants. He limped laboriously over to cast a shadow on my face. I wondered how often he had to have a new cane made.

Oktar waved his hand, and two of the guards grabbed me and hauled me to my feet, exhibiting me to Carovor.

His eyes were a dull grey, their windows leading to nothingness; I could see nothing behind them, like his soul was empty, a deep, never-ending hole.

"Mm-mm." His eyes went up and down, as he inspected my face, my breasts, my thighs …

A smirk slithered across his face.

If Oktar smelled of death, his king must be death itself. I wheezed, turning my face, and tried to hold my breath. He smelled offensive, like a putrid decay, festering. The malodour shot through my nostrils in a stinging attack, lingering. My body's defences answered with a well of water in my eyes, and a slow stream down my irritated nose.

"Why do you refuse to accept me as your king and god?" His breath was so foul it tumbled upon my face like a thing of substance.

I found myself heaving, overwhelmed by his odor. For an instant I reverted to childhood and shrilled the first thing that came to mind, "I want to go home."

"This is your home!" Carovor bellowed.

"This is my prison," I cried in a pained tone.

He sucked his teeth, pulling on the ends of his lengthy beard.

"You think you are brave but you will die a coward's death," he stated in a matter-of-fact way.

I looked him in the remaining good eye. "I am not afraid to die."

The king hissed and jerked his head. The men holding me released me abruptly. I was on my knees once more.

"Who do you think you are? How do you expect this to end? Let us suppose you escape, you cannot survive any way you turn. These forests are not your terrain, little bird. You want to fly, I see it in your eyes. Yes … it is the same way my toucan's eyes glint when she stares upwards, towards the windows of the menagerie. But you will learn as she did. I will tame you as I tamed her and all of the other wild things that once resisted me," he rumbled.

My lips trembled as tension moved through my face. He looked at me like he was asking in earnest. Like he genuinely could not fathom why I was not grateful to be here, in this place.

"You have nothing, and you have no one to protect you. You are all alone," he sneered with a sly, ugly smile.

The answer came to me on fresh, remembered bird-song, the echo of my father's voice from beyond death, the feel of the Mother in all things bright and wonderful: "I am not alone, I am not alone ..."

Carovor interrupted: "Who, then, is with you, little bird?"

His eyes continued to examine me, tracing inch by inch of my body with intrigue, disgust, almost curiosity.

"Even wild things can break," he leaned over uncomfortably, gripping his stick.

"You have made such a spectacle of yourself, you tiny little ant standing beside a mountain. I see how people look at you, the reactions you cause!" his bottom lip stretched downwards as he overemphasised the last word, like a hissing snake.

He reached out and poked his index into my chest roughly a few times.

"What is it inside there? Inside you, in this, this little frame, that makes you so foolishly bold?"

I wanted to have honest answers, not for him, for me. Who did I have? And what made me like this? The honest answer? I had me, and this was just me being myself. I locked my jaws and I kept silent.

"Mmm," Carovor twisted his jaw and looked like he was musing over something very vital.

"Tomorrow you can have your freedom. You will self-immolate. If you do not, in our kindness we will help you," he pronounced.

SEVEN

Alone

W here's bloody poison when you need it? At some point during my abuses I had lost my vial. And though it had been filled with a killer brew, it had been something from my village life, linking me to all I used to know. It had held a thing made by my mother's hands.

She had brewed vats and vats of herbal concoctions for medicinal purposes, and the more concentrated states that were lethal. I used to watch her as though she were making magic. I learned that way. At times, she graced me with her words; like there, in her kitchen, weaving drafts of spells, my mother could not help herself from wanting to pass on the knowing.

"The ornamental-seeming Oleander flowers, so beautiful in shades of pink, red, yellow, purest white, dancing around undulating edges: we use the seeds and leaves when treating wounds; but if eaten, this delicate-looking flower is sure to kill," murmured my mother.

Now, thinking about it with all lost and all gone, I wonder if she might not have just been talking to herself … not me at all.

My mother, so beautiful and so able to bring death. Like the flowers and plants she loved. Like so many things.

I remember really, really liking the idea that delicate things could be deadly, too; that if flowers didn't have to be one or the other, so could other things be. I admired that about Nature.

"A drop or two from the essential oil of the deceptively decorative yellow Jassamine Vine will ease severe pain: making it a popular choice for toothaches especially. And it calms the nerves of the anxious; sedates the sleep-deprived. But one drop too many, and this innocent-looking darling will bring on violent tremours, paralysis and organ failure."

I nodded at my mother's lore sharing ... though she never looked to see me nod. Was she looking at me now, from wherever she may have fled this world to go?

Out in the wild I could have found any of her poison flowers if I wanted. Now I needed them, and all were out of reach. Shit ...

I had never given much thought to exactly how I would die. But burning? I imagined what it must feel like, closed my eyes shut, fought to shake off the sensations.

Hours later I was returned to my tiny cell. I was amazed to find that it had been cleaned, and someone had left a wooden bowl with some sort of brownish soup and a cut of bread. Beside that waited a small basin of water with a washcloth. Another larger folded fabric had to be a white dress, like the one I currently wore had once been.

I stared, and the seconds stretched into an eternity. *Ohhhh ... that's what it is!* A final meal, granting a little dignity, perhaps. Well who knew, even the wicked could be kind. *-ISH*.

This is it, then. No more possibilities: to dance with the wind in feathery fields; to skin my knees and forearms while climbing a tree; to get caught in the white rains while running through the forests, with the mud squelching between my toes, trying not to slip and fall.

Yearning hit me so hard I doubled over with the feeling of loss and yearning. What I would give if I could only smell the fresh waters of the rivers again, just one more time. Then once more lie on her soggy banks and gaze into the free-flowing currents, letting them pull me into their dreamy otherworld. Down there I imagined it was kinder, safer and more free. Perhaps …

Something rigid bumped my back, and I stumbled forward into the open cell. The guard behind me grunted inaudibly. Back in the now, I could hear birdsong travelling on the winds. The caged bird outside was singing. The song fell through the window like a shaft of sunlight out of clouds. In that instant I named the little bird Sunny.

This begrimed little cell, with its closing-in walls, had become habitat. I was already like those animals in Carovor's collection. But I was not, too. I was human, and I needed to talk to someone. I needed interruption from the memories, the nightmares, the pain, and even the numbness I sometimes succumbed to. So I had taken to talking with wee Sunny, through the hole-of-a-window, which funnelled my whispered words to the open air. Maybe he heard me as clearly as I heard him, though I always whispered, fearful of being discovered and having my feathered friend be removed.

My small bird friend's yellow head was such a beautiful shade of the colour, it reminded me of the sun, daffodils too, and the sweet pulp of ripe mangoes. But mostly the sun.

I pulled myself up to the window. The sun was setting against a backdrop of orange and pink sky. Sunny was swinging and singing. I wondered how long he had been in a cage. If he was born in captivity, like the black toad Papa reared for fishing, or if he'd been caught wild, like me. I imagined it was the former; he just seemed too comfortable on his perch.

"Well, guess this is it, Sunny, boy. Tomorrow, ah going home. See you when you get there," I said.

"Hope it won't be as soon as me," I added.

The bird continued trilling, oblivious to my pending execution ... perhaps even oblivious to my existence.

Later that night, I ate my last meal and scrubbed myself off as thoroughly as I could with the cloth and basin of water (I did gulp some of it, and it was fresher than any drinking water I'd been given so far). I changed into the clean dress and folded myself on the floor. Sleep did not take too long a time to come. Sleep and dreams.

I HAD A BABY BOY. *I know he was mine because I carried him with such affection. It occurred to me that I didn't know where we were, but the place felt familiar. And I felt safe. As I carried him along a long winding road, I pointed out the lights visible on the surrounding hills, and I delighted when I saw his joy. People bustled around us, and everywhere was brightly lit. It seemed a happy time.*

Yet, as we carried on it got dimmer and dimmer, and we left other people behind till we were all alone. The road led up a hill that bore no lights. I walked upwards, straining ever more as my baby boy got heavier, hurting my arms. The hill became more inclined, getting steeper and steeper, until it suddenly morphed into a ladder. I screamed as we slipped, grabbing desperately. One arm clutched my babe, the other holding on to a rung for dear life, until I got my feet on to the ladder as well.

I managed to make it close enough to where onlookers had gathered and were peeping through a window. I passed my baby to safety and climbed higher. Near the very top, an outstretched hand reached for me. Gratefully, I stretched to take it, looking up into the face of ... my mother! I almost let go of the ladder, but our hands met in the space between us. Realisation hit me: my mother was not trying to pull me to safety. Instead, she was pressing something into my hand. It was a vial of poison.

†

I DON'T KNOW if it was sensing that death was meeting me halfway, but when I awoke in the morning, I felt pure and weightless.

Sunny was not singing at the time, but I had a song in my heart. When they came for me I was already humming a song that Papa used to sing to me throughout my childhood. It was about a mountain that stood isolated, telling Mother-God it must surely be a mistake for it to have been made to stand alone. But, Mother-God told the mountain that everything in this world was made exactly as it should be, even those who might seem all alone.

But even so you ain't alone, ol' mountain, ye tall and strong one, ye tall and strong one,

I have moulded you as you are, as I imagined you, to touch the heavens,

So you can feel the rain hard, and the sun bold,

You stand amongst the rivers and valleys, ye tall and strong one, the rivers and valleys,

And you stand amongst the skies and its dwellers therein,

The squirrels and the wolves, the birds and trees, the tributaries and the bees all look to you,

Yes they all look to you for shelter and nurture, ye tall and strong one,

See you are not alone, never alone, ye tall and strong one.

· · ·

THE CHIEF WHIP WAITED OMINOUSLY, with his weapon of punishment and accompanying militants. I got up and walked out on my own. Freedom was coming. I continued to hum my father's song.

The morning was young, and as we walked beyond the building that had caged me, on towards my death, many women, men, and a few children, stopped to stare. I thought that they were scrutinising me because they knew my fate. But perhaps they wondered about my carefree attitude, for I was now singing my song aloud for all to hear. I did not fear death. It was life that terrified me — being trapped in this crazy world, without my Papa.

I still wanted someone to pay for these wrongs committed against us, these wrongs that had tossed us into chaos, like inanimate objects thrown by the force of a monster flood. In the absence of revenge, I accepted death as a better outcome. Better than living a shackled, meaningless existence. Better than being an alien without a home.

At the square, I thought that they had made too much of a fuss for me. The procession was met by a crowd of followers bearing lit candles. At their idol's feet, they had erected a wooden cross, encircled by a pile of dried kindling. While they strung me to the cross, my heartbeat thumped against my chest as if in protest. I gazed into the flame of a candle held by a young girl with a heavy hair fringe and fat plaits pinned atop her head.

"I pray for you," the girl said, looking me straight in the eyes, and a woman next to her rested an arm on her shoulder.

"Why?" I asked, wincing when the rope was tightened and knotted around my wrists.

"Your soul will be tormented," she said.

"I am already tormented" I said, in a flat matter-of-fact tone.

"Because you refuse to accept Lord Carovor" she took a small step forward, and her eyes widened. "Accept him, all will be well."

I paused.

Was that the sound of a drum? Boodoop boodoop boodoooopppp…

I snatched a mouthful of air and felt it filling my chest. It was my heartbeat that thundered in my ears while it wore down my heart's walls.

"When I die," I gasped for air, "I will not rest until I've haunted every one of you sadistic monsters," I declared.

The girl didn't say anything. She didn't need to. Her frowning brows said it all.

Some heads turned, hushed whispers passed opinion.

The horns sounded, and the mad king made his way, limping, to my sacrificial spot. The gathered bowed in reverence, before Carovor proceeded to address them.

"Sometimes we are reminded of why we must make sacrifices. It is the only way we can rid ourselves of curses, famine, war, impurity. Sacrifice is necessary. Our old world had turned to chaos because THERE WAS NO ORDER!"

His right hand emphatically gesticulated towards the audience; his every word growing more powerful by the syllable.

"We LET the impurities among us SPREAD. Like a virus. Until we *almost* destroyed our world. But WE, can show them a new way!"

His voice trailed off on one of the wind's wings. I saw it go in a blustery flurry, felt it brush against my face as it passed … right, upward, left, upward, upward, upward …

I followed it until my head was tilted toward to the skies. Mother Goddess was not happy. She pitched a flash of brightness across the heavens, which must surely have made every pair of eye here blink. She roared, and a cacophony of thunder rumbled. The blue of sky was crowded out by bleak, burdened clouds on the verge of bursting open. I stared into their roiling, ever-changing mass ... and then I saw his face.

"Papa," I muttered, and my heart felt full. Even when the clouds changed form once more I was ok, because now I knew papa was here.

In those last moments, I could hear every second pass in pace with my hammering heart. I wondered if time had slowed because the universe knew I was departing. The exact day, hour, moment no one knows, but everyone expects. Until the very second you stop being here; when even time itself halts, very briefly, to acknowledge your departure, as you transition from one realm to another. You, I, each one of us, are after all just another thing, element ... part of this universe. Never really going from it — only transitioning form to somewhere other.

There was rushing now. The twigs and branches at my feet were set afire. As they caught and blazed, my mother appeared at my side. She waited.

"You — you've come for me?" I asked tearfully, but mother didn't answer.

I waited, but she still did not answer. In death, as she was in life. Fucking fabulous. I sulked. Was I always her disappointment? I blinked and she was gone.

The flames were being fanned by the wind that had come riding on the dark clouds. The fire licked at my feet. I screamed, but more from anxiety than agony.

How long would it take for the flames to set my feet alight? The light material of the dress was the real danger, just a spark could set it ablaze. Undulating smoke began to close in on me, entering my nose, stifling my breaths. My throat burned. I wanted to instinctively crouch over and cover my face, but I was tied up and the more I shifted around, the more apprehensive I became.

It would take a long time, this exact passage into death. Choking, heat, flesh catching, charring, being stripped away. I might yet be alive through much agonising suffering, begging for mercy, too late, with a lipless mouth.

These people had caught me like an animal, caged me like one, had tried to control and subdue me like one. Now they would roast me like one. It used to take so long to roast meat back home. At least that meat had been already blessedly dead.

It happened in a split second, while my mind was turned to my racing thoughts. More thunder bellowed, and I thought the earth shook, that the thunder had made fissures in the earth, that would spread until we were all nothing.

There was screaming, a sense of panic … I had shut my eyes when the skies lit up again, and then I felt it. The torrential rains did not ease in. They came on suddenly, pelting down like stones from the heavens. Heavy, cold droplets of rain that pricked icily at my skin at first, but after a few minutes it felt more like a battering, each drop playing to a rhythm in a celestial orchestra.

Through the white distorting rains, the blurred figures of people dashed for shelter, away from the open square which felt vulnerable to Nature's attack. Smoke rose up from my feet in little plumes until there were no flames. There was nothing but rain.

I was still here. Now. As the smoke cleared, I made out the figure of a displeased looking king and a handful of his people looking to him for instruction. He walked clumsily towards me, muttering to himself, one arm raised over his head like it could shield his face from the downpour.

When he was close enough, eyeing me from the corner of his eyes as he paced back and forth, I noted that the showers had washed the edge off of his stink. He glowered inches from my face.

"Death deserves better than you!" he growled, pointing his finger at me, and left it hanging mid-air.

His mouth made awkward shapes as he fumbled for words that did not come. The whole time his finger was still pointing at me, bopping ever so slightly as he clenched his teeth. I imagined fumes coming from his protuberant nose. He was raging.

He turned and walked back as the rains eased gradually. As the air cleared, I saw that Oktar was now standing with three militants to one side, and to the other was the Chief Whip, his bald head glistening after the deluge, his whip lying lifeless in a massive puddle.

King Carovor looked to Oktar and the militants, then to the Chief Whip. Left then right.

"Who checked whether today was fit for a burning?" The king shouted.

The armed men looked to and from each other bemusedly, and no one spoke up.

"Did no one check the weather?" grumbled the king.

The men responded in a chorus of muffled, inaudible sounds. The mad king wobbled over to the Chief Whip, who stood like a statue with his rigid upright posture and emotionless face.

What the hell is going on?

As the rains had temporarily lightened with the promise of more to come, Carovorians trickled back into the square to see what was happening.

The king grabbed up the Chief Punisher's whip, turned and walked back towards Oktar and the three militants. He threw his arm over his shoulder and with great effort lashed the whip out towards the group in a rage; but it was clear he lacked the skill to wield the weapon. The men did not move, still the lash was enough to cause piercing whelps to escape their lips like the sound of wolves that had been hurt badly, quite suddenly. Oktar gritted his teeth and not once his eyes reached to meet mine.

The mad king flung the whip to the wet ground towards the Chief.

"Must I do everything myself to get things right?" blurted out the king. "There cannot be a burning if there is rain! What shoddy planning!"

He shouted, "This cannot go unpunished. Someone always has to pay, you know that!"

"Sire," called out one of Oktar's militants, and Oktar's face distorted in disapproval.

"Respectfully, we did not recommend a burning today," said the young militant.

"You didn't?" Asked the king innocently.

"No sire," answered the man.

"Who is at fault then? Did you advise me against it?" asked the king.

The militant gulped, and his two colleagues flanking him eyed each other.

The king let out a heavy sigh. Just then another round of thunder roared.

"Someone has to pay and today it will be you lot! You will whip each other, finishing with the girl. But you will start with him!"commanded the mad king, pointing to the Chief Whip, who up until now had said nothing.

The older man did not move. I thought back confusedly to how he had been the first to bring me food and medicine; about the look in his eyes when I told him he was nothing but a glorified slave. I believe the Goddess opened me, opened my mouth.

Without thinking I blurted out.

"Ok, I'll do it! I'll do it!" I had to shriek repeatedly to get Carovor to react to me.

"You'll do what?" his eyebrows raised, but his ravenous eyes fell to travel down the outlines of my dark body, revealed to almost nakedness by the sodden, clinging, thin white dress.

"I will pledge allegiance to you. I will leave my old life behind," I confirmed.

A shudder ran through my exposed body and all of me sagged. Carovor could not fail to witness it. More than my words, the involuntary convulsion demonstrated I'd been finally, thoroughly subjugated.

The king's sight scanned me scornfully from head to toe.

"Was that so hard now?" he gritted through his teeth, then looked worn out from his searing rage.

Carovor started walking away, calling commands: "Perform the repentance ritual; then put her under the watch of Elder Darja. Leave her here for the rest of the day and night! The rain will do her some good."

Then, almost as an afterthought, he added, "Shave off her hair. All of it."

My blood ran cold.

"What? No wait! I said I'll bow! Please don't take my hair! Please! Please!" I screamed even after I could see him and his escort way off in the distance.

I broke into ragged sobs as the rains came heavier again. Under the deluge, they chopped my hair off and shaved it clean. They left the rain to wash the hair off my skin. My fat, long plaits were snagged amid the blackened, bedraggled wood around the foot of the cross, with the wild wind dragging at them, to eventually take them even farther from me … to Goddess knows where.

They took my hair. My hair was home, and home was in my hair. It was the same hair my Papa had touched with such love; the same hair I had washed in our river and streams; the one thing about me other villagers had admired and envied; the hair that had been a profound part of my identity.

My hair. No longer. This, too, Carovor had taken.

I felt naked to this world. Stripped and abased.

Better you had just let me burn.

EIGHT

Not Even Death

T took a beating from the pelting showers, as the heavens reopened up without restraint during the evening. I stayed there overnight, exposed to the elements, bound to hard wood, practically naked, shivering, weakened and defenceless, with my thoughts reeling from the pain of the burns on my feet. They had left my shaven hair amid the charred wood on the ground before me, like a kind of mockery: *Aye, look what we ripped from you, even this is no longer yours, look at it. Look!*

And I looked. Overnight, in the rain and soot of part-burnt wood, my fallen hair was not my own. The plaits lay limp, lifeless, and devoid of the music, laughter, love, and pain of my former life, that it had held securely among its strands.

It would no longer shield me, cover me in the ways that I felt it had. I could no longer smell it and catch the river's breath on it, or touch it and feel the fortitude flowing from my sinews through to every strand.

There was one good thing in all this dread: Papa never left me again. He stayed and he sang, and he kept me alive.

My mother had departed the second the fires beneath my feet went out.

The rains were so cold my body hurt from shivering. When the clouds dispersed, I thought that it was Papa who had cleared the sky, and brought out the stars so I could see them. He had named me after a rare shooting star, after all. I didn't spot any kind of shooting star that night, but the ones I saw shone on me. They shone hard.

"Papa? See what they have done?" I opened a part of me that I only ever used to let my father see. The rest of the world was never allowed to see it.

Without reason, the world of man had cast me aside almost from birth. Now it had taken my home, my family; robbed me of my virtue, and even compelled me to renounce my faith. I hadn't really, not in my heart. But though my lie had been necessary for the sake of survival and safety, to buy the time I needed to plot and grow strong again, it was still a lie made against the Mother Goddess and my deepest beliefs.

The world wanted to break me … Imagine what it would do to me if it knew I did have a feeling heart under all the granite?

"Why did you have to go, Papa?"

But my father didn't leave me with that thought. A curling current of air brought his voice to my ears.

Idzorah-Ulka, as sure as the sun rises and sets, nothing can separate you from my love. Not even death. I will be with you in all things good and sustaining, even until your last breath, and beyond. Even when your eyes cannot see me, I will be there, holding you.

I had never been an obedient child, but I always listened to my papa. I listened to him now. This would be the last time I'd ever utter words of Papa *physically taking leave*. His disembodied words had reassured me in a way I desperately needed, if I would endure beyond these tribulations.

Throughout everything that had befallen me in this life, Papa had always spoken truth to me. So I reminded myself of that, and took him at his word when he pledged he would be here, watching, guiding and still loving me ... even if I didn't feel it.

In the morning, a woman crowned with a head of neatly rolled hair, white like a coconut's jelly, made her way to me accompanied by that pitiable girl from the crowd, who had come to pray for my soul, even as her words had damned me to hell. The woman's slanted eyes inspected me, a distinctive mole rested on the tip of her thin upper lip, her stern face devoid of any expression. Her eyes moved to the girl beside her.

"My name is Yishmai," said the girl, who looked a few years younger than me. She was a dainty thing with voluminous plaits snaking elegantly around her head. "Elder Darja will show you the Upright Way. You'll see there's nothing hard to it really and —"

Her shrill voice had trailed off in the wind.

"I don't care, I don't care," I was muttering, but when she didn't seem to hear me, I screamed, "Shut up!"

And she did. She didn't say another word to me for the rest of the day. Elder Darja didn't flinch. She lifted her chin and stared hard, as hands busied around me removing my bindings.

‡

THE CARRIAGE DIDN'T TAKE TOO long to arrive there, but their residence was still a good distance from the square, the homes, and the main hubs of activity. It was not difficult to read into this; they wanted to keep those like me from "infecting" everyone else with our "evils," until we had been deemed fit to be around others.

New converts lived in this area, littered with a string of buildings walking distance from each other. Commune 12, where I was to be housed, was the very last, spaced out about three buildings from Commune 11.

Commune 12, I would later learn, housed the "troublesome" ones. Four of us if you didn't count Yishmai, who seemed to live there with Elder Darja and round-bellied, blonde-haired Elder Dawn, who mostly repeated Elder Darja's orders, rarely giving instruction of her own. She had a lighter disposition and walked around humming, with a faint smile on her face.

We stood in a straight line, one behind the other, outside the building. Darja stood tall at the head, then walked beside the line, with Dawn in her shadows. She paused and looked at the lad at the very front of the line.

"Tuli," she said to him.

No answer. He didn't move his head to look at her from the little I could see from where I was standing at the very back.

"Your-name-is-Tuli," she tried again in a staccato rhythm. "Say, Yes Elder Darja."

"Ye-yes Elder Darja," said a fine voice.

"Das right" said Elder Dawn trailing behind, nodding.

Next in line, a woman of seventy years or so, who looked fit in stature but couldn't hide the years written on her face. Years or hardships.

"This one here is a recent from de old world," chimed Dawn, hands on hips.

Darja stared at the woman. Tilted her head, said, "Mary," and walked onto the next in line as the woman answered, "Yes, Elder Darja."

Right in front of me was a thin, clean-shaven man with pale skin. His head was small, and he bore a silver piercing that went through the top bit of cartilage in his left ear then connected through the lower cartilage of the same ear. When I'd first arrived I'd noticed he had other piercings too — one through his brow, and another noticeably through his nose, which was crusted with blood. But these things I noticed last … after the X tattooed across his mouth.

Darja turned to look at Dawn and lifted a subtle brow.

"Dis the one that don't talk," said Dawn, nodding her head. "A mute."

Darja looked his way again.

"What shall we call you?" She thought aloud. "Noah," said Darja lifting a finger to the air, while stepping towards me.

"A nod will do for you," Dawn said pointing her finger to Noah, whose head made a movement I hardly saw.

"You will be called Wren," said Elder Darja, looking at me. I was still staring at the back of Noah's head.

A hand grabbed my chin roughly to the left, my eyes meeting Elder Darja's. "You remind the king of the bird, Wren" she said, in a tone lacking highs and lows, passion or apathy; like she believed words could convey meaning just as well without vocal expression. A slight twitch of her mouth made me think she was trying to sound complimentary.

She then slapped me hard in the face—harder than someone who looked like this had a right to slap. I got the message: *It was not a question.* The woman was simply letting me know that whenever she said that name, she meant me.

"Yes, Elder Darja," I answered, feeling the sting in my cheek.

She pushed my chin back to the front, and walked ahead of the line again as Dawn began reciting a list of rules.

"Do as you're told and everything will be merry," said

Dawn with a hearty smile. "And do as you're told means, do *exactly* as you're told," she clarified.

"Our word, our Law is what King Carovor commands. He has the wisdom. He saved us from the Old World and established this new order that spares us from destruction," she beamed. "To understand what it means to be Carovorian you must strive to live like us. Don't question your elders, they are the mouthpiece of the King. Do as you're told, take only what is given to you and do not question your King. Understood?"

"Yes, Elder Dawn," a half chorus of lack-lustre voices answered. Dawn was happy all the same and clapped her hands loudly.

"Right, time to scrub up!" She grinned, leading us inside.

‡

WE'D BEEN RUTHLESSLY scrubbed clean, dressed and brought before Elder Darja in the quarters where we would now be housed.

A narrow walkway led from the front doorway of the well-kept wooden building, into a spacious room that smelled mildly of vanilla. As we walked into the room, I trailed my finger along the smooth planks of tanned wood, until it caught on a splinter. A dot of bright red, like a lily-leaf beetle, appeared on my finger and quickly expanded until it was running down my index finger.

"Tiny buggers," Papa used to say, carefully hand-picking the beetles from his bulbs. Whenever the flowers died, I knew he was fretting on the inside by the way he'd grind his teeth while staring at the holes left by the tiny pests. How could a bug, a mere bug, so small, so fragile and easily crushed, wreck so much havoc on our plants?

Every time I asked Papa, he'd shrug it off and say with a smile "No bother, we'll start again. Get them next time." I would smile back, assured.

Today there was no smile, only horror as the red on my finger morphed into a rapidly expanding pool on Papa's chest. He lay bleeding out, dying before me again in our family hut, as the red took form and started coming towards me.

"Wren!" A voice pulled me back to the present. Elder Darja's head was tilted as she stared at me, hands on waist. The new converts were huddled together on a bench, Yishmai and Elder Dawn stood to the side, all staring.

She handed me a piece of clean cloth. "Wipe that up and sit down," she looked to my red-streaked finger, before pointing to the bench.

We sat quietly listening to Elder Darja go over the rules and house chores. A faint breeze blew through a nearby open window, and for a moment it was so quiet I could have forgotten where I was.

Elder Darja was intimidating despite her diminutive stature. Her facial features were pointed, and she bore a frown with pursed lips. I don't think she was trying to frown. I think that's just the way her face stayed. She walked upright, but with stiffness. Her eyes were the grey of metal knife-blades and just as cutting when she sliced them down your cheek. All the new converts feared her. Her orders were rarely challenged, whatever they were.

Us new converts in this building reported to Elder Darja, who was to "teach us the enlightened ways of the upright society." I tried to imagine what that could mean. Fleeting visions of slavery, human trafficking back to the old world my parents had long escaped, and new societies with inhuman practices flooded my mind's eye.

I shuddered to think of what else they could threaten me with, having already dished out such cruel punishments to me in my early days. Whatever it was, I didn't want to find out.

I had to find a way to regain my strength, find my equilibrium and be ready, so that when the time was right, I could run far from here. Leave this place and figure out my next move. But I would need them to trust me. I would have to behave, to pretend that I was fine, and not yield to the raging anger and engulfing pain bubbling up in my belly.

I had a plan; and I was so desperate for it to work that I would not even whisper it to the night winds wherein Papa resided, for fear that my words or very thoughts would sabotage me somewhere along the way.

We would sleep in a hall of small beds lined up next to each other in rows. That was adjacent to the main room where we were to congregate daily for instruction. The kitchen was at the back, and to the other side of the building was the washroom and latrine.

Every day we were awakened at 5 a.m. by the jarring clangs of a large, hand-held bell rung enthusiastically by Elder Dawn. We were expected to follow the exacting regimen set for us with promptness and efficiency. The day began with an order to wash and change into clean plain garments.

There was little privacy in those first months. In the washroom we stripped from head to toe, while Dawn observed us. We then sat in a row and recited commandments after the elder at front: "I accept King Carovor as my king. I will obey my king and his vessels. I will honour him. I will not seek any interest outside of my king's commands." And so it went.

After that, we scrubbed the floors, hand washed the house laundry, picked crops from neighbouring fields, weeded the garden-beds. I felt, as a personal punishment, I was always one of the girls Elder Darja assigned to fetch chopped wood for fire. Some of the buildings in the compound were fitted with solar panels but there was none such in Commune 12. I think that was intentional.

I used to be strong, but my physical endurance had been relentlessly eroded by the suffering I'd faced since capture by Carovor's people. In those early days, in Commune 12 we only ate a small meal comprised of some of the collected crop, and only at the end of the day when all converts had completed their chores. If someone didn't complete their chores, then none of us ate. It took a few days to figure out, but it was a kind of clever thing they did.

Neither of the elders intervened in the beginning, and I wondered why, waited nervously for the ensuing punishment. But none followed. First it was silent Noah who had refused to move from his cross-legged position in bed to do his chores, so we didn't eat. The rest of us still toiled, only to realise at dinner time that no food was coming, with Noah's chores undone.

Second day, same thing. By the end of that evening, one could see steam seeping from Mary's pursed lips as she side-eyed Noah, still sat cross-legged on his bed, while the clinking of bowls and scent of warm food sailing into the room from the kitchen tormented us.

Day three, before Elder Dawn could ring the murderous bell before the crack of dawn, I turned in bed to see a shadow at the foot of Noah's bed. I sat up. Tuli was already sat up looking. The shadow moved to Noah's side, and I made out that it was Mary. She nudged Noah hard. He sat up, rubbing his eyes. Mary leaned over and whispered into his ears. When the bell went off Noah got out of bed, and proceeded with his chores like the rest of us.

Besides that one time I saw Mary whisper into Noah's ears, back then no one said anything to the other; every convert was for self, each suspicious of all the others.

Another time, as Mary sweated profusely from a fever, the three of us stood around her bed looking at each other unblinkingly. Elder Dawn had earlier rung the bell, saw us all wash and dress and never prodded or poked Mary or commented on her state. After she assigned the chores accordingly she strutted out to the kitchen humming like nothing was amiss.

"Right, time to go," beamed Yishmai, who strolled into the room from the stairwell. She looked around at us three then went, "Well, what yer waiting on?" More exchanged glances among us three.

I walked away briskly to the storeroom and brought back three cocoyea brooms made from the coconut tree's long-leafed frond. I said no words, but extended two of the brooms towards Tuli and Noah, who glanced at each other. Noah took the broom from my hand first, then Tuli. We would do Mary's chores before our own to make sure we ate that day.

I tried to keep my head down and to renew my motivation to keep going every day. But it was hard, like laboured breathing, living in a loop: day after day, repeating the same tasks, in the same space, in silence, not knowing what was going to happen or whom to trust. It was a different kind of punishment.

It was like you felt an air of unease that some morbid thing was in hiding, waiting around the corner, but you didn't know which bit of the day, or week or month it would finally occur. So when something in our daily routines changed, anything or anyone new appeared, the unease and tension it brought became nearly physically palpable.

One day, after chores were distributed, Elder Darja

informed us that when we had proven our faith, we would then be assigned community chores: duties at the private homes of other cult members who were too ill, too old and frail, too busy or simply too above the work to do it themselves. Some of us would be accompanied/chaperoned by other Carovorians at first.

Yishmai was assigned to be my chaperone. She wasn't a new convert. Apparently she was Elder Darja's "daughter," and she was made to follow me about to ensure I remained obedient and virtuous, in step with their ways. Every day she gave a report on my performance and general behaviour to Darja.

By then I had stopped counting days. I wasn't sure it served a purpose any more, since I accepted it might be some time before I got any opportunity to escape. This made the days seem longer and harder. Even with Papa's presence I felt profound loneliness. I was in a house of new converts, but none were from my village, and in the beginning there were rarely opportunities to speak, with hawk-eyed guards or elders constantly monitoring us, and suspicion among us rife. At night when the lights went out, I could hear the musical symphony played by crickets and company outside. Everything else remained silent.

It bothered me that I had not seen a single person I knew, particularly my younger twin sisters. I didn't want to talk to anyone in this corrupt, twisted place, and from the looks on many of the other converts' faces, it was evident they felt the same.

But my growing desire for company or some familiarity had clearly become a sort of food I needed for survival.

It didn't surprise me, then, when one day I found myself responding in like manner to Yishmai's sociability.

On the way back to the main building on that day, I stumbled and dropped the armful of logs I'd been heaving under. Exhaustion had cracked my dogged determination, and when the wood dropped from my suddenly sagging arms, I had gone down, too. I was slow to rise.

I felt faint and flagging, the heat of the sun sapping my energy still further. I closed my eyes and let my head hang down. Then the light dimmed. I opened my eyes. There was a shadow lying along the ground, crossing over my own. When I looked up, Yishmai had moved near me, her body shielding me from the sun's rays. I waited for a rebuke, but she extended her hand ... with a smile. I didn't even think. I took it, and she pulled me carefully to my feet.

"Come on, I'll help you," she said, in that child-like voice of hers, bending to gather the scattered wood fuel. She was so healthy and spry, that by the time I had lifted two logs, she had picked up all the others.

As she stacked them deftly in my arms, she declared, "It will get easier, Wren, and you will see it's not so bad. When they see that you are sorry, truly, and that you understand our ways, you'll only get community chores — lighter, easier work — and more opportunities to get to know our people. You'll even have some time for yourself each day." She smiled again.

"Thanks," I muttered, indecisively.

We fell in step side by side. I could see she had slowed her strides to not overtax me again. It might seem small, but having been so long deprived of legitimate, living human kindness I was grateful.

Elder Darja is your biological mother?" I asked after a while.

"Yes. She's a good mother," Yishmai replied.

"So you have both been a part of this ... society for a while?"

"I was born into it, like Elder Darja herself. It makes it a lot easier for us I suppose; but I've been here from the start of my life, so I know it's not that bad."

I considered her cheery look sidelong, and almost envied her naivety.

We were making our way into the building where I had to drop off the wood when Yishmai touched my shoulder and whispered emphatically, "I *am* sorry for everything that happened to you. I didn't think it would be like that."

She turned and walked away, to report her adapted version of my day's labour to her mother.

‡
‡

I WAS surprised at how fast time went by after that. The days had always felt agonising, owing to the combination of loneliness, heat, heartache, and heaviness of enslavement. Being in Yishmai's transformed company somehow made my varying levels of pains bearable.

Enduring this existence was crucial. In spite of the fact that there was too much happening inside me and around me, despite the fact that I was repeatedly at risk of losing all constraint, I had to endure this way of living being inflicted on me.

Most days I wanted to float up into the blue skies, to ride on the back of the clouds, to be lifted higher than even that by Papa's loving arms. That never happened. I was stuck in this mortal world fighting for a chance to live free.

I hadn't figured out how I would do that yet, but I needed to have a chance. That meant a few things.

There was no time to process the pain of my earlier nightmares: my ruined village; my dead mother's eyes gazing back at me; my lost seven-year-old sisters; the theft of Papa's physical presence; the violation of my body and mind. My stretch of resistance had made me too much of a spectacle. I had earned notoriety to my detriment — eyes were *always* on me. Most likely.

I hadn't seen the devil that was Oktar since the attempted burning, but I expected that he knew my every move.

I had to learn to survive the days again. I was wild on the inside. I was still the same me that used to run with the wolves, me who hunted in the dark, and let fly arrows so that any one would hit between my target's eyes. These skills would serve me out in a forest full of Nature's challenges. But for now, in this "Godman"-made place, I had to look to less conspicuous means of survival. Routines. Well I had those whether or not I wanted them, I just had to embrace them.

I had to make myself blend into the crowd better. I had to appear *tamed* (How I hated that word!). I allowed Yishmai to help me achieve all these things. Enough that others noticed, too.

It was to be my last morning doing this particular routine for new converts: waking, washing, reciting commune rules, assigned chores, dinner, bedtime. After my very public morning wash, Elder Darja pulled me aside to where Yishmai waited good-naturedly.

"It has not gone unnoticed that you have altered your insubordinate ways to align more closely with ours, Wren" began Elder Darja.

"As a reward, you will be permitted to stay in a room behind the workhouse, and you will be assigned two hours for your own personal use daily. You still have work to do as regards your spirituality; but I do not doubt that spending time with Yishmai in these coming weeks will help that."

The elder must have read the question in my eyes as to why "these coming weeks" should be much different from the ones I'd already spent in her daughter's company, because she expanded, "You will assist her in the special, essential work to be done as we prepare for the God-King's Annual Togetherness Festival."

I managed a smile that, thankfully, passed muster as I turned my eyes on Yishmai. She beamed back, seeming as assured in my delight as her own.

I cleared my throat. "When does the festival start?" I asked.

"Three months time," the girl said gleefully, egging me on to follow her so we could go to the market to begin gathering elements and particulars to prepare for the event.

"Imagine glowing lights under the evening sky, music, dancing, food and drink, everyone dressed up in fancy costumes! Ohh! It's like a dream!" exclaimed Yishmai, gesturing ardently with her hands.

"We celebrate everything we have, make new appointments, grant exceptional members awards and gifts, and show our thanks to the king for bringing us out of the havoc of the Old World into this new one."

Yishmai wouldn't shut up about why it was a privilege to partake in preparations for the Annual Togetherness Festival. It sounded too good to be true.

As we ventured towards the market, we stepped more into the heart of the town. The frequency of buildings, houses and people increased, but there remained something natural about the place. Perhaps it was because I could feel that at least one river ran on its perimeter, or because the forests were within reach. *My* reach.

Yet no matter how far we moved from the buzzing market streets or the king's court, the true nature of this place couldn't be escaped. It was heavily ordered, and not only by the people wearing uniforms. It thrived off rules, enforcement, threats of punishment, and public examples made of those who broke the order.

Yishmai skipped along ahead of me, swinging a wide-open, rounded basket. Her innocence was almost revolting. Her tiny stature made her look like a child — from behind, if I overlooked her pale skin and straight hair, she appeared a slightly more grown up, taller version of my twin sisters. This matched her demeanour and child-like voice too.

Ahead, we could see clusters of people buzzing about, a sea of pure white, so calm, so deceiving.

Yishmai, though, was not looking ahead. She had stopped, and was peering up into one of the nearby trees. Tall trees, with wide spreading branches of light wood. They were bedecked by ornate leaves the colour of turmeric root stains on my mother's fingers, mixed in with swirls and speckles of brown the shade of her skin.

"Sweet king Carovor!" Yishmai exclaimed, jaw dropped open.

I quickened my stride and hurried over to see what she found so exciting. Slithering along one of the branches, minding its own business, was a dark brown snake with yellow stripes. I laughed.

"It's just a snake. Come on," I pressed, trying to walk on. She looked at me with disbelief.

"Just a snake? It's incredible, Wren! Never have I seen one this up close. Elder Darja usually makes me walk on, says they're dangerous," she explained.

"They're not."

"No?"

"Ribbon snakes are harmless."

"Eek!" She squealed and her voice went higher the more excited she got.

I looked at her, this girl so guileless and in wonder. Something in her amazement moved me in an affable way. Without thinking, I began climbing, my hands and feet instantly remembering this skill, taking me capably upwards. It was like going home. The rough bark against my limbs, catching at the light material of my dress as I shimmied up, reminded me of everything I missed.

A smile crept its way onto my lips as recollection settled on me, like particles of dust: I and Yanu racing up the sycamore trees to finally clear up our longest argument. *Which of us is the best?* And the best simply did not mean the fastest, because Yanu and I, the greatest tree climbers among all in the village, knew that climbing a tree was an actual art form — an assessment.

Tree climbing was *the* absolute mother of all assessments. Were you strong? In body ok, but what about your mind? How did you reason? Could you focus and aim right under pressure? What kind of a risk-taker were you?

"What are you doing! What — Wren, no! Come down! I mean, what —" Yishmai's whiny protests sucked me back into the present. The girl was lifting to her toes, then hopping from one foot to the next in agitation.

"Wait," I reassured her. I sat on a branch near enough to the fairly small creature, reached out and gently picked it up by its midsection, supporting its thin body with my hands.

I could hear Yishmai whimpering under her breath. She seemed sincerely frightened for me. The snake's body was dry and warm to touch, felt comfortingly resilient; and in the afternoon sun, there in that tree, a flicker of something warm sparked in my belly.

"See?" I said. I started to smile down at Yishmai's girlishly giggling form. The smile stuck hard, and I almost tipped out of the tree, taking the hapless snake with me. I saw him coming. Oktar. He was attended by two of his forceful-looking militants.

I'd always known he was around somewhere, but the sudden sight of him caused my hearing to go for a few long seconds. The tree felt rising and falling under me. The snake picked up on my fear and tightened its coils around my wrist.

When my hearing returned, I made out Yishmai hissing up at me, looking alarmed but trying to not attract attention, "Get down! Come on, now!"

I can't move.

Oktar's men stopped at attention a few yards from the tree. He continued on and moved in closer, with a repugnant grin that shifted the tattoos on his cheeks.

Even before Oktar had ordered his men to stop where they were, Yishmai had spun and pelted off ... without me. His callous gaze had not followed her flight, but held me in his sight as if to fix me to the branch I wavered upon.

"Not so long out of your cage and you're back to your feral ways, wildling. Fly to me, little bird," Oktar compelled.

"No!" I snapped, looking all around me, shaking inside. The snake was trying to slip away from me, unsettled by what I was emanating.

"Don't make me come up there. That will only make me angry; and you know what I'm like when I am angry," he snarled.

I had survived till now, and up to this point I'd thought that there were few things left capable of evoking terror in me. Somehow this demon of a man managed to do just that.

I could hear and feel my hurrying, hammering heartbeats. They seemed to judder my unsteady body. I couldn't seem to get enough air in, so I opened my mouth. The more I gasped, the faster my heart banged on inside my chest walls. I pulled in mouthfuls of air at a controlled pace, trying to steady myself.

I looked out over the far distance I could see from my perch in the tree. No sign of Yishmai. *She left me.* Swift as lightning riding on that realisation, it struck me that I could do something other than cower in a tree.

"Ok, I'll come down," I tried to sound compliant and cowed.

Oktar began to laugh, beckoning me down with his fingers. I lifted my hands slowly towards a branch, as if to lay the snake down. Instead, I flung it at Oktar's upturned face. He was visibly startled, but instantly clawed at the unfortunate creature. Those were the only bits of his reaction I got to see.

My body grated harshly against the bark as I slid, then sprang out of the tree, landed with a thud, upped and ran.

NINE

A Quiet Place

T could feel the weakness in my entire body as I pushed myself forward towards the bustling market. My lungs had caught fire. I didn't have to look back to be sure they were following me. I could hear shouting behind.

I rushed into the marketplace, my expression surely wild with desperation. I wasn't going to let Oktar mess up my mind or ruin my plans. People cried out in surprise as I bounced off them, but no one moved out of the way. I knocked a few people down, and each setback made me rage internally.

"Out the way!" harsh male voices shouted in my wake.

I risked turning to see how close they were. In that instant I smacked into a man pushing a wheelbarrow of apples across my path. He wasn't much bigger than me, so we both went down in a tangle of limbs, overturning cart and flying fruit. Past my pain I had the presence of mind to try and crawl on all fours, rather than risk twisting an ankle by stepping on one of the many big apples rolling around. I crept and wriggled maybe four feet beyond the muddle, before a heavy booted foot pushed me flat down.

I started hyperventilating. I was sprawled and helpless,

all energy draining out of me as adrenaline ebbed and raw panic returned.

Oktar stooped beside me. Everything slowed to give me enough time to suffer the gloating on his expression. What that look made me feel was heavier than the boot pressing down on my spine. Oktar said nothing for some time.

"Who do you think you are, mmm?" he finally asked.

My mouth started moving, like I was chanting again. Except I couldn't hear much of myself, as the sense of sound diminished, leaving only a painful, buzzing vibration.

"You might have them fooled, but I know better," he bared his teeth.

At a nod from Oktar, the weight lifted off my back. He turned me over himself. His two companions were hovering over me, their machetes pointed at my face. Oktar dragged me roughly by the ankles behind a stall.

"Move!" he barked at a man who had been standing there. As the fellow scuttled away, Oktar loomed over me, unbuckling his thick belt.

"No, no!" I whimpered, instant realisation twisting my gut.

I tried to lift myself up off the ground. He shoved me so viciously back down my head whacked the cobblestones. It almost rendered me unconscious.

"Move, wildling" he rumbled, "and a machete will go through your throat. I promise."

I flopped onto my stomach, all I could manage in my current pathetic state, and tried to crawl away. Oktar trod on my nearer hand, then used the same foot to push me over prone.

"Do you know why I turned you over? Hmm? So you could look me in the face. So you will remember who is boss," he spat.

And like no one was there watching, he reached for his

trousers. I looked away and waited, but nothing happened. After a long moment, I dared to move my eyes back in his direction.

Oktar had paused, a look of uncertainty on his face. His expression contorted and took on an uglier appearance as he kept looking down at himself. He was limp. Horror: that was the look on his face, horror.

I waited, watching him for his next move.

Oktar zipped up his trousers in a rough tug and dragged me to my feet. I tried to protest, but that was stopped by the hand he slammed to my throat. He clamped his fingers roughly around my neck. I gasped for air, drool spilling from my gaping mouth.

My hands scrabbled desperately at Oktar's, trying to lessen the pressure on my neck. I couldn't draw breaths. I was passing out. Darkness was descending over my sight. My arms were going limp, my hands falling away from slapping at the choking hold. Past the shadowy fog, I thought I heard Yishmai's high, piping voice calling my name. That couldn't be ... she had left me. Stranger still, as the gloom descended and took me deeper in, there came the unmatched clipped tone of Elder Darja snapping, "Unhand the convert, Oktar!"

++
++

I SEE HIS FACE. *Soldier*. Why is he here? Surely his own powerful royal family would have negotiated his release as soon as they discovered he'd been taken. He should be long gone out of this hell-hole. But ... here he is.

Soldier comes to me, his hazel eyes alight with warmth as he looks at me. Up close his eyes are a universe of their own. Around their golden rim, I see hues of green leaking out into a mesmerising pool whose colours shift with the light — like the glinting waters of the Truro pools near to home. Papa, Yanu and I would hike there sometimes on lazy days, to stare into the enchanting waters.

Soldier must know I am weak, tired and hurt, because he lifts me. His arms feel so good and strong around me. So does his heartbeat, when I lay a grateful palm against his chest. I wanted to say, *Take me from this place.* But I stop myself, momentarily irritated that I'd even think to ask anything of him. *He is your enemy Idzorah-Ulka*, I chide myself.

Soldier, though, reads my deepest need. He turns and begins carrying me away, his eyes smiling down into my own. We are surrounded by radiant white light, with a sparkling ray of yellow-gold shining on his handsome face. His movement is so light and unhindered, like he is a being of air and spirit. Yet, his voice is firm and bold, when he bids me, "Tell me your name." I open my mouth to answer, but can find nothing to let out.

I've forgotten my name.

"Wren? Wake up, Wren," a voice calls as from a long way away.

I start to ask Soldier who he thinks it might be, but the voice grows louder, more insistent, "Wren! Open your eyes!"

I jolted awake and instantly clutched my head. It pounded fit to explode. I slumped back, hoping that would make the room stop swirling. Elder Darja was sitting at my side, wearing her characteristic scowl. Yishmai approached with a bowl. She sat on the other side of me and rested a cool wet cloth upon my throbbing forehead.

"What were you thinking? I specifically said, 'Go straight to the market and come back.' What is all this about climbing trees and making a commotion in the market!" Elder Darja said, lips trembling startlingly.

Yishmai tried to intervene with, "But Wren only —"

"Both of you!" Elder Darja shrilled, "You were given instruction. 'Go to the market, get these things and come back.' That means no detours. Do as you're told. This is what happens when orders are not obeyed!"

"It was my fault, Elder Darja!" Yishmai blurted again. "I wanted to see something, and Wren was just trying to be good to me, like we're told to be with each other."

"No, no!" I interjected, finding that I wanted to spare Yishmai any blame. All she'd done was be impressed by the snake. Nobody but me made me climb that tree.

Elder Darja was having none of it. She had been shaking her head, but now lifted a halting hand in my face. She got up and walked to the door. She turned back to eye her daughter and me, her expression unreadable like it mostly was; then looked out the open doorway and directed, "Bring her here."

Confused, I was about to ask Yishmai who her mother was talking to, but two soldiers strode into the room. They came straight to my bed, hauled me out of it, and carried me, feet dragging, outside the door. They dropped me on my knees in the grass.

"I take no pleasure in this, but it's for your own good," said Elder Darja. She spun and took a rough grip on Yishmai's shoulder. The girl, who must have endured being grabbed that way before, didn't look too taken aback, until her guardian griped, "People will say I cannot control my own. Kneel down next to her!"

Years of compliance to her mother's will meant Yishmai never thought to protest. The lashes stung dreadfully, the rod cut from a bush was sturdy yet flexible, like the ones my own mother had used when I disobeyed her. I bit back every bitter tear; swallowed them to help fill the sea of hatred and malice that kept rising and rising in my heart toward these people. One day ... one day I will have strength enough to drown them in that sea.

After just the first stroke, Yishmai yowled, then sobbed profusely. Both times after, she did the same. When it was done, she hunched over and hugged herself as she wept on. Yea, I thought nastily for a second, *it's not so bad.* Then I felt sorry for her.

Elder Darja had stood in front of us the whole time and never so much as flinched.

I stared up at her as Yishmai cried. I traced the fine lines that ran around her eyes, making her appear frail and vulnerable. But she was far from either.

My lips trembled as anger bubbled up inside me.

"Shhhh," Yishmai shushed, before I could say anything. I don't know what I was going to say. I was just upset.

"I beg your pardon?" Darja spun around.

"Nothing," I answered.

"Nothing what?" She looked furious.

I looked at the ground, trying to hold my tongue. An unfulfilled tear trickled down my cheek.

Elder Darja lunged and slapped me hard across the face.

"That will give you something to cry for."

"After all I suffered today, you still kneel me down to whip me?" I complained.

"It was your disobedience that got you into this mess!" she bawled. Tremors shook her sagging cheeks.

"My diso-"

"Shhhh!" she grabbed my face between her calloused hands. "Oktar needed to teach you a lesson. Punishment is what you get when you don't obey the rules," she sang the last few words like they were a fun melody.

"And the next time you question me, Wren, you will get

ten lashes more than these, heavier and more painful than this time!"

She straightened up, and scowled at me and Yishmai.

"You — your recklessness, your folly will be the end of my daughter!" Elder Darja exclaimed, pointing an accusatory finger at me.

Elder Darja's pointy, stern face twitched. For a moment she was the most expressive I had ever seen her. Even Yishmai was affected by it, because she stopped crying, her eyes riveted by her mother's visage.

"Make sure the market goods are acquired before the end of the day. Both of you! Yishmai, you will have no dinner this evening." With that, the Elder headed stiffly back to the hall.

"Yes, Elder Darja," mumbled Yishmai, even though the elder was gone out of hearing.

Silence took over for the rest of the day, until I was well enough to venture out with the girl, who had come back to help me.

++
++

"YOU INSULT ME! And I am your only friend!" Yishmai squealed at me on the way to the market.

"You are?" I asked dryly.

"Yes! Do you know what they say? Some whisper that you are of unsound mind, and they fear it will infect them. And how can I argue? I've seen what they've seen — the things you do. I can only try to elicit some sympathy, some … pity on your behalf," she enlightened.

"I am obliged, Yishmai; but please don't trouble yourself with trying to get pity on my account."

"You're so arrogant!" she shrilled again, her lips trembling just like her mother's had not so long ago.

"Me? No. I am many things, but proud is not one of them. I am sad for you," I shrugged.

"Your arrogance makes you speak out of turn, Wren" she snapped.

"No, really, it is I who should pity you. You have eyes but you cannot see."

She said nothing, but pouted and breathed huffily as she tramped along beside me. Her basket bounced against her knee in what seemed a peeved sort of way.

I stopped and turned to her. "Yishmai, who will remove the veil that shrouds you in darkness? Who, but you?" I asked, but she never responded and that was the end of that.

‡
‡

DREAD SETTLED on me as we approached the market. Yishmai must have reverted to form and softened up. She rested a hand on my shoulder, softly; but I jumped a mile anyway.

"Elder Darja had a word, he won't bother you any more."

I should have said "Thanks," or "How can you be sure?" or "Why would he listen to her?" But I stayed mute and moved along.

I was feeling so many things, relief not being one of them. I found myself anticipating Oktar stepping out from every shadowy corner. Whenever someone shouted suddenly nearby, I twisted around and half-crouched, momentarily sure I'd heard his voice, ready to dart for cover and hide. A stabbing pain started plaguing me in the centre of my chest whenever I drew breath. I stopped often to grip there. Was I having a heart attack?

"Take deep, slow breaths," Yishmai said, her hand on my back. "In for four, out for four." And though they were painful at first, after a few of them, the ache eased away like a fading bad memory.

Any anxiety I had shifted focus as we passed the square bordering the market. A bloodied man had been strung up to a makeshift pole. He drew all my attention, and I carefully examined his face. He looked thin and weak, unkempt with long facial hair. His white clothes were dirty. Yes ... I recognised him; at last I recognised someone, even if he was just one of *Soldier's* men. He had guarded the entrance of the tent I'd been kept in, before the Carovorians had drugged then incarcerated us. He looked so beaten down, I doubted that he would last much longer. I doubted, but who knew? I had discovered the strength of human will. I was still here after all; maybe he might make it, too.

"They say he tried to escape," a man buzzed to his female companion, who was carrying a small babe, as they walked past close to us.

Our path would take us past where Soldier's man languished. Many carried on like he wasn't even there. When people did stop to peer, I assumed that they were newly indoctrinated. Yishmai said nothing about it, either, but when I turned to walk away I saw her steal a glance when she thought I was not looking.

"Come on," said Yishmai, after she saw what she saw. She sped briskly up so she was walking ahead of me.

In the heart of the market, the many sounds blended into one all-encompassing mass of noise. Was it my imagination that many faces all seemed to be looking right at me? Were people pointing? I shook my head and tried to breathe the way Yishmai had taught me earlier. It had helped then; it might again. But there were so many faces, and Oktar's appeared among them in several different directions. Impossible for him to move so fast, be all around.

Don't think of him. Don't! Look at something else. Look for something else. Papa's voice filled me with relief. I obeyed. I made myself consciously look around me, into faces of people here, to perceive that they were just going about their business. I started sifting through them with my forest-trained eyesight, looking for someone to concentrate on: perhaps someone who I knew from some other place than here; someone who wasn't strung up, in pain and dying. Even someone like *Soldier.*

"Fresh from the north, get your soursop right here," belted out a loud female voice, that lifted free even from amid the other market noises.

"Here," called Yishmai, pulling me by a finger to the stall owned by the powerful-voiced woman. She was voluptuous and sunny, with long, thick blonde tresses haloing her face. The abundance of hair on her head made me more conscious of the absence of my own.

"Let me see this one and that one," Yishmai indicated two of the large green fruits with knobby spikes along the exterior.

The seller cut the fruits in half to reveal their smooth white interiors for our approval. As the woman was bagging them, Yishmai began poking at other items on sale. That's when I heard a familiar voice.

I swung around, and scanned the faces streaming by, stopping and going. At last my sight lit on the face to match the voice. At a stall mere paces away, my village's Oracle was beckoning customers to a table heavy with fruit and hand-crafted baskets. I didn't take my eyes off her, for I feared if I did she would vanish into thin air like she'd never been there to begin with.

"I'll get the thing for the thing from over there," I mumbled to Yishmai.

Without checking if she had heard me, I crossed to the former seer's stall. As I drew near, I marvelled that I had recognised her — she looked like she had aged ten years since I saw her last. Maybe if I had not first heard her voice, but had only glanced her in passing, I might have continued on and never looked twice. But, I would have known her voice anywhere. I had heard it many a time, including that unforgettable moment in my infancy catastrophe. Some people contended that it was impossible for me to recall that. There were a lot of things they deemed impossible ... but I'd done them anyway.

Her thick, braided hair had gone almost completely grey and was unkempt. Her face was pinched and careworn. She was vocalising her stall's goods, but her eyes never looked up. I was standing against her table, and still she never looked up.

"Oracle," I said in a hushed tone.

Her gaze at last lifted to meet mine and widened with immediate recognition. I had always felt I despised her, but looking into her dark eyes was like looking through an open window and seeing my village. Her lips parted, but she offered no words.

"Oracle, it's me, Idzorah-Ulka!" It elated me, after so long, to gasp my real name to someone who already knew it. Still she said nothing. She just looked at me, or through me like she was a ghost in a shell. Or I was.

"What do you see? Tell me!" I demanded.

I was growing markedly desperate, leaning almost halfway across the table. I knocked against some basket handles, flopping them over to the floor. She did not shift to retrieve then. Neither did I.

Yishmai came over and linked her arm with mine in a

friendly sort of way. "What thing for what thing were you getting?" she asked. I neither replied nor looked her way.

I refused to take my eyes off the Oracle. The seer who had damned my life before I even had a chance. She could have hidden the truth for the sake of protecting an innocent. She could have revealed the augury to me when I was older, in a kind way, and offered to guide me so I would grow from the challenge, not die from it. So much she could have done, this "wise" woman.

But what did the past matter when at last here was one person from my village, maybe with earthly news or divine insight into what had happened to our other tribesfolk, to my small sisters, my friend Yanu.

"What is wrong with you! Why won't you say something?" I ground through my teeth, anger making me fist my hands.

"I do not know you," she whispered coarsely.

"Oracle!" I cried.

"Oracle!" I cried again.

Yishmai had had enough and pulled me away by the arm. She was tugging me along, surprisingly robust. Still I craned backward at the woman who had looked into my future and closed doors before I'd even reached them. Her face was turned away, but I could see her watching me leave from out the corner of her eye.

Some distance away, Yishmai dropped her basket and gripped me by the arms. She actually gave me a sharp shake.

"What was that? What is *wrong* with you! Do you have a death wish?" she snapped.

I shook my head. "No, I only want to live ..." I said.

In silence I added, *free*.

Her hands fell away and a moment passed in which neither of us seemed to have words.

"Come," Yishmai reached for me and she never let go of my hand until we were back on our side of the town.

We turned in the produce to the kitchen cooks. Yishmai led me toward the hall, then with a quick look around, snagged my dress and tugged me with her. We ducked behind the bathroom stalls. I'd never been back here. It was damp and dotted with soap-scummy puddles that smelled fairly ripe after a day of unhurriedly evaporating under the sun. We tiptoed round the edges of the mucky pools, then followed a wire fence down a path running along the back of several more buildings.

The sun was setting by now, and the air began to smell a different kind of fresh. I recognised the scent. I could hear the sound of wide-running water.

The building Yishmai stopped behind was old, large and unlit. There was a break in the wire, lower, near the ground. Yishmai stooped and took hold of some links there. She hauled back on the wire and exposed a gap big enough for us to squirm through.

"Where are we going?" I asked.

"You'll see," Yishmai grinned.

I followed her through the breach. We went down the hill and left the compound behind. Halfway down, the land evened out a little before continuing on at a steeper incline. We stopped on that natural ledge. I took a good, long look around. I could see a large river running alongside the lands to the north, that were bordered by grassy fields. On the other side of the river was a forest. A forest!

Yishmai sat on the ground and wrapped her arms around her knees.

"You'll have to wait a bit longer to get your own hut and your two free hours now. But just be really good and Elder Darja will unfold. I've seen it before."

Yishmai looked very pretty in the sweet hues of the sun going down. Was it a reflection of what she was like inside for real? It was hard to reconcile this side of her with the girl whose first words to me included: "Damned to hell, you are."

"I figured you mightn't really know what to do with your two hours of freedom every day, when you get them; seeing as how you have no other friends and all." She looked around as if taking inventory of our surroundings before adding, "It's just somewhere to be sometimes."

It *was* somewhere to be. The evening sky had painted streaks of oranges and pinks across the deepening blue canvas, and the stars were already beginning to show themselves.

"Thank you," I said. "Do you come here often? To fish? Or —"

"No. These waters look nice from up here. But they're deep ... and inhabited by dangerous creatures. No one likes to fish here! Everyone prefers the fish brought in from our sister towns in the west. A few have drowned here before as well!" Yishmai's already large eyes widened emphatically.

I wondered if she would next tell me there surely must be ghosts here as a result. But, no ... she'd not be sitting here if she believed that.

I sat beside her, counting in my head. I wanted to ask many, many questions: about the "dangerous creatures"; about the river's depth and flow; about the forest on the other side. It might seem suspicious if I suddenly went from my taciturn tendency to blurting out a bunch of queries, so I determined to work my way up to it. I knew I was brave, but I had to start being clever.

I realised Yishmai had been absorbing the intensity of my expression. I began to try to deflect, but she spoke first, in soothing tones, "It will get better, Wren. Just lay low. Try not to get into trouble."

I looked at her, not knowing what to think. She had

been angry with me just earlier in the day. I didn't say anything, so she spoke again.

"He used to be nicer. Oktar, I mean. But someone has to be tough around here, and make the choices no one else wants to. He used to smile. I remember he used to smile. But he is the king's front man. The king cannot do a lot of it himself. He is too ill and needs to preserve his health for us.

"Everything we have acquired and achieved is because Oktar was there on the front line, leading our missions to new lands for wealth and converts. He has lost his innocence," she laughed a tad sullenly, "but he has given us much more."

I couldn't look at her. I wanted so badly to tell her to go fuck herself. I bit my tongue. Sometimes, I'm learning, it's better not to speak. We sat on and let the silence embrace us, able to roam amid our own thoughts for a while.

I couldn't help being angry. Maybe Yishmai couldn't help being what she was, either. She was damaged for sure ... to not be able to define right from wrong; being "less nicer" from flat out vile. But she had not damaged herself. This place, had done it; as surely as it was damaging me. We were both victims. If I let myself hate her for what our assailants did, that would be something like giving in and becoming like them. I would fester. So I tried to change my thoughts. At least toward her.

It seemed safe to ask, "What is the purpose of the King's Festival?"

Yishmai came alive again. She bounced about to turn more to face me, before gushing, "We wear costumes, dance and get drunk. And we exchange gifts! Oh, and we procreate."

"You ... what?"

"Procreate. Well, I mean, the aim is really to find a

mate for the night and *try* to procreate. It is how our society comes by its many children."

What many children? Was she smoking something, or had I missed the throngs of children entirely this whole time? In my time here I had counted only a handful of children under 16.

"Um, ok ... go on?" I urged her.

"Yeah, so, it's illegal to remove your mask while in the act," she said.

"Masks?"

"Yeah we wear masks with our costumes. It's to avoid any attachments to your mating partner. That can complicate things. Only the king can assign one a husband or wife. But anyway, during the festival there are no rules, except a few exceptions, like keeping masks on. It's total abandon!

"On the third night, twelve people are chosen by the king in a draw. They become ambassadors, who go forth to faraway lands to educate others about the greatness of our society. They, in turn, identify special individuals and offer them a place here, to live as we do. Being blessed by choosing is an honour we all dream of," Yishmai concluded.

I huffed.

"What?"

"And this is a tradition?" I asked.

"Yes, it has gone on for many generations."

"How do you know?"

"I just know," she said, conviction in her voice. "Please tell me what you are thinking, Wren. I'm starting to know that look on your face."

Yes, I was starting to know her really well, too. I looked at her, innocence and all, and I thought it best not to trust her. It didn't feel right. Even if she was a good person, being so guileless and committed to her community's ways, she might sell me out without intentionally trying to bring me to harm.

"I'll make you a pretty mask and —"

"I'm not going."

"Yes you are," she argued.

"No-I-am-not!"

"It's decreed by King Carovor. You'll be *punished* if you don't go."

I shot her a hard look, and growled, "Oh sure, I'll just go to make it easy for Oktar to find me and force-fill me with a baby!"

"You'll be wearing a mask!"

I frowned and turned my thoughts inwards.

She tilted her face as she considered me.

"I see what you mean, Wren. Look it was blip ok? Somehow, you got under Oktar's skin, but Elder Darjan spoke to the King. Oktar won't harm you unprovoked. 'Sides, you'll be wearing one of my pretty masks, no one'll recognise you."

"You don't say," I smirked.

Yishmai crawled in front of me and sat back on her heels. "Who is Papa?"

Her question staggered me. I looked away as the world tipped and slanted briefly. I was trying to mask my emotions, but the fact that I felt myself working so hard told me I was failing sadly at it. Yishmai snatched my hand up and against her heart. She promised she wouldn't tell a soul.

"How do you know about him?" I husked.

"You kept calling for him, when Elder Darja and I took you from Oktar in the market this morning" she revealed.

Right. That was only this morning. It already felt like several days had passed.

"Who is that?" she insisted.

"My father," I gave wearily.

All the recently broken places in me were hungry for some kind of release. I could let this much out.

"Is he here?" she asked.

"No, he's dead," I choked.

This peculiar girl showed little sympathy all of a sudden. Like dead was better to hear than that he was captive, maybe converted, too.

"Don't worry, our king will find you a new papa!" she said, her eyes brightening up.

I clenched shaking fists. How was it even possible for someone to be that ...

So much for not hating her. To keep from throttling her I took the talk somewhere else: "Yishmai, what is the real purpose of the King's Festival?"

She seemed mystified. Like I'd asked a question in gibberish. "What do you mean, Wren?"

I wished she'd stop using that name so much. I looked up at the stars, out in full now. The sun had hidden its face from us completely.

"All societies have traditions and every one of them has a purpose," I began.

"Well I told you —"

"I mean, why doesn't the king just choose his twelve ambassadors without all the drunkenness and sex and everything?"

She paused. "It's just a festival where lots of different activities happen. That includes finding ambassadors and helping us procreate impartially, to ensure our society continues with strong, healthy offspring. Did you not have festivals where you come from?"

I looked at her candid inquiring frown, and couldn't find anything sinister in her asking. Yet, I knew this conversation was not supposed to be happening, since I'd been sworn to leave everything about my old life behind. I hadn't known her long, but it seemed curious for Yishmai to be breaking rules.

I glanced about suspiciously.

"Well, yeah. Everybody has festivals," I conceded.

"Like what?" her eyes were lighting up again.

I sighed heavily. This girl wasn't going to give me a break.

I looked up to the evening sky again. The stars blinked back at me, but not with uncertainty, with calming allure. I lay back and folded my arms under my head, so I could gaze properly into the evening sky. From the corners of my eyes, I saw Yishmai mimic my actions.

Up above, the sky projected familiar sights that I had witnessed from my childhood before all this awful came. Among the stars I saw my young sisters, Kajri and Qarnai, dancing with colourful strips of cloth, as a group of our people cooked in communal pots in preparation for a ritual breaking of our fast.

Papa sat with elders, smoking a prized plant in long-handled pipes, echoing chants and prayers to our nurturing Mother-God. She was being solicited to bless our lands and rivers with an abundance of meat for us to hunt in the coming year, so that we could nourish ourselves and loved ones without disturbing nature's balance. For the lands, rivers, and trees were our brothers and sisters, and draining them would be no different from cutting off our own hands and spilling all our own blood.

We danced, prayed, and made sacrifices for seven days. All year round, we never starved or wanted for.

"Please tell me more," Yishmai begged, bringing me back to the present. I had lost myself in the stars and in the memories of things lost.

"Yishmai."

"Please. I swear I'll tell no one what passes between us," she vowed.

I sat up and looked at the curious soul beside me.

"Maybe another day. Besides, I don't even have my two hours of freedom yet, so whatever this was must surely be coming to an end?"

She nodded unenthusiastically, as though I had stripped some of the colour from her world. I punched her playfully on the arm, and she, even more playfully, pretended to tumble over from the blow.

"Shucks, Yishmai," I chuckled, pulling her up after me. Her and those mood swings.

"I'll share my secrets with you if you share yours with me," I offered. And she was smiling again.

As we walked back up the hill, I stopped to look to the skies one more time. The image-echo of my once simple life remained there, both tormenting and encouraging me.

Looking at it playing out, I realised this was the first time I'd recalled Kajri's and Qarnai's faces since this whole horror-filled life transformation. I really had tried to conjure their appearance, but nothing came clear. Had mentioning Papa openly to another person unlocked something in my memory? Or was I seeing them because they were dead like Papa and Mother? I didn't want to think about that. I wanted to hold on to the belief that they were still somewhere out there, perhaps not alone, waiting to see a familiar face to run to and smile at ... like I've been waiting.

"So what time will you take your freedom hours, now that you have somewhere to go besides the market?" Yishmai asked, as we reached the top of the incline and worked our bodies through the slit. Yishmai used her shod foot to push the wire once more closed, and we retraced our original path, back to the lodging.

"I'll ask Elder Darja to have them right after the sun sets"

"But it'll be dark. You'll miss all the good stuff

happening around the place," Yishmai said; bewilderment, and maybe some disappointment, underlying her words. Had she wanted to share time with me?

"I like late evenings. It's quiet and still. It would be nice to go back and watch the river and reflect," I explained.

"You're strange. You'll hardly be able to see the river, except under bright moons. Ooh, it looks so lovely then," said Yishmai, "so all right!"

I was happy she had talked herself into seeing my side. It saved me having to do it. Hopefully Elder Darja would see, too.

More than being "quiet and still," and watching the pretty moon on water, late evenings were perfect for something else: planning an escape.

TEN

A Familiar Face

In the weeks that followed, I worked harder to blend in with this society's way of life, pretending to follow orders now, fully aware they were punishable if I failed to carry them out. I went about my business, acting at ease; though with every step I took, I remained ever watchful for Oktar to spring out of a shaded corner. It never happened. Yet, that made me worry *even* more.

I had been spending my two hours of freedom each day in the tiny, wooden room assigned to me all on my own. I had meant to spend my time at the ledge above the river, planning escape. So far, I hadn't been able to bring myself to use my precious free hours in that worthy activity.

On the first three nights, I had made it down the slope to the spot where Yishmai had taken me, but turned back for my room almost at once. The first night it was out of fear. So much fear in me now. The second night, I had resolved to surmount the fear.

Though I was uneasily glancing around me as the evening dark deepened, I was managing well enough ... until my mother had appeared, cloaked in a shallow nimbus of dim light. I jumped a mile in my skin. She beckoned me to her, then pointed to the deep waters beyond. I fled. The third night, my mother's eerie, silent, gesturing form sent me running away again.

My sleep was no more comforting. In my dreams I climbed a never-ending tree, summoned by Papa's voice calling, "Come home, Idzorah-Ulka."

But every time I thought myself almost to the top, where I would at last meet him again, I suddenly discovered there were more branches to climb. Exhausted, I scaled persistently on, until a branch snapped under me. I went tumbling down, down into a great abyss.

I awoke to a ray of sunlight streaming through a small hole in the galvanised roof of my room. Its expanded light hit hotly across the top of my bed, and I gave up any chance of staying in sleep any longer. I got out of the bed and the cool floorboard beneath my feet protested quietly with a sound like a deflated chirp. I stepped off, then on again; off, then on again. Each time the board whined.

I stooped and inspected the woodwork, which was shoddy compared to the fine floors in the other buildings I had seen so far. Still, I was not anywhere near heavy enough to make any kind of floorboard creak. I gave it a proper stomp. The board loosened. I dropped to one knee and pried it up with my hands. There was a narrow dusty space under the floor. I reckoned a skinny person could fit in there lying sideways. But it wouldn't be for a person. I fitted the board back in properly and pushed the small cot bed over the spot, to cover up my new concealing place.

No sooner had I done this, Yishmai let herself in. Place of my own? Right. I wasn't allowed a lock on the door. The loose latch on the inside dangled ineffectually from a nail.

"Should get that fixed?" Yishmai fiddled with the hanging bit of wood.

"Morning to you, too," I sniffed.

She grinned, before tossing an apple at me.

"Come on. Got a different job for you this morning, after you collect the firewood for the kitchen."

Yishmai led me down a path I had not walked before. We passed into a prim residential area, crossed a field and through some alleyways, to eventually come out above an entrance to the bustling market area that we'd never used before.

My heartbeats raced off, thumping loudly, drumming in my ears.

I stopped, my breaths short, sharp, to regard Yishmai with a betrayed look.

"Ok, ok." She threw her hands up defensively. "I knew you would be sour if you knew we were coming here. It's for a good reason, I promise."

Just inside that access, the market's meat vendors were selling everything from pigs, goats and cows, to chickens hanging upside down on thick wooden rods, and other less identifiable types of animal protein. Yishmai grabbed my hand and led me past that section, on through dense crowds, to outskirt stalls.

The air was fresher here, tame winds able to drift through from the open air just on the other side. The stall we stopped at seemed bedecked by streams of cloth hanging freely, billowing in the breezes.

"You get to pick whichever you like," she said with a huge grin.

"What? Yishmai, I —"

"I know you don't have any money, but you have to wear something nice to the King's Festival, so I'm getting it for you. Don't even think I'll stand for you rejecting my kind offer! Now go on," she prodded warmly.

"So there's no firewood to collect?" I asked.

"Sure there is! But we're doing it *after* we buy your dress material."

I stared at the young girl trying to be my friend, extending me the only kindness I'd seen in this place, and I wanted to feel bad. I wanted to feel bad that she couldn't see it was all a lie: my docility, my obedience, my acceptance. Well, for the most part. She seemed all right; but I wasn't her friend. She was simply someone I was stuck with, maybe even a means to an end.

I smiled, and threw my long arms around her neck, laying it on thick. "It's gonna be great! Thank you Yishmai, you're the best!" I gushed. I let her see me concentrate and consider carefully for a while, before pointing to a sheer midnight blue fabric with shimmering gold dots speckled all over it.

"It's so beautiful, Wren! It's perfect for you. It matches your complexion so well! I'm gonna sew you the most gorgeous dress. You're going to be the envy of all the girls!" she burbled, towing away a manageable bolt of the cloth over her shoulder.

At another stall, Yishmai gave me a choice between a golden-yellow or midnight blue mask for the King's Annual Togetherness Festival. Seeing that I didn't want to stand out and all, I went with the latter. She seemed happy either way, and never stopped prattling about how good it was going to be.

I followed closely behind Yishmai, looking around to see if any eyes were peering at me. Men, guards, women … besides a passing glance, no one seemed too interested, but I still felt like eyes were watching. I tried to stay close to my companion, but there was no threat of losing her; I simply followed the bolt of blue cloth.

Then I saw *him*.

A butterfly unfurled its wings in my belly.

I mean *him, him*.

I stopped in my tracks and stared at *Soldier*. My breath took leave ... the world went with it. He was just standing there at a stall. So near. My heart began racing, and I parted my lips to get some air inside. He no longer looked like a soldier, with his common white clothes, tousled hair and stubble on his smooth, pale skin. But as I would have known the Oracle's voice anywhere, I'd know his eyes.

He looked up and his sight caught on mine. *Will you remember me?* The way he continued to stare was my answer: he remembered me all right. Time did not feel passing, so long we seemed allowed to gape at each other. I opened my mouth, but what could I say? He opened his mouth, and silently formed my name. In that moment, this was like another beautiful dream of him. So it made sense to face another rude awakening. A smiling woman wearing a regal alabaster-pale dress stepped close up behind Soldier and touched his arm. He began turning his face to hers. His eyes lingered on mine to the last, till eventually obliged to look full away. The eyes focused on my face were fleet-ingly replaced by the dazzling woman's. Such a look! Such eyes. Her hand stroked down Soldier's spine. I continued to stand there, until Yishmai butted my head with the bolt of material and asked me what I was doing. She drew my attention for a second only.

Yet, when I looked back, it was like Soldier had vanished in plain sight. I swayed on my feet, then pulled myself together. As I fell in step behind Yishmai again, I saw no sign of *Soldier*. Thinking of the illusory quality of what I'd just experienced, I questioned whether I had in fact seen him at all. *You did!* something in me asserted ... Yes. Yes! It hadn't been like how I'd seen Papa or my mother. He was alive; and the sight of him had sent heat and blood rushing to all the parts of my body that had gone cold and numb in this diseased place.

Later, Yishmai was folding away the cloth in her room

while I sat hunched in a chair by the open door. Done, she gave me her attention, "What's the matter with you? Been more muted than usual since we got back from the market. You didn't run into *him*, did you?"

My heart skipped a beat, and I looked at her in shock.

"I don't —"

"Oktar. Did you see Oktar at the market?"

The relief was so immense I had to fight to hold it in, and not let a huge breath of air rush through my mouth.

"No! No, I didn't see him."

"But you did see someone you like, eh?" she grinned, punching me in the arm.

Ugh. Like? Pffttt. I mean why would I like Solider, I thought to myself. *Wait, did I like him? Oh Goddess no. No, no , no!* I did not like him. I was just surprised to see him there. Right? Right! Why would I like him? After everything that's happened.

An intense wave of emotions rolled over me — confusion, anger, surprise. More confusion.

Shit. I resisted the urge to hold my belly, where the butterfly fluttered about under the thought of him. *Shit, shit, shit!*

"Good one," I feigned a smile.

"Oh, don't pretend. I saw you looking at that handsome man. The one that just got paired with Cora, the daughter of Elder Roman. Luckily for you, a man can have more than one wife here," she poked.

"Lucky me," I said, scratching my neck. I cleared my throat, and ventured as casually as I could, "I've never seen him before."

"I have. His name is Mickhal, a new recruit," she revealed, pulling out a measuring tape and looping it around my waist.

"Mickhal," I whispered the name, only to realise that it couldn't be his real name.

"He's a good looker, ain't he? Won't it be lucky if you were to see him at the Festival when you're looking all prettified?"

"Prettified? With a mask on my face?" I joked. "Yeah, I guess that would be lucky."

After Yishmai measured me for the gown, I went out and fetched the firewood, delivered it to the kitchen, and had an early dinner of a dried-up piece of chicken and half an under-boiled potato. My thoughts never strayed far from *Soldier*.

Where has he been this whole time? How can he be married? How has he, a former prince, been faring in this place? Why hasn't his family come to take him home? What was that look he gave me at the market? What was he thinking at that exact moment?

Too many questions. I shouldn't be so curious about him. What happened to the vengeful rancour that I once held in my core toward him? Thinking about it prompted remnants to start seeping back to the fore of my feelings. But the questions remained, overshadowing all.

"You are troubled, my child," my father uttered, as I later settled down in my wooden shack.

"Why would you say that, Papa?"

"You always answer questions with questions when you've no desire to answer with answers, Idzorah-Ulka," Papa pointed out, with a hearty laugh.

I grinned back, my mood lifting. I took a good look at Papa. He looked as real as Yishmai, whom I'd seen just minutes before. He sounded as real, too.

"You have always followed your heart, daughter. You should not betray it now," my father declared. So assured, he sounded, but ...

"What are you saying, Papa?"

"You wonder how a man you hate could arouse something so fantastic in you. There is no easy answer except

135

that you only betray yourself when you act against your heart."

I considered him. Papa looked exactly the same as he did when I last saw him alive and happy: wearing a beige tunic, his wooly grey hair wrapped up messily in a bun, like those delectable ones mother baked in the dirt oven outside our hut.

That last time, he was stood at the foot of the tree beckoning me down, following the dinner debacle with Yanu, his parents and my melodramatic mother. I hadn't come down but I'd glanced at him briefly, deeply. I saw that even though he was worried, his narrow eyes smiled, like he had known everything would be ok: that I would come down out the tree; and the next day would come; and the next and the next, and somehow everything would be okay.

If only it were so.

"Papa? When we get vengeance, will you leave me?"

"I will never leave you, my little girl. As for vengeance, it is not for the dead. It is for the living."

"Eh, Papa?"

He chuckled, and I lost myself in it. His hand caressed my face. I tilted my head into the spirit-touch and let go of my worries.

"Men exact vengeance for themselves, even when they say it is for the lost and the dead. But vengeance brings no peace, neither does it awaken the dead."

I sighed in frustration and pressed, "But are you not here with me now because you need vengeance to rest peacefully, Papa?"

He did not hesitate. "No, my child. Vengeance breeds hatred, and hatred more hatred. I am not here for revenge. I am here only for you and because of you. You need me, my Wild Child. I will rest in peace when you find peace," he enlightened.

"I will find peace when I reap vengeance," I rejoindered.

"Who are you talking to, Wren?"

I spun. Yishmai was standing behind me, holding an apple. "You brought along the apple I gave you this morning, but you never ate it. So I brought it again to you. Who were you talking to?"

I looked back over my shoulder. Papa was already gone. My smiled felt sad as I whispered, "Only myself."

✠✠
✠✠

AFTER YISHMAI LEFT, I took a walk down to the river bank.

The evening was young. Night was slowly encroaching on daylight's territory, forcing its darkness into the oranges and yellows left by the sun's dipping trail. My feet sank into the soft earth. The river brought a smell of something refreshing and clean to this grotesque land. The whistling wind caressed my face and kissed my nearly bald scalp, playing light fingers through the bit of hair that had grown there. The waters moved steadily on, making music as they flowed to their destination, wherever such a place might be for a river. I thought of the place I might be destined to go to, but so far could not find or reach.

I moved close to the river's edge and sat waiting. I waited and I waited, until the natural sounds became insufficient for my heavy, feeling heart and I began to sing.

It was a song to the river, a song I would sing again and again, asking her to subside, to let me pass when the day for my escape came, to love me as I loved her, to be for me as I was for her:

Oh river, clear-watered sister,
Flowing through the bosom of Mother Nature,
Love me, like I love you, like I love you
Sustain me, carry me, like the giant water-lilies and our brother manatees,
Riding the sacred flow of you
Carry me home
Clear my path, my fluid sister,
When shadows lurk with seen and unseen dangers
Oh, love me, like I love you, like I love you

MY SECOND TURN into the chorus, a familiar countenance eerily emerged, causing a chill to crawl up my backbone. A large black toad surfaced and stayed afloat, as it waited for what I had to offer. I grabbed the closest living thing that moved before my eyes — a wriggling earthworm. My voice took up the river song again.

Dear river, my sweet sister,
home to botos, black toads and barracudas
Love me, as I love you, as I love you
You hear our call, dear sister
Life great and small,
The otter, nymph, and piranha, all equal in your sacred halls
Ribbons of water bind us, where your love finds us
Carry us home
Oh faithful sister, love us, as we love you, as we love you

I EXTENDED the worm toward the toad. It inched a little closer and devoured the writhing offering, before submerging beneath the dark waters as uncannily as it had surfaced.

I'd had no pin to put in the creature's head (and probably wouldn't have had the stomach to do that anyway), so it probably wouldn't come back. But I felt — *good* about having made something resembling ritual sacrifice after such a long time. If anyone saw me doing this, surely it would mean Elder Darja's birch ... or worse. Was it worth the risk?

I quickly stifled a startled little yelp as something splashed from the water and landed near me. It was the black toad. It had returned! In its customary disconcerting fashion, it regurgitated two fish, still amazingly flopping, beside my toes. In that instant, I felt my father's presence all through me, as if to say, *See, you learned this from me. You are like me. You are mine. Forever.*

Deeply moved, I sang in thanks:
Dear river, thank you sister
Nurturer and sustainer,
You are life, oh living waters of Mother Nature
I love you, as you love me, as you love me
This is how it was meant to be
Whatever comes, you see me through
So in the dawn I look to you,
Take me home, and love me as I love you, as I love you

I MOVED IN CLOSER, for food was not what I had come for. I let my song die on the wind. I contemplated reaching into the toad's wide mouth to tempt its fine, poisonous fangs. The creature never took its bulbous eyes off me. I hesitated, not being able to shake the chills the creature gave me, and sat back on my heels. The toad and I remained there together for a bit. In time, I worked up the nerve to reach out. It stayed perfectly still for me to pat it gently on the back. As I withdrew my hand, it suddenly gave an admirable back spring ... and disappeared into the deep, shadowed waters.

As the ripples its dive had made grew smaller and

smaller till all gone, gloom descended on me once again. I regretted not trying, at least, to milk the creature's poison, as I might yet have need of it later on.

I looked up. The sky was full of bright stars. In a rush, all regret departed like grey smoke on an untamed wind. I would sleep well tonight.

++
++

MAYBE I WAS the first person to ever make an offering on her banks; but as if inspired to continue showing me its generosity, the next time I was at the river, I discovered it had even more to offer.

The days had lengthened, I realised, because there was still a good bit of light out. Stood on the edge of the river bank, I tossed fresh bits of yesterday's fish in the shallows of the water and waited. I sniffed my fingers instinctively. The smell was strong and I knew it would take lots of washing to get it off. But I wasn't complaining. It was exactly the kind of smell I needed to linger in the water.

It had been some time since I last saw a stingray. But there it was, seeming to flutter in the clear shallows within sight of where I had stopped. Had it been deeper out, and the evening darker, I might have failed to see it at all. The sight of this gorgeous creature made me ecstatic.

I reached for a small fishing net that I had strung together on a fallen branch and carefully tried to trap the ray. *Don't break, don't break*, I whispered to the branch. A few mishaps here and there as I tried to maneuvre around the ray and get it within the net while steering clear of its barbed tail. When I finally got it, my heart skipped and I backed out of the water, hands extended with the net in front of me as the creature slashed its tail about violently. I despaired in doing this, for it pained me like I knew the thing personally.

Shhhhhhh …

I took a few quick breaths in, and carefully moved the net around, looking at its movements until I got the stingray on its underside. He calmed down massively.

Shhhhhhh buddy … Biting my teeth, I took a sharpened stone and cut the tail off clean. More thrashing about.

Sorry my friend. So sorry.

I let the severed tail fall through the net on the wet earth before returning the stingray to the waters with a song of good health, long life, and a new tail.

Good. Given the opportunity, I would try to do this two more times, to feel satisfied that I had enough venom with me to account for unforeseen circumstances. A smile broke free on my lips. My plan was coming together, and no one was going to get in my way.

ELEVEN

The House on the Hill

The days wore on flat and bleak. I harboured a fear that inertia would take me over again and mire my intentions of achieving my freedom, finding my sisters, and getting us all home.

I had ruled out death as an alternative, but in the recesses of my mind and deepest chambers of my heart, I heard her tempting whispers beckoning. And they were tempting.

But time flowed forward, even in this forlorn land, and with every passing day that temptation to give up, give in, let go, shrank, while my will to keep living grew.

Looking back at the times when death had seemed very viable in the face of all the odds, I realised I had temporarily forgotten myself. I had been mourning inside. The pain felt too big, too tall and too wide to contain within me. That was what had driven me to that point of despair. In that empty place of misery never consoled, death took the opportunity to be near me, always there, offering an open door to a place where my captors could no longer hold me, where nightmares would cease, and I could meet my Papa and family again.

I have heard people say that the human inclination is to live, to *want* to live. At that time, I wasn't at all sure about that. Living, that once used to be effortless breaths drawn while having free reign in my heart-home wilderness, had taken a murky form that required only painfully sucked down, unwilling breaths. Living had become hard. Too laboured.

There was something inside me even at the worst of time, though, that resisted. As much as I had wanted to be with my Papa again, my obstinate inner voice had warned me I *should* be afraid to die.

Move on from the only life I had ever known ... not actually knowing what lay on the other side of death's inviting door? *Would Papa, my mother and sisters (if they had, indeed, travelled on) be waiting to greet me? What if there was a chance they could elude me in death, too? What if my spirit could not find theirs and I spent an eternity lost, wandering an unknown realm without my family? What if!*

Death was an undeniable gamble.

Ironic it was, but when I had considered running into death's arms, it showed that in some ways I was already dead. The true Idzorah-Ulka, who faced animosity and aloneness, but persevered and found happiness within herself, had been so damaged by loss and shock that she closed her eyes. Life was a flower that had wilted, turning grey, its petals on the brink of falling off but never quite getting there.

My family was dead but what really was the truth? And who knew it? Perhaps they were simply in another place, maybe even more alive than I was in this world with my pain. I had nearly let my enemies kill me. Thank the Goddess that things had never quite gotten there.

Yes ... that was then; but life — my life — was in the now.

"So, what do you need ribbons and feathers for?" Yishmai asked, her probing eyes tracing my face.

"I just wanted to make a decoration for my hair, as it's growing out." I forced my lips to curve upwards, aiming for a genial veneer to conceal the depths of my abhorrence over their act of shaving off all my hair.

Her face lit up, like I had undergone some sort of approved transformation that *they* were waiting on.

"I'm truly pleased to hear that, Wren! I will get you the prettiest things I can find."

She was about to bounce away, but paused and cocked her head at me. "It's not bad, you know."

"What's not bad?" I asked, confused.

"Your hair. I can tell you're troubled about it; but it actually looks really nice. Suits the shape of your face, brings out your jawline," she gesticulated around her own jaw. "Maybe you will start a new fashion among the girls" she said.

Quick, construct fake smile. "Yeah, maybe," I said.

It was a typical morning of obligatory chores upon chores upon chores. My months of servitude in this prison-society were so unbearable that I wondered at how these people did their duties so effortlessly. Like breathing, following orders seemed a natural thing to others here.

Yishmai had just accompanied me on my task of gathering chopped firewood for the kitchen. As we were dropping the load off, Elder Darja appeared with her distinctive stern expression and posture so upright, she looked as though something had been shoved up her backside.

"How are you two girls getting on with work?" she asked.

"It's all done," Yishmai replied.

Elder Darja's look pierced me.

"Yes, all finished now, Elder," I added.

"Good," she said. "Because I have another job for you.

144

One of our new recruits needs help combing her hair. The texture is a little like yours, Wren, but a fair bit thicker. Not to mention she's not right in the head, so no one else wants this chore."

"Will I go with Wren, Elder Darja?" asked Yishmai.

"Yes, you may go, but you need to be back soon. There is a mountain of work in the kitchen."

✝

YISHMAI WALKED with me past the market to a side of the village where I had never been. It was less developed than where we lived, but construction works were in progress everywhere, creating an unbearable cacophony. The houses were scattered in no structured fashion, making it a maze for a first-time visitor like myself. We passed some dirt-covered men in hardhats, digging what appeared to be a well. They stopped and stared as we walked by. A couple of them whistled at us and made sexual remarks. Their lewd words made Yishmai visibly uncomfortable.

One of them pronounced an indecent comment on how he would have his depraved way with Yishmai. I stopped in my tracks and spun around. He was taken aback, but pulled himself together and sidled up to me with a confrontational swagger. Yishmai bolted back to meet me. She grabbed my arm and tugged at it.

"Come on, you have to keep out of trouble. It's not worth it, Wren," she beseeched in a sulky tone uncharacteristic of her usual jaunty self.

I turned to her. "They should have respect," I declared, gritting my teeth.

145

The man, almost ten years our senior, was chewing on a piece of grass, daring me to act. The muscles on my face were twitching erratically. My heart had started hammering. I looked him up and down, then spat at his feet, before turning to walk off with Yishmai. Her hand was shaking as she gripped mine, but she pretended that she was fine and strong.

I turned and looked back to see a thin man shuffle through the group of men; he forced his shovel into the ground hard so it stood on its own, before pulling down the cloth covering his nose from the dust. He pulled off his hard hat and wiped the sweat from his brow in one swipe. It was Noah, the pierced-up mute from our commune. He had been at assembly at the commune this morning but it was hard to properly look at anyone when we were stood in a line.

Now that I faced him, he looked less haggard than when I first saw him, with crusted blood around his nose piercing. He was handsome even. Shit. It took time to register. I hadn't forged any decent kind of relationships with the rest of the commune, so I didn't know where Noah stood. Would he rat on me?

I stared him back, trying to decipher the look on his face. *What was that look?* But of course he didn't say anything. He turned to the older offending man, still stood there chewing his grass, and Noah, staring the man in his eyes, roughly pulled his shovel from the dirt and walked back.

A sharp tug of my hand and we were walking away.

"Why did you do that?" asked Yishmai.

It was a good question, and I asked it myself before considering what stories I would spew to the girl.

I glimpsed at Yishmai. Today her hairdo against her pale skin made me think of her as a river nymph. A centre part separated two front plaits, which framed her face

146

beautifully, almost covering her little ears as they merged into one bigger plait. It made her look cute.

Wait, little ears? Cute? What the hell?

Come back, quick!

I cleared my throat and matter-of-factly said: "He deserved it. More than that actually; but as you say, I need to keep out of trouble."

"Hmm ... so what would you have done if you didn't have to worry about getting into trouble?"

The question and thought brought a smile to my face, a real smile. I knew the me forged from the wounds of war would have revelled in kicking the bastard senseless.

"Best not dwell on what we might have done," I said.

We ventured to a slightly sloping lane, which led to a house on a hill. Isolated from any other, it seemed to stand majestic, though was fairly humble. Hanging on the door was an arresting circular ornament made primarily from small, beautiful beads I had known growing up. They were a striking red with a black spot on them. A warm feeling swelled in my stomach, and made my eyes watery. So watery, until my vision blurred then cleared, like a fog, to the past.

"OK, OPEN YOUR EYES!" *squealed Yanu, in a tone so high he sounded like an entirely different person.*

First, I saw his wide grin — he couldn't look any happier, except for the sore looking bruise under his left eye where small-boned Maie had punched him the day before.

He asked for it, I mean who would try to cheat Maie, expert negotiator and trader, out of anything? But Yanu didn't want to hand over his marbles after losing the game. So Maie punched him and walked off.

"What do you think?" His eyes looked down to his hands extended before me. A fine looking bracelet made from red and black

beads. I looked up at his face again, he was still grinning. I burst into a chuckle and reached for it. He pulled his hand back.

"Uhh, don't put it in your mouth"

"Of course dum-dum, I'm not stupid," I screwed my face at him, and he burst into a short guffaw before signalling for me to extend my wrist, where he tied the beautiful beaded bracelet he'd made me.

A SOUND of knocking brought me back.

Yishmai knocked on the door, again. Then she looked at me, to the ornament and back to me.

"They're made from the rosary pea, the beads. So pretty, aren't they?" she asked.

I smiled again, another genuine one. "They're remarkable," I replied.

"Ok, well I will leave you now, but I'll see you when you get back. Yishmai said.

"Why are you leaving?" I asked. "I might get lost on the way back."

"Yes, true; but Elder Darja looks overwhelmed by the work in the kitchen. Just, if you get lost, ask someone for help," she said, adding emphatically, "And stay out of trouble!"

"All right," I reassured.

As Yishmai walked briskly away, the door opened.

There the Oracle stood, unkempt and impassive, her mass of thick hair puffed up in the air around her head. A tide of shock trundled through me and before it could roll out again, I was swamped by hurt, pain, and confusion. My breathing became laboured, but I tried to hide it as best as I could.

Up close, I could see a distinct cloudiness in the lenses of her eyes. I stared hard. Cataracts. The woman who saw far into the future would have problems seeing the present. This woman had pronounced good or bad fortunes on the fates of others in a past life. A life that seemed so long ago gone. Yet it hadn't been that far past a time when we were all still living in our village in the Baiuchi Forest. So much had transpired from then and there to here and now. Too much. Was there no going back?

The Oracle looked as worn down as that first time I saw her since the village destruction — another version of herself. A far less empowered version. But she was wearing a necklace made from the same beads decorating the door. I wondered how she managed it without either of them being confiscated.

"I'm here to comb your hair," I said, stepping inside.

She pushed in the door shut behind me and, for the first time since my arrival, looked at me properly. Her eyesight really had declined, for it seemed to take a while for her to take me in fully.

I looked away. Her lodging was roomier than mine and more improved with furnishings. "Could you please sit here for me?" I asked.

She never stopped looking at me, moreover, searching me. She foraged past my own eyes. What might she be looking for?

She finally slumped onto the chair. I got behind her, and considered her truly thick head of hair. Yes, our hair was similar. But that did not mean I wanted to touch hers. Still ... I used a large wooden comb to part down the centre of her hair. Before I could pass the teeth through her tight, springy curls, she spun suddenly around and regarded me with almost bulging eyes.

"You will live," she uttered.

"What?"

"You *will* live" she repeated insistently.

"Look, woman, I was told to come comb your hair, and

that's what I'm here to do. I'm not interested in your sense-less ramblings," I minced.

Since our last encounter in the market, when she denied me outright, I had written her off. I had vowed if I ever saw her again to be as cold-hearted and rejecting toward her. But here she was, while we were alone, spewing hot air, just like on the day of my naming ceremony.

She looked around nervously, then leaned in closer towards me.

"Idzorah-Ulka," she whispered.

The comb fell from my hands. I stepped back and went stiff. I tried to stop my head from swimming. It was strange hearing someone else call my name, my true true name. It's exactly what I had hungered for upon seeing her at the market. Now that she had given it, and I experienced my reaction, I was almost grateful she had not acknowledged me before.

"You will live," she repeated a third time.

"*You* said I would die. Your prophecy has ruled my entire life. What's changed? A few shackles and a war changed your mind? A little too late, lady," I spat out.

"Not all of us are steeled like you," she looked down. "War breaks us. It tears many of us from our true selves when we have stood in its ravages. It is a test. And I am sorry … I have failed. But before I go, you have to know that you must live, because you will live."

"I don't understand," I hissed.

"Some destinies are too strong to be directed by men. You make your own destiny. My time has come to meet our forefathers. But you, you will live. Only, sometimes, to live we must first die," she announced.

I felt an eruption of something strike up to my head. It threatened to flip me off my feet, so I gripped the back of the chair she was sitting on for support. My throat felt restricted. I opened my mouth and could only gasp. I realised my cheeks were wet.

The Oracle seized my hand in her own. "I am sorry. I am sorry," she said.

I took pause. A flood of emotion threatened to burst through the walls of my heart. I gripped my chest, and took a deep breath. I nodded and nodded, but couldn't find any words.

In this, she was right. War had touched us all in different ways. It broke us in unique ways, altering the strongest parts of our humanity.

I spent the next couple hours combing her hair in rows of plaits along her scalp. Little was said, but more was not needed. There was a silence of understanding between us, camaraderie. It made me feel re-energised for whatever fights lay ahead.

Finished, I stooped in front of her. "Where did you get those Jumbie beads?" I nodded at her necklace and at the front door.

She gripped the piece of jewellery and swept her hand past her shoulder, "Out back."

"Could I?" I asked.

And she smiled. "I am glad. The ways of our people have not left you, either, despite all their efforts to break them from us," she said.

I went out back and found the Jumbie beads peering like eerie red and black eyes from out open, desiccated brown pods, on a plant just outside the Oracle's back door. I picked a few handfuls carefully and bagged them, before tucking that safely under my garments.

Back home in our village they were used to ward off evil. They were worn as jewellery by our men, women, and children. Yet, they contained one of the most fatal poisons known to us. Deadly, but they were so glossy and gorgeous — beautiful secret weapon.

But it was not my people's way: violence.

I thought about this, as I stood by the plant that used something eye-catching to protect itself even as it continued its existence So different from my people.

They had wanted to talk things through. That was well-intentioned … but we lived in dangerous times. With the world on the brink of collapse, we never knew who else would make their way into the Baiuchi Forest. Back in the old world it was a savage fight for survival, and humanity had lost its way. The elders' descriptions and stories of murder, corruption and deception sounded horrifying. Yet, the best measure we had come up with, to protect ourselves against travellers coming our way intending harm, was to keep ourselves secret. *Avoid fighting.*

Sometimes shaking with fear after hearing the awful descriptions of the Old World, I used to ask, *Where had all the good people gone?* To me, our village seemed not much better: a people who did not want to fight with strangers, but outcast one of their own.

I understood Papa's explanation, that people are products of their environment, and even if our people were good, the frightening things that had happened around them had made them hyper-vigilant, overly cautious, superstitious at times and oh so afraid.

As much as I hated to admit it, some part of me now felt some understanding about how any news or pronouncements of gloom would spook a people who had escaped the murderous society of the Old World. How anything that seemed full of the volatility of it could look like a threat. They hadn't hated me. They had been afraid of me.

It was a sobering thought.

I looked down to where I had hid the bag of poison beads. Maybe my fellow villagers had cause to fear me. I was, indeed, quite different from them.

I had work to do. Inside me, a volcano was shaking off dormancy and bubbling to life and might. I thanked the Goddess for her recent gifts. She was showing she was with me. That meant my mission was just.

I bade the Oracle farewell, wishing her courage to face her final days, and strength to travel to her ancestors. I somehow knew I would never see her again.

As I let myself out, I was graced with a last vision of her. The Oracle lifted shaking fingers and ran them caressingly against the plaits my own deft digits had crafted. In a way, it was like we were touching hands across a divide.

TWELVE

The King's Togetherness Festival

I stared at the new black satin ribbons and peacock feathers that Yishmai had brought me. The ebon fabric folding and unfolding in a beautiful way on the table looked like death overlapping itself, seeking something. Or someone. She had apologised for not finding me a *prettier* colour. Her word, not mine. But what could have been more fitting than black? Black is the night sky; the deep hole inside me ... the terror I would unleash on this place before I drew my last breath. Black was triumph personified.

The King's Togetherness Festival felt, to me, as though it had come upon us far too quickly. Over the last two months I had been as good as could be, demonstrating a measure of burgeoning thrill over the Festival that was like wine to Yishmai, making her almost drunk with gladness over my altered attitude.

I felt that despite all I had actually fashioned in secret labours, there couldn't possibly have been enough time for me to prepare everything I needed. I couldn't shake the dread stirring in my stomach.

Today was the day when I would learn, one way or the

other, whether I had actually got my preparations right. It was the day of the King's Togetherness Festival.

I had been waiting for Yishmai to return from the market. She'd insisted that she had some last-minute "bits" to get, to make us "beautiful" for the event.

Earlier in the day, when I had been out myself with her, Yishmai was so preoccupied by the coming festival she seemed one big bundle of animated nerves; and so had everyone else.

The market square had been transformed — lanterns and candles everywhere. Many small white tents had been assembled over an expansive area; apparently to give couples a degree of privacy if they wished to further their kingdom's cause by procreating. My stomach churned fretfully at the thought.

Meanwhile, Yishmai, totally misreading my expression, had insisted I couldn't even begin to imagine what the place would look like, based on what was there in the middle of the day.

"Tonight, seeing it all completed will be an entirely different experience, Wren! You won't even recognise this place," she had enthused.

As if any of that matters at all, I thought, as I edged the bed back and carefully removed the loose floorboard it concealed. One by one, I extracted and inspected my secret treasures. There was a neat slingshot of my own crafting, just like Papa had taught me. I'd carved a sturdy tree branch to create the Y-shaped frame, then attached two strips of excellent rubber to the upright, forking ends. It was strong and supple, as need be, yet I took it up delicately, like lifting a fragile, but lethal flower, and tucked it neatly into my bosom.

Next, I removed the little bag of Jumbie beads. As I shifted it from one hand to the next, the contents softly clicked along each other's hardness, as though making a grim muttering to me, a secret rallying call.

Next, I pulled out the two stingray tails I had succeeded in collecting. I couldn't have been sure this would work, but I did everything I could to make sure it would. I had cut the sheath around the rays' spines and carefully scraped the mucus and venom off with a bit of broken ceramic I'd kept after Yishmai knocked over a vase in the kitchen. After storing the venom in a tiny herb glass, I sun dried the tails' barbs, that gleamed and felt similar to teeth.

Once dried out, I inspected them keenly: serrated edges, so beautiful with their zigzagging design, also sharp, long and strong. Handling them carefully, I dipped an end of both barbs into the collected venom. It had gone a bit dry so I added a little water to the bottle to get it fluid.

After setting them away in a safe place, I worked diligently on carving and polishing a beautiful wooden ornament, the kind I would have worn to keep my long hair in a roll. It used to be that with one pull of my hand the slender artful pin would come free, and set my plaits tumbling against my shoulders and back.

Women with shorter hair used to wear these in my village, too, but as part of a handmade head-dress: ingeniously affixing the carven decorative artwork to other ornamental bits, like bright feathers, beads, shards of shiny shell and sometimes even seasonal eye-catching leaves and berries.

The latter design was my aim, but beauty was not my intention. The wooden ornament I carved was hollow down its entire length. In that secret crevice I cautiously inserted my two poisoned barbs, to nest there until I hatched my plan for revenge.

That done, I set to making the deceptive head-piece. The ribbon was intricately plaited into a firm head band which would sit on my forehead. On one side, to rest just to the back of my right ear, I affixed the three glorious peacock feathers Yishmai had happily bought, in response to my feigned excited pleas. They were shimmering with every turn in the light, casting hues of blues, greens, copper. I attached the carved piece and it was striking, yes, but looked perfectly innocuous: a vain woman's finely-wrought trinket and no more.

When I tried on the head-dress, the peacock feathers flared outwards above my ear, calling and alluring with their dazzling display, perfect complement to the nearly copper-hued wooden carving rising from amid their splendor. No one would guess that I was concealing deadly weapons amid such beauty.

I obsessed a bit over its positioning on my head. I would have to be able to get it easily when I needed it. Still, I would make certain I had a backup.

The bag of jumbie beads called to me again, reminding me they were there. Everything would be ok.

‡
‡

MY HAIR HAD GROWN about three inches from my scalp. It was still upsetting to instinctively reach for my heavy, reassuring plaits, only to suffer the abrupt and rude awakening that they had been taken from me.

As I crushed the jumbie beads with a rounded heavy river-stone, I sang a song of protection.

In a culture fixated with fates and the idea that many spirits dwelt among us, it was imperative to seek protection against any unkind ones, and from other evil eyes that may intrude. The beads were worn as a constant shield: the lone black dot on their otherwise complete red turning each one into an eye. Strung on a bracelet, necklace or ornaments like the one on the Oracle's door, they could "see" all sides, making approach by malevolent forces difficult. My need for them now differed from their customary use; still, in a way I was seeking their ultimate protection from a society that had taken everything from me.

With every movement of my hand grinding the hard beads, my body felt release. Each pound a clear intention I set out into the universe. *Hear my heart Mother Earth, Mother Goddess, Holder of the Universe, Maker of all, Keeper of my soul, and the truest, purest embodiment of Love.*

When I had finished grinding, I thought of Sunny, my yellow-headed bird-friend who had kept me company in the days of despair spent in that poky cell.

Yesterday, I had gone seeking the little one out alone after I'd finished my chores. I was cognisant of the possibility that I might encounter Oktar. I had not; but his men were everywhere, as always.

It was hard to go anywhere unnoticed. Perhaps it was all my perception ... or maybe people really did remember me. I always had that sense of being stared at, whispered about, like I'd learned to identify back home from my earliest years. Thankfully people were always busy in this place, so there was little opportunity for them to dwell.

That was the cover I used — acting as though I was still in the middle of my duties. I'd made my way to near the prison block, but angled down an airy path that would take me around to the area almost directly behind the cells. A narrow, deep drain separated the blank, sheer back of the prison from the garden-path that ran parallel to it. This was Sunny's garden. When I saw him from afar, my heart tripped over itself with relief and gratitude. This little fellah had kept me living when life itself had felt as though it were draining away from me.

As I drew near his cage, I'd heard that Sunny was singing, as though he had never stopped since last I heard his song. I looked around, making sure that everyone was about their own business. Swiftly, I flicked his cage door open and stepped away. The bird didn't budge or seem bothered by my presence. After waiting a while, growing more nervous by the second in fear of drawing attention, I started to doubt that Sunny wanted to leave his prison. Perhaps he had grown used to it. Perhaps he had forgotten how to fly. Could he have forgotten how to be a bird?

Deeply saddened by that thought, I turned to walked away. Sunny shot past my ear and veered higher, headed for one of the distant trees. I stopped gaping like an idiot and tucked my chin down; but as I walked on, I glanced repeatedly up into the open stand of trees with my forest-sharpened vision. I saw when my bright-hued friend left the tree on his glorious wings, never circling back.

"That's right, Sunny," I whispered. "You fly on, and don't you ever get trapped again."

I wondered if I would be like him one day — with the wind under my wings. For now, I would soar vicariously through Sunny's escape.

On my way back through the market I had seen the Chief Whip for the first time in a while. The older man's face looked careworn, but his body was still strong. He stood in the distance staring at me, and I wondered if he had been trailing me, and witnessed my earlier act. I kept walking, picking up the pace, nervous about Oktar popping up somewhere near, as the two men never seemed far from each other.

"You've blended in nicely," I heard from behind me.

I looked anxiously over my shoulder, and there was the old man with his whip. I kept walking, aware that he kept following.

"You can fool them, but you cannot fool me."

I didn't turn around again, but he had caught up and gripped my arm firmly.

"What do you want?" I asked, and I suddenly recalled him lifting me out the cell after Oktar's first assault.

Fine lines curved around his eyes in patterns that I had never noticed before. They were not easily visible on his copper skin, which made him look younger than his years. Despite his muscular frame and stern demeanour, there was vulnerability in his face. I still couldn't tell what it was or why it was there. Was I the only one who could see it?

His was unlike many other faces here. Unlike Oktar, whose face lacked humanity, with a vacancy that could not hold empathy or love or kindness. Oktar looked even more dangerous with the two tattoos of daggers under his eyes, curving elegantly down his cheeks to pointed ends. But this man, the so-called Chief Whip, was a different type of dangerous.

He stared into my eyes with conviction. I waited for him to say whatever it was he intended. But he said nothing. The Chief Whip squeezed my arm tightly before roughly letting go of me.

"You don't frighten me," I said.

"You should be frightened," he snarled.

I walked in closer to him till we were only inches apart.

"I've told you before you're no different from me. You're a glorified slave, is all," I said.

He slapped me in the face. It stung but didn't hurt terribly. I had gotten used to the feel of being slapped — it almost revved me up. I might have grinned at him, or bared my teeth like a feral thing. His brows furrowed and he took a step back.

I had left him there in the market, doubtless watching my receding back as I made my way cautiously to my lodging.

++
++

I HAD FINISHED CRUSHING the last of the jumbie beads and carefully placed them in the phial I'd filched from a vendor at the market. Today, for the first time, it would not go into the hiding place under the floorboard

I couldn't think of the best place to secret it away. I needed them on hand for any arising opportunity, but out of sight till then, like my stingray tails. I hated the idea, and was almost revolted by the act itself, but I eventually inserted the smooth, strong, minute bottle up into myself. I had just finished situating it when Yishmai breezed in the door.

"Shit," I muttered to myself in a fright. "A knock would be nice," I said to the girl. She carried a large parcel.

"Oh yes, you said before; but it's not like you have something to hide now, so it don't matter anyway," she huffed in an offhand manner.

"You're right," I agreed readily, trying to smile.

Yishmai had brought both her dress and my own for the festival. We were to get prepared together ahead of the evening's commencement.

She never tried to contain her excitement as she undraped her creation for me. The blue chiffon dress had a deep, sensual heart-shaped cut at the front, and the long voluminous sleeves gathered at the wrist in wide cuffs. The flowing skirt, though falling a few inches above my knees, looked demure and delicate covered by a floor-length outer layer of transparent blue chiffon. The shimmering dots added an allure to the overall effect. The gown would hug my figure temptingly.

"It's very gorgeous, Yishmai, thank you," I said, feeling discomforted that I was about to wear something pretty and enticing in such a disturbing place. I had worn nothing but my same drab white shift since I had come to Commune 12.

"I told you, you will be the envy of all," Yishmai said with a big grin.

"Don't you think it's a bit revealing, though?" I squinted.

"Well that is exactly the point! To attract the other sex," she harped, like it was a perfectly natural thing.

"Right," I said. "Well, go on, let's see your dress now."

Yishmai made a show of foraging through the parcel, like there was so much there besides one other party-gown. At last she withdrew a bright yellow dress, with a full flared skirt and thin straps. She slipped it on effortlessly. Its hem landed just under her bottom.

"You look amazing," I expressed honestly.

A Cheshire Cat grin emerged on her face, before she twirled around and around in imperfect circles, making a show of herself.

She returned to digging in the bag, proving she did have more in it besides the gowns. Her hands emerged holding two masks: the shiny midnight blue one that she had gotten for me, and a deeply purple one with a vivid yellow star for herself.

"You look exceptional," Yishmai continued to assure me, as she powdered my face and painted my lips. "And I like what you did with your hair, very inventive."

"So how does this festival work, now?" I said trying to avoid getting powder in my eyes, while also distracting her from looking any closer at my head-piece.

"Well King Carovor will open the festival. There will be food and music; endless amounts of drink, and smoking of special herbs for the three days. No *real* rules, just care-free abandon. Keeping masks on, of course!

"Even the guards will take part. If you see someone

you fancy, go talk to them, or they will come talk to you and, well, the tents are there for, you know, stuff," she tittered.

"Nobody really goes home; you're expected to stay at the festival for the three days," she said.

"Wait, so I have to stay in these clothes? What if I need to wash myself?" I asked.

"Oh, well, if you really must you can. There will be communal wash areas that you can use to tidy up over the three days. You'll be expected to put your fine garments back on, always with the mask. No one should know who you really are," she stressed.

"Sounds incredible," I snipped.

"Don't worry. You know what I'm wearing so just find me if you need a little help with talking to a love interest. But, don't call me by name!" she chuckled.

I smiled, and it was surprisingly sincere. I felt strange, like a different person wearing this beautiful gown in this sordid place. Yishmai placed the mask onto my face and held up a mirror. I stared into it.

"A diamond amongst ashes," Papa whispered, face glowing, from behind Yishmai.

This time, I flat out grinned.

The big smile dropped away, though, as I gazed back at the stranger before me. I didn't recognise the person in the reflection as me. Nothing on me said *Idzorah-Ulka*: not the dress, the frills, the makeup the ornate, head-dress (hiding secrets), the hair … or lack thereof.

My sight moved down my forehead to the eyes behind the mask. Ahh … they were mine — still my familiar feral eyes. In them I saw the wild creatures of the land, sea and air; I saw hurricanes and swaying trees; rivers running free, and birds flying high. I saw me.

"Shall we go?" Yishmai asked at last, happy to indulgently let me stare at my transformed self.

I linked my arm with hers, and we went out the door together.

⁺⁺
⁺⁺

YISHMAI WAS RIGHT — I didn't recognise the main square at all. In the dark of night, the place was lit up with lanterns of all design, and candles of all shapes and sizes held safe and protected in hanging glass orbs. Like many others, we roamed among the bedecked tents before the carousing began, just taking it all in while we were comfortably able. There might be scant opportunity later.

The lights behind the white tents gave the place a surreal ambiance, reinforced by the mesmerising sounds flowing from instruments played by expert musicians. It appeared that in every tent food had been laid out: meat, fruit, delicate pastries and sweets. Yishmai reminded me that everything would be replenished till the festival's end.

Barrels upon barrels of alcohol held station between many of the tents, for easy access by revellers. Food attendants busied themselves rolling ground herbs in special paper, to be smoked by those wanting to assist themselves into an accommodating mood.

Yishmai explained that women past child-bearing years would serve as the main attendants, along with "unproven" females, who had been deemed barren. There were men who had shown themselves to be impotent or judged sterile, who would also not partake of the festivities except in the role of workers. Members of both sex with a physical or other birth issue would also toil, but play no other part in the three days of frolic, lest they threaten to pass on their "deficiency" to a next generation. None from among these would go masked. It's how those committed to trying to procreate for king and future would know not to waste their time. In an almost literal sense, unmasked translated to undesirable.

There had to be workers, though, to serve food, clean up spaces, fetch and carry, among other things. Some would be required to linger around, bearing ready trays heaped with various narcotics rolled in paper for smoking. In bags slung across their bodies, they bore herbs and other necessities for rolling fresh 'smokes' upon request.

Looks like everything's been thought of, I mused sourly.

Garlands of flowers, festive wreaths and thick, rainbow ribbons festooned everything. I had never beheld anything this grand in my life. For moments at a time, I almost forgot my woes and felt something akin to delight. Imagine, if that could happen to me, much less a girl like Yishmai.

Waves of sound rolled out from a gong, and resounded through the night air. Yishmai dragged at me, and we practically tumbled our way to the outskirt of the square where the launch assembly would take place.

I held tightly to Yishmai's hand when first confronted by the large mass of people whose faces I could not see. The air was fecund with laughter and cheery lifted voices. Despite this gay atmosphere, my stomach churned. I could not stop myself from imagining Oktar skulking behind any one of these masks.

A podium had been mounted for the king's speech, and he would certainly have a large audience. Even the King's Guard wore masks, standing by a bit more idly than normal.

King Carovor stepped up on the platform wearing a golden mask and long tunic, reminiscent of the golden statue in his likeness at the front of the settlement. *The place*

I had almost lost myself while committing allegiance to a lily-livered god-king.

I jerked, and looked around anxiously. I was so small and alone amongst all these enthusiasts. Their tide could easily engulf me, drown me in their sea of belief. How had I held off for this long? Even now, an avalanche of their enthusiasm almost buried me.

As if in answer, reminding me that I never walked alone, there in the crowd I saw Papa looking calmly at me. Of course he had no need of a mask. None but my eyes could behold his visage. My father nodded reassuringly, and I felt a little better.

After all the exultant noise, absolute silence descended eerily. It made me look from Papa to what everyone else was fixated on: King Carovor himself.

"My people!" the king began, "We are gathered here tonight for my annual Togetherness Festival." He paused dramatically amid thundering applause.

"You love your King?" he asked the crowd. They screamed an uncannily unified affirmative.

"Well, show your King love by showing each other love. Participate wholeheartedly, dutifully, in this most critical aspect of our culture. With this sharing of each other, you worship me. Thus, you ensure us future generations to worship me by your present acts of adoration. You will strengthen the knots that tie us together."

As if emotionally moved, a murmuring travelled through the masses, and the King's Guard did not seek to silence it.

I took the chance to turn to Yishmai, whose face was lit up with anticipation. I started to whisper her name, but stopped myself in time. Instead, to get her attention I squeezed her hand and queried, "What does the king do during the festival?"

166

She leaned closer to my ear without looking at me, "King Carovor participates like everyone else."

"But everyone knows who he is, he couldn't hide it," I indicated.

"Well, no, he couldn't. He's God. He makes the rules. His rules *have* to be different for Himself, Wren. When the God-king summons anyone who catches his eye, or the eyes of his Guard, in taking that person it is a great blessing he bestows," she cooed.

I felt sick thinking of that *man* in an intimate act with anyone: blobs of actually stinking fat resting on some horror-struck woman. *Ughhh!* I thrust the thought aside before it made me physically sick.

Following the king's speech, one of his scribes appeared on the stage with a scroll highlighting the do's and don'ts of the festival. It was all but comical: "Do engage in merriment. Do seek out the attentions of the opposite sex. Do engage in acts towards procreation for King and realm ..."

It all seemed like a dream — the loony, lurid kind.

No sooner had the king's herald blown his overtly large horn to signal the start of the festivities, than people promptly turned to drinking, eating and having sex — in the tents, outside the tents, under the trees, sometimes practically underfoot.

I had been forewarned that this would all be considered customary, but it was incredible to actually witness no one batting an eyelid.

I had lost Yishmai almost instantly. She was somewhere in the middle of all this madness. I gathered that was the point. Everybody had their something.

Few and far between I happened upon people simply talking. I saw Mary, the 70-year-old convert from my commune, serving a platter of minute pastries. She was wearing a white gown without a mask and barely looked up at all. I recognised Tuli, the young lad from my commune, by his characteristic posture of sulking while trying to look busy. It struck me that people must certainly be able to identify those they were familiar with, just as I had made out Tuli.

Other times I saw same-sex couples brusquely separated and shoved bodily in the direction of the opposite sex.

Everyone meant business, except for the odd person who was on their own; and I imagined that they were "new" like me.

I tried to blend in, always ensuring that I had a drink in hand —though it was the same drink I kept swilling in the fancy glass, "unintentionally" sloshing some out every now and then so the level went down. Then I'd get it topped up and begin the routine all over again.

My body had filled out again these last months, almost to the lithe curves I used to have. Men's eyes appreciated my long neck and legs, and seemed to equally enjoy everything else in between, sheathed in the shimmering blue. Several had approached me already, seeking my attentions and, doubtless, more. I brushed them off coyly and kept moving as I tried to figure out my next move.

Papa had disappeared some time ago in the throngs' initial dash. I was overjoyed when he reappeared.

"Papa!" I almost called out to him; but that might attract the attention of the many people within earshot of me, even if they couldn't see what I could.

Instead, I sent out a pressing word-thought, "Wait!" and elbowed my way toward him.

But Papa turned and went on beyond me. He just kept walking ahead, deeper into the crowds. I had to rub and slide against bodies in shouldering a way through, and eager hands kept rubbing and sliding across every exposed inch of my skin possible.

I lost sight of Papa altogether at one point, right

outside a tent where a couple, stark naked, was hard at it. The entrance of the tent remained pinned up, and I got the full view of them before I realised what I was seeing.

I was intrigued by this act. It was curious to see two strangers in masks interlocked in each other's bodies, fuelling such passion, with such strange rhythmic movements. So longingly they leaned in … with such lust. They wanted it, craved it and more.

It was different, say, from watching macaws in a primal mating ritual or rabbits thumping dutifully. I continued to watch, waiting to see what would happen next. Only when the woman's eyes fluttered open and languidly locked with my own did I manage to shake myself out of the trance. I quickly hunched away.

A short while later, Papa re-emerged, in a rare open space between two smaller tents. I followed in his wake, not unlike a ghost myself. He finally stopped and was waiting ahead for me. As I approached him, he pointedly looked to his left.

A man in a rich beige robe and matching mask stood talking to a woman whose hands roamed up and down his arm and chest. I halted and looked to Papa, questioning with my eyes. He was still there, answering with his eyes in turn, prodding me to look on at the near couple. So I did.

As the woman reached up to kiss the man, his eyes behind the mask shifted and looked fully at me. Like an arrow I'd once seen pierce a fleeing doe, a fierce energy propelled straight through me to the chest. Even camouflaged by costumed finery, I could tell those eyes apart. I knew those enchanting hazel eyes, that shouldn't belong to any earthbound creature. The *look* in them fanned a spark inside me, urging it into a great fire that spread through my body … to places I blushed to acknowledge.

Soldier rested one hand on the woman's chest and slowly pushed her away, easing himself out of her grip at the same time. I did not see what she did — she did not call out or follow at least — because I only had eyes for him. He walked towards me.

Despite it all, I willed myself to step back, run away. I looked to Papa, for some kind of confirmation. When he gave none, I opened my mouth to shout at him, *Why have you led me here to my enemy*? But in a blink Papa was gone.

With each step Soldier took, my heart did a somersault; my hands fidgeted, my lips trembled. And here he was ... right up to me, his face inches from mine.

Allowed by the freedoms of this festival, Soldier cupped my face in gentle hands, leaned in and kissed me. The warmth experienced when I had seen him before filled me up again; so much it threatened to spill all over everything. His roaming tongue sought out a sweet surrender from my mouth. It was with such passion that his lips caressed mine, I accepted hazily that he didn't realise who I was.

But any doubt lingering within me was put to rest when he stopped kissing me and, with his lips still touching mine, whispered, "Idzorah-Ulka."

THIRTEEN

Soldier

T slapped him so hard my palm stung. Soldier was slow to react. When he did, it wasn't in any way I expected.

He showed no anger, no surprise at my aggression towards him. He straightened his knocked askew mask, then spoke calmly, with ease and familiarity, like we were old friends.

"I deserve it, I know. But eyes are everywhere. I have to keep up appearances," he explained softly.

Why are his eyes smiling at a time like this?

His words prompted me to look cautiously around. Everyone was frolicking, seemingly caught up in their own affairs. But — and I hated to admit it — Soldier was right. No freedom was true in this place.

My former captor took my spasming hand and drew me toward a tent. *Ughhh!* I wanted to rip my palm away from his. I wanted to throw a fit of rage, and scream in his face, at his face, all day long. But that was not all. A part of me longed to grip his hand tighter, to interlock my fingers into his, to feel his hand's touch and every-thing in between, and never let go in case he disappeared, like a little sunny bird on the wind. I was in an emotional tug-of-war with myself, pushing and pulling parts of me in different directions with powerful, compelling emotions, and I wasn't sure which one would win.

Finding an empty tent initially proved difficult. At least we were able to realise this even upon approach — by the sounds of pleasure emanating from within. We were, thus, often saved from having to lift flaps and glimpsing ...

At last Soldier flipped an entryway up and gestured for me to enter. I wasn't sure about anything I was feeling, so I focused on trying *not* to lose my focus — which I was absolutely in danger of!

Inside the tent, there were undergarments and two half-finished bottles of liquor discarded on the woven mat lain across the grass. There was a low table with platters of food evidently eaten from; some throw-pillows propped up as though to create comfort, and a lantern whose dancing flame, beneath prismatic glass, cast eerie shadows of ourselves that kept our company.

I gulped. *What am I doing here?*

Soldier lifted his mask. The sight of his face was like a blow. I turned away, actually clutching my gut. He didn't share my apprehension. I felt his hands upon my shoulders and he made me face him. My heart jumped high when both his hands rose and brushed against my neck. *Soldier* gently eased the mask up till it was resting over my brow.

"What are you doing! We could get caught," I hissed.

He smiled a charming smile, and caught the hands I raised to pull the mask back down. "Trust me. Everyone's busy."

I shot him a gimlet eye. "Why are you even here?"

His brows curved downward briefly, then relaxed. "Here, as in, with you? Or —"

"I mean here in this crazy society! Why have you not

gone home? Why hasn't your all-powerful family thrown its gold about to buy your freedom!" I pressed him hard.

No answer was forthcoming. He just gazed at me with his beautiful hazel eyes, like their willpower would silence my questions.

"Why hasn't your family come for you?" I asked again, fumbling to sound rational.

"I failed in my quest," he said in a flat tone.

My insides turned sour.

He should be dead. Dead like Papa, and mother. Dead like Maie, and Melon, and those other Baiuchi villagers who fell while no loving eyes looked upon them, and no soothing voices bade them safe journey to the place beyond. But he, the instigator, was still here, and it wasn't fair. I could fix that though, I had the means.

But I looked into his hazel eyes and saw no malice. Just like Papa's eyes held none when he had led me to this man. Why, I didn't know but I owed it Papa to stay and find out. Sigh.

"What does failing have to do anything?"

"I … I believe I've been disowned. That is what happens when a prince fails a royal quest such as mine," he muttered, the earlier light in his eyes finally dimming.

I stared him up and down, down and up. He wasn't joking. Was I supposed to feel sorry for this — this "converter"? *Not even for you, Papa.*

"I tried to make contact with my family, but with no money or men, it has proven difficult. I promised payment to any messenger who would deliver a communication to my father. Several took up my offer. Whether my father received the message is a mere guess at this time. I've not heard back. If help was coming it would have been here already.

"At least one of the messages was intercepted, and I was flogged in the square. The messenger was taken away

173

to the King's Court for punishment and never seen again. I — I think no one is coming for me," he rasped. He looked forlorn.

I relaxed my shoulders, and stared up at the canvas of the tent. It was patterned by dirt and wear from previous usage, but looked so pristine and unsoiled externally. Was it at all possible to know the very heart of a thing just by how it looked from outside?

"How long have we been here?" I finally asked.

"I'd say just under a year" he replied.

"A whole year," I muttered to myself, deeply distressed that another year might pass, and another, until I was an old woman with no hope left of escape. Maybe I would decline into the likes of Elder Darja, labouring away to twist the minds and hearts of girls who longed to be free ... girls like me.

Soldier was about to take my hand, I gathered from his movements. His eyes sparked when I grabbed his first.

"We have to escape!" I declared.

"Yes! But how? It's heavily guarded and —"

"I know. I know. But every problem has a solution," I advanced.

"You've found an answer to this problem already?" he asked, half hopefully.

"Yes. And no! Our best chance is to leave before this festival comes to an end: while everyone is high on hard drink, sex and the delusion of freedom."

The more I spoke of it, the more I grew convinced my plan was sound.

"What of the King's Guard?" Soldier asked.

I sighed in exasperation, "We need a distraction. A worthy disruption."

"What do you have in mind?" As if he wasn't already close enough, he leaned even closer.

174

I met him halfway and ground out, "I'm going to kill the king."

He pulled back in surprise.

"You? You're going to kill the king?" He asked, staring at me intently, searching my face as if it hid secrets that would come undone under his piercing look.

"Yes," I stated matter-of-factly to his questioning face.

More staring. *Why the hell is he looking at me this way?* Soldier took a quick breath in and said, "Let me do it. I can —"

"No," I sounded sharper and colder than I had intended to.

"Idz— "

"I have a plan."

The colour drained from his face and he stammered out, "It's dangerous. For you especially. And I don't want ... I mean ... you don't want to have more blood on your hands, trust me. I put you in that position once before. So let me do it —"

I looked away and abruptly put my hand up to signal for him to stop. I didn't want to hear it. But now I couldn't unhear it; and as fast as his words had taken form, they conjured up haunting images of the bloodied stone he wrested from my dirtied hands. I saw again, next to me, the blood that I had spilled, oozing from the corpse of his soldier — a perpetrator, not too far from the body of my sweet, sweet friend Maie — an innocent.

Soldier ignored my call for silence. "The more blood you spill, the more it will chip away from you. Coming back from that is hard. It's so hard," he stuttered.

The more blood you spill, the more it will chip away from you. His words echoed through my ear canal and lingered. I closed my eyes briefly and tried to shake them away.

"If you go off the paved path past Commune 12, there's an old disused building at the edge of the property,"

I described. "Meet me behind it by the chain fence tomorrow, when the moon is at its fullest. I don't think we'll have another opportunity like this anytime soon, what with everyone being drunk and, yeah, horny.

"Bring food — as much as you can carry," I instructed, racking my brains for anything else. "And any weapons you can find."

That Papa led me to Soldier here and now, it must be for this. It was the perfect opportunity that I'd been waiting for: a sidetracking festival with drunkenness and sex; and company to make my escape.

Why did I need company? I wasn't sure. Maybe it made it less scary? Seeing Soldier stirred a flickering flame inside of me. For whatever reason, he was fanning this flame, and I took it as a sign from the universe and Mother Goddess. The time was now.

One of his thick eyebrows made a sharp arch, "Where will we escape to? Do you know these lands?"

"I don't. But we will go to the forest across the river, and continue northward, I think. We may be able to find my cousin's village high in the mountains."

He searched my face, for what I couldn't know, and my heartbeats sprang about uneasily.

"You don't know how to get there, do you?"

"No. But I'll be damned if I spend another year in this hell-hole," I barked defensively.

"I understand, Idzorah. However, our chances would be better if we try to find another, nearer civilisation? There must be neighbouring villages besides those run by this king. Don't you agree?" he posited.

Anger steadily edged back into me as I watched Soldier. I backed away from him, my hands sliding from his to hang at my side. They started shaking again, I was so furious now. I tilted my chin and let my look at him run down my upward tilted nose. He wanted my opinion? I'd give him it.

"Do whatever you want! I am not going in search of any other so-called civilised societies. If they are near here, Carovor holds sway over them, and what happens here must surely happen by their acceptance!

"All I've seen committed by these murderers, rapists, and child-stealers— well if these are civilised ways then I am truly a savage. I embrace it!" I pronounced, enunciating every word.

Soldier regarded me silently, poignantly, like ... a star had fallen in his lap. His words were as heavenly to me, "And I embrace you, Idzorah-Ulka. Whenever you go, I will go, too."

I should have been confused. Confused by what he had just said. Confused by my own words, and why I was bent on making a plan to abruptly leave with him, of all people. Maybe it was that I had no one else, and he was better than no one? But his words opened my eyes to myself, to what had become the sharp, clear, sudden truth in me: it wasn't just that I had no one else. I wanted to save myself, and I wanted to save him.

For myself?

"Why should I trust you?" I asked suddenly. I knew I was actually asking it of myself.

"Idzorah, not a day has gone by that I've not regretted deeply what I did to your people. I've learned so much since —"

"Look! Just don't think that you're good in my book because we're working together on this. If I had someone else," I lied awkwardly, "I wouldn't choose you!"

He nodded. "I know. I understand."

"No you don't! So stop saying that you do! You have no idea the hell I've been in while you've been here enjoying the finer side of life in this evil shit-hole!" There was no mistaking the vitriol spewing out of me now.

Soldier turned away for a moment, clenched his fists then turned back to me. He drew a shuddering breath and began, "You're right. I have no idea what it must have been like for you. But I saw you suffer. I — I *felt* your suffering.

My narrow look doubted him to his face.

He rushed on: "I saw them chop your beautiful hair off; shave you bald, and leave you in the rain. You could have died. I picked you up and carried your half-dead body when Oktar almost choked the life out of you. I imagined, if this is how he treated you publicly, what he must have done to you in private," he choked up, and I thought I saw tears well in his eyes.

Had I, though? I was too focused on trying to prevent a river spilling from my own to confirm his.

"You carried me? You were there in the market when ...?" I asked, looking away as shame stole over me fast.

"Yes."

"I thought it was a dream," I said, feeling befuddled.

"It was no dream. It almost broke me, completely realising if I'd never done what I did, you would still be in your village with your people, and none of this would have happened to you.

"I almost rushed in; but it was the old woman, Darja, who warned me it would be worse for both of us if I did. That I could only help you by staying alive. I *am* responsible for your suffering, Idzorah-Ulka. I will never stop until I make it like it was." Soldier fell silent.

I fervently wished there was some way to make things over as they had been. I had crossed a decrepit bridge, which collapsed after I reached the other side. There was no going back.

"It is a nice thought. A nice dream. But you cannot

make this right. You have permanently altered my existence" I felt a single teardrop roll down my right cheek.

He wiped it away with the back of his hand and touched it to his lips. His fixed his gaze on me. "Then I will spend the rest of my life at least trying."

I looked at the man before me. His face bore stubble but it wasn't unbecoming on him. It made him look more of a man, less a soldier. As I stared at him, there was a war raging within me. On the one hand I wished to fight him, kill him in cold blood like his men had murdered my people. On the other hand, I felt compelled to ... love him.

The thought repelled me, but my feelings were there nonetheless. Still, I called myself stupid, weak! I told myself it was because I had no one else; I tried to make myself wish there was someone else to escape with me. But that we had been brought together, two opposite beings now caught up in a common purpose, could only be fate at work.

"I never stopped trying to find you," Soldier said.

Don't ask why, idiot girl! He'll tell you, and you don't want to hear what you know he'll say.

"Why?" I asked anyway.

"Because," he whispered, "you are my redemption. You're the only one who can save me."

"What the hell are you on about? You must be confused!" I barked. His words, so close to what I myself had thought, had struck a nerve, making it ring bitterly.

I blustered, "Save you? I should kill you where you stand!"

"Is that all you want?" he asked.

Slap!

"Ouch," he murmured, touching his face.

"What's wrong with you?" I demanded.

"All I am saying is that I am in your debt, and will remain so until you release me," he replied.

"You are released! Now stop this!" I hated saying the words, and I hoped he couldn't tell I didn't really mean them.

"Not like that," he said, a subtle smile playing across his lips.

I sighed. "It is a fool's errand seeking forgiveness, *Soldier*. Men cry out to debtors, 'I forgive you, I forgive you'; but in their hearts bitterness rules and is seated behind the true, unacknowledged human inclination to seek justice for the wrongs endured."

He listened attentively, never once interrupting.

"Most of us do not speak of wanting justice, but in earnest, this is among our strongest desires. We think that justice will somehow restore the something snatched from our souls. That it will make our tormented lives somehow more bearable," I said with a faded smile. I wasn't certain where the smile came from, but I suspect it was at my own recognition of the folly behind that way of thinking.

"You mean to say that your need for justice is standing in the way of you forgiving me?" he asked, after a bit of contemplation.

"Yes," I said unequivocally.

"Then take it," said Soldier, extending his arms wide in surrender. "I am here and I will not resist."

I quaked. Could I really take my vengeance? Someone had to pay! But, I was ashamed to admit, I didn't know if it should be this man.

"If only it were that simple. You have spun an irrevocable web of catastrophe that has led to lives being trapped and devoured. It cannot be undone. Do not live in hope of my forgiveness. Ever ..." I said, my voice trailing off.

He sighed, then glanced away. Something like disenchantment etched itself across his face. "All right. All right. Then tell me, what can I do to help us escape?" he asked.

"Well, you are a soldier. You can fight, can't you?"

"Yes. But Idzorah-Ulka, the king's men, they're everywhere."

"They're not everywhere. Leave it to me, I have a plan. Just be ready to fight if need be. Be ready to really fight. Remember, tomorrow night."

"I won't forget."

"And just to be sure, don't say anything to anyone, not even that woman, okay?" I asserted.

I saw that he was about to ask, "What woman?" but then stalled.

"Oh. No, of course not," was all he replied.

"Is that all?" I asked, a spark of jealousy flaring in me.

"Is what all?"

I feigned laughter. "Who is she, Soldier?"

"I was married —"

"Married? Wow!" I exclaimed, pretending I didn't already know.

"It never meant anything," he chafed.

"I'm sure."

"What's the matter with you? You hate me, but you don't like that I'm married to some enslaving woman?"

I rolled my eyes and grimaced. Soldier's pretty eyes went round.

"Look, I didn't have a choice! They *married* me to this woman. She saw me and asked the king's permission. It was against my will, and I certainly don't recognise this king's authority, so it means nothing to me. They *force* things on us, these people!"

I looked away, feeling ashamed. I, of all people, should know that.

Soldier took my hand in his, brought it to his mouth, then kissed it. I wanted to pull away, to spurn him and run off; but I didn't. I let him continue to hold my hand until it dawned on us that we should leave the tent. We both slipped our masks back down and walked out.

A drizzle had begun, but the festival attendees weren't bothered. The rain was fresh and so light that no one seemed to notice it. *Soldier* walked away into the dampening crowd, half glancing back before stopping himself and striding on.

I was left to ponder on the how and when of my plan. I had to look for the right opportunities and seize them before the moments passed.

I walked in the other direction, feigning smiles and a look of drunkenness, to scope out the rest of the festival activities and guard allocation. It wasn't hard.

I lingered past the last string of tents nearing the square, where I once saw a man strapped against a pole, and saw groups of people stood, sat and lay down next to two camp fires, smoking fragrant herbs. The air was hazy and replete with it. The atmosphere was different, like stepping into another level of this place — like I'd crossed over past an unseen veil. My gait slowed, as did time.

Throngs of people danced like possessed figures, alone and together, twirling skirts, unbuttoned shirts, in a high fever, arms and hands making rhythmic movements in the air. Colours dazzled and merged, vibrations dipped then surged, with a thousand laughters in different notes, a chorus of insanity infecting this age of inhumanity.

I had paused to watch, and it was the beating of drums here with varying depths that made me do so. I felt the hollowness of the sound pull me inwards, like I was sucked into a space between here and there, where the music took shape before release into the world. I stood for a while, in a trance, then walked away unsteadily from the drums to the nearing sounds of a band with flutes and stringed instruments, coming from the southern side of the property.

I walked aimlessly but with knowing, still inside myself

as the festival happened around me. No one persisted when they approached me, and I simply walked on with my feigned smile. Here and there, hands passed across my shoulders, my back and one tried to hold onto my hand. I was struggling to steady my gait. I followed the sounds of the flutes and paused again, then looked up to see the idol of King Carovor.

I was back here, the golden idol still standing, masses around it drunken, dancing, drifting with the sounds and in the mood of the festival.

Mary, the eldest convert from Commune 12, was serving drinks on a tray. She wasn't wearing a mask and her posture had a certain kind of 'confident but don't care' air to it. Once I even asked her about it. She said it was down to "the wisdom of age and not giving a shit about the things that don't matter." She had said it with that intriguing lilt in her accent.

"Can ah pour you a wee drink lass," she said with a serious face, but there was a sincerity in her eyes.

"No thanks," I muttered, examining the tray of cups and bottle of drink hanging from her neck.

"Sure?"

"Yeah," I said, as I examined her face and wondered how she had managed to stay calm the whole time I'd known her.

She reached into a brown satchel slung across her shoulder and handed me a drinking pouch. "Water. Filled it mihself. Stay hydrated an' don bother to drink the stuff we serving tomorrow evenin'. Tis no good for a little lass like yerself," she said. "Yer hear?"

I nodded.

"Good lass!" said Mary, as she walked on to offer drinks to a group opposite us. They cheered as she started refilling their cups. I plopped myself on the grass to sit a bit and stared curiously at the small pouch Mary had handed to me. I opened it and took a whiff. Water. Just water. I looked up at her, still cheerfully serving drinks to the avid attendees. A small space in the raucous crowd cleared and a familiar face appeared. Noah the convert was stood there, staring at me intensely.

‡
‡

THE SKY WAS overcast but the sun shone brightly through a break in the clouds. I took it as a sign from Mother-God that deliverance would come in these perilous times.

I had tried sleeping in a tent near the square once my wooziness had eased, but Noah's piercing eyes kept bothering me, so I snuck back to my shack and dozed in and out of a restless sleep. If anyone asked, I'd say I had wanted to freshen up.

Not wanting to raise any suspicions, I headed back to the festival in the late morning, and was surprised to see that some people were already socialising and drinking, while others were asleep in the open spaces and tents.

Some were unashamedly cleaning themselves from buckets with washcloths in the open areas, while others headed to the public wash areas. Festival attendees were clearing away rubbish from the previous day's festivities and preparing to replenish food stocks due to come in from the kitchens.

I poured myself a cup of mint tea from one of the food tables and sat in silence as I watched the band of drummers coming back to their instruments. I looked like any of the people nearby who were waiting for fresh food to be brought.

Half hour and a hot bread-bun later, the drummers

were in full swing again. People seemed reared up by the rhythms while getting hot food in their systems. The food stalls were fully stocked with cooked meats, bread, nuts and fruit and drink. Attendees like Mary and Tuli were walking around everywhere, offering nibbles from on their trays to those awaiting their chances at the stalls.

I was gazing at everyone, and trying to name that strange feeling like the world was happening to me, around me, and I was just a bystander, except for when people needed a villain, then all eyes were set upon me. But even then it still didn't feel real. My reality might have been a dream. As I pondered, I noticed Yishmai stumbling towards me with a red-headed guy in tow.

"Ohhh, jeeere you are!" she slurred.

I smiled at her. "Perhaps you should sit down for a bit, Yishmai."

"No, no! I brought you something," she said, looking to the fetching fellow next to her.

The fine specimen of maleness smiled at me engagingly and, seemingly confident in his own charms, extended a ready hand towards my face. I pulled back.

"Whash wrong? Is he not to your liking?" Yishmai lisped out. "I can find you someshing else to suit you. Just tell me what you want."

She whirled none too steadily to call out to a blond man in a golden tunic walking by a few paces away, the red-head forgotten.

"No, Yishmai, no!" I snapped.

She stopped at once at my sharpness, and regarded me with pouty lips, "What is the matter, Wren?"

"I appreciate it, but I don't want to. I've — had enough for now," I clarified.

"But it's your duty," she argued, swaying from side to side.

"I know, I know," I lied. "I'm just tired, taking a little break. Not used to … so much," I grinned.

"Uh huh," said Yishmai in a lingering tone with a dash of doubt.

"What?" I asked innocently, but as Yishmai opened her mouth to respond, a familiar voice called out.

Elder Darja approached in the company of two armed men.

"A word?" She said, turning around to walk back in the direction she came before Yishmai could even respond. The girl scuttled behind her mother, turning around briefly only to mouth, "I'll be back, stay there."

The red-head looked at me, as Yishmai was walking off. He shrugged his shoulders then wandered off the way they'd come.

As I watched Yishmai trying to catch up with Elder Darja, the sounds around me layered up on one another. The drums and flutes rose up; the shuffling of human movements, laughter, words being spoken aloud, the clanking of cups and activities stirring up again. A stridency of sound, that grew and grew, and the higher it went, the queasier I began to feel in my stomach, like something wasn't right.

I twiddled my fingers while waiting for Yishmai to return. The festival was in full swing again, with some revellers looking as fresh as if it were day one.

The crowd cleared a space with pace, then filled it back just as quickly, like a murmuration of starlings, to let ten of the king's armed men march through in rank file, headed in the direction of the new convert commune buildings. Revellers stopped to look for a minute, but as soon as the guards passed it was back to business as festival usual. I continued to watch the soldiers march on, tasting a bitter unease.

The glint of bright yellow caught my peripheral attention. *Yishmai*!

I readied myself with the realest fake smile I could muster and was about to say hello as she walked straight toward me; but she just linked her elbow onto mine and kept on walking at a pace.

"Uh, Yish — what's going on?"

Nothing.

"Hey, can we stop for a moment?"

Still nothing, but her heavy breathing.

"Ok stop!" I brought myself to an abrupt halt, forcing Yishmai to stop beside me.

She could barely get a word in between her panting.

"We have to go see the king," she said.

I unlinked my arm from hers and took a quick step back. "What? Why?"

"Can't explain right now," she said.

"Well try."

"Something's wrong," she looked around us in both directions. "There's word of some sort of plot."

"Plot? What kind of plot?" I asked in shocked horror.

My insides twisted. *Did they know about me? They couldn't.*

"I don't know. I'm not sure, but it's bad. And the king is vexed. I mean, real vexed. Elder Darja says if no one owns up to it, the king will start picking people at random to punish. Starting with the new converts," she said.

I paused to think. This development had thrown a spoke in my plan.

"Okay, okay, so why … why do we have to see the king?" I tried not to sound nervous.

Stay calm, stay calm, stay cam …

"*You*," she stressed, "have to take the lead, make an offering, or … or pledge to help him find the true culprit," she said.

"What kind of offering? I asked in confusion.

Shit, shit, shit …

She shook her head and shrugged while mumbling beneath her breath, "Well, what do you have?"

My stomach churned.

"No. I don't have anything worth offering the king. No," I shook my head in a quick motion.

SHIT!

Yishmai gripped my arms and moved in closer to me to whisper. "You have to try."

I pulled away brusquely. "No — I …"

The idea alone was making me nauseous.

I knew why she was saying it. I was the perfect scapegoat. I had managed to keep my head down, but didn't put as much effort in pretending to integrate as the other converts. I had used up all of the energy I had left in secretly planning.

Just as I opened my mouth to put up more pleading protests, a gong bellowed out from the main stage area. A familiar voice started to speak over the speakers and everyone hushed.

"Fellow Carovorians, it appears that one or some of you have crimes to answer for. It might be nothing, let's hope we're wrong; but just to make sure, the King in his kindness offers you a chance to come clean and there will be no punishment. If no one comes forward, I'll start picking people to pay at random, starting from among the newer converts."

A nervous wave of murmurs passed through the crowds, and though we were nowhere near the stage we could tell something was happening.

"Starting with this one," said Oktar over the speakers.

The wave of whispers and murmurs passed word through the crowd, that one of Commune 12 had been detained. Tuli, the quietest lad in my commune, had been identified as the one to pay in the stead of whoever was plotting against the king.

Oktar paused with a heavy breath over the microphone. "If no one comes forward by sunset, Tuli of Commune 12 will die."

"Please, please," Tuli's pleas could be heard just off the loud speaker before it went dead.

Yishmai and I looked at each other.

"If you don't do something now, tomorrow or the next day that might be you," said Yishmai, suddenly sounding angry. "What is wrong with you, Wren?"

"What's wrong with *me*?" I asked, caught in genuine surprise.

"Yeah. We've tried to keep you alive, to give you a future, and you won't even try to help yourself."

"Excuse me?!" I sounded more shocked than I had intended to.

I could see she was frustrated, but I genuinely didn't know what Yishmai expected from me.

She threw her hands in the air and shouted, "Do what you want!" before bolting off into the crowd.

A cold chill ran across my body. I felt it, like invisible hands making the hairs on my arms and neck stand upright. Poor Tuli. What would they do to him? Next it could be any of the converts from the other communes, or Mary, Noah or me — any of us new ones. Maybe they would hurt anyone belonging to a commune they'd pulled converts from to punish. Maybe they would hurt Yishmai.

I ran after her. "Yishmai, I'm sorry! Yishmai?" I shouted, but she had disappeared into the throngs of lasciviously cavorting festival-goers.

"Yishmai, I'm sorry," I whispered, if not for her ears, for my own.

I decided I had to look for her. I suppose in this pernicious place, where the gulf between me and these people was very wide, Yishmai had given me something to hold on to. She had showed me some degree of goodness that seemed absent everywhere else here. Out of gratitude, for that at least, I owed her an apology.

I ran through the crowds in my long dress, which made me clumsy as I tried to navigate abandoned, frolicking revellers and their detritus. For brief, brief moments I glimpsed familiar faces and silhouettes in the crowds. Or I thought I did.

My sisters. Kajri and Qarnai, had a knack for manoeuvring brilliantly through crowds, mazes, and the sorts of things that adults in my village were tripped up or injured by. There were two girls ahead of me now, their laughter reaching impossibly back to my ears, weaving their way through the clusters of people, tents, liquor barrels and fallen decoration. They trailed strips of coloured cloth that waved in the light winds, streaming the songs of our Mother Goddess in their wake. It called me on; alit my feet with haste, and I abandoned my search for Yishmai.

"Kaj? Qarni? Wait!" I called after them as they led me through the old side of the market area, now transformed into mass lovers' nests.

I ran as fast as I could, which was very fast. I ran like the Idzorah-Ulka who had grown up chasing the wind in the vast forests bordering my home. I ran the way I used to when I had the feel of the earth under my soles. And as I ran, I remembered: wet or dry, the earth was mine; never an obstacle, but a propeller when I needed a push forward.

At the edge of the market square, the laughing girls disappeared. The revellers were dispersed here — spread out amongst the various forking paths. The glitter-covered couples seemed to be taking breathers: mingling, flirting, dancing drunkenly as the sounds of music floated, fainter here, on the breezes.

I skid to a sudden stop, staring at a path that made its way through to King Carovor's residence.

A pang of something reached in and hit my heart hard. I threw myself on my knees to catch my breath and beg for strength. I closed my eyes for a moment then looked up to the skies. The rain that was not quite rain had cleared, and the sun peered through the lifting veil of clouds like a promise of good to come.

"Where are you, my sisters? Were you even here?" I muttered.

My time in these Veridhakth Lands had bared me to the rough, gritty nature of pain. I felt its sharp edges daily, like razors cutting me enough to hurt me and strike fear; but not thoroughly enough to kill me. So I lived on always with the anticipation of more pain to come. I just never knew when.

Yet, whatever I had suffered, whatever I had endured, the burden of not knowing my sisters' fate hurt deepest of all. It was a load that doomed me to search endlessly, with little hope in sight.

My thoughts were interrupted by a glimpse of familiar bright yellow in the distance. I knew that dress. Yishmai? She was headed to the king's residence.

FOURTEEN

Flightless Bird

I shadowed Yishmai until she strolled through the huge gates and right up and into the double front doors — strangely standing wide open — of her king's residence. Tall golden pillars and two guards flanked either side. Carovor must have been quite confident in his people's devotion, to leave his premises so lightly guarded.

My thoughts whirred at the thought that Yishmai was about to report me to her demon of a king. All of this plead your innocence with an offering made no sense to me at all. And what plots were they suspicious of? This distraction wasn't good for my escape plan, especially as it turned the focus on the new converts. I had to find out what was going on.

Suddenly, I was grateful for Yishmai's blatherings about the king's "glorious" abode every time we'd had to pass on the road outside its gates. I had listened indifferently, certain all she claimed to know first-hand was most likely gleaned from things Elder Darja, apparently a frequent visitor here, had spoken about to persons other than Yishmai herself.

I hunted through my memory and was rewarded.

There was an alley that led to near the king's chambers. Servants used it at dawn to discreetly dispose of Carovor's very human nightly waste. I located it, and ran through to the back of the building, to what I assumed would be the throne room.

Much of the building appeared to have undergone renovations, with no one sparing a thought for its rear outer exterior. The work there was rough, and moss was growing through fissures, which went unnoticed to the passing eye. The funny thing about cracks in a thing, is even if it's too small to notice, at some point the crack gives way to a weed of some kind. A destructive weed that grows and grows, and by the time you do notice, it has already had some negative effect on its surroundings.

I rolled the light flared skirt of my dress up to my thigh on one side and knotted it. I did the same on the other side. With my legs thus freed, I proceeded up the wall, as I had scaled many a tree in my homeland. Before I reached the window with light emanating from it, I could hear lifted voices carrying on the clear evening air. Gripping onto the blocks and nooks in the wall for dear life, I peeped through a small ventilation gap.

Ah, it wasn't the throne room, but a temple of sorts. Human-sized statues in the king's likeness stood in the four corners of the room. The space was lit by many tall candles, and populated by silver-masked men in long purple robes. They appeared to be praying.

In a chair on a dais almost central in the room, King Carovor sat with his two hands opened upwards, as though he was about to receive something sacred. He was still wearing his opulent golden robe, topped by a crown of striking jewels.

A guard approached and whispered in the king's ear. *Damn it!* I could see but I couldn't hear a thing.

Yishmai was ushered in and half-bowed awkwardly

before the king, holding the edge of her dress with her arm extended in a demure way, though the pose actually revealed more of her lower body under the short hem. I could see they were speaking with each other, but that didn't last long. Soon, Yishmai moved in closer to the king's chair, then closer still, till she stood directly before him. And then the old, disgusting man took hold of her and kissed her!

I had to cling to the wall more tightly, as repugnance almost made me lose my hold and fall. The king embraced Yishmai closely, petting and fondling her. In his arms, she looked more like the little girl she was. I felt sick.

Carovor put Yishmai from him to give her a drink brought in by a servant. She sipped obediently. After, he brought the same place where her lips had touched the cup to his own lips. While he drank, watching her keenly, Yishmai pulled the thin straps of her dress off her shoulders one after the other and let the glittery frock fall to the floor.

One of the king's robed men anointed her with something out of a silver bowl. He put his hand in the bowl then his hand to her face. After that, he made circular gestures with his hands as he walked around her saying … Singing? Something.

Yishmai never turned around from facing Carovor. My heart bucked and sped up, as another of the King's Guard, toting a spear, moved behind my young companion. Without warning or hesitation, he rammed the spear through Yishmai's diminutive frame!

The life felt sucked from me hard. I gasped for air, and a burning current enveloped my entire body.

My last vision of the king was him biting roughly and without any restraint into Yishmai's limp, uplifted hand, from where she had fallen to the floor, gushing blood.

Carovor tore her flesh away with blood-stained teeth. My fingers let loose from the walls.

I fell with a heavy thud on the grass, and pain rippled along my spine. I lay there staring blankly into the sky. Staring, but not seeing. *Am I breathing?* A wave had hit me. I felt it tumbling me over and over, and I found myself unable to move against its force. As if stuffed full of water, my ears had stopped working … the former distant sounds of festival revelry and debauchery shifted into nothingness, into clean white silence, which encased me.

Move, I tried to will myself. *Move!*

I had no idea what words had been exchanged between the king and Yishmai. But that paled in weight to … She had been speared in cold blood! Oh, my Mother God. Oh, my …

This is a society of cannibals.

Something about those words was like a slap. My thoughts began to slowly return as I lay there — Goddess knows how long — in shock. As my thoughts gradually cleared, I felt deep regret at what I had said to Yishmai — a girl, just a girl, only doing as she was told, as she'd been taught to do her whole life. Just a girl who had been amazingly kind to me, despite those teachings. The truth was I had done nothing to ever really thank or befriend her.

Now I truly wanted to weep, but my mind was too messed up to even get that right. I might have lain there longer, but my papa appeared with no words, only an outstretched hand. He pulled me up out of my stupor. I found myself running again, running.

I had to tell Soldier. We needed to expedite our plan. We couldn't wait another day. Back in the market square among revellers, I was brought up hard by the realisation that I didn't know where to look for him. I didn't know where he lived or where he had gone. Only that I had told him to meet me near the workhouse the following day, when the moon was at its highest. Damn it. *Damn it!*

The drunkenness of the festival didn't have time for a bleary-eyed, unsure girl. As I walked around with cautious steps, my heart beating in my mouth, it became more evident that the fruit was rotten on the inside. As I took in the sights of vulgarity, everything seemed to slow. I watched the women with their breasts out, sharing the laps of men. I watched the lurid imbibing of alcohol and hoggish devouring of excess food, sometimes right off the ground.

I recalled the dearth of compassion I had encountered during my worst times of suffering here. This now, was the true face of these people; not the demure souls wearing white going about productive days and restful nights.

The macabre construct of this culture made me think of a bitter truth: some things, only fire would cleanse. The society that professed to be a paragon of righteousness for others was rotten, with worms eating it from the core.

A delayed reaction to what I had earlier witnessed — an innocent lamb devoured by a conniving wolf — but what little I had consumed earlier erupted unrestrainedly out my unprepared mouth. I fell to my knees and let it be done. At the end, I found I had little strength left to continue to pretend I was a part of this deviant scene.

It was with much effort that I made it back to my wooden shack, my body acting instinctively. Thoughts raced around in my head, too much to process, too fast to stop. I was fearful of stepping inside, but had to, figuring there was nowhere safer. Should I have gone to the Oracle's house? Back to the Commune 12 common hall?

I aimed for the bed, but was unsteady and ended up on the floor, trying to slow my thoughts, my breathing.

In, one, two … Out, three, four…
Yishmai. Oh … no.

"Papa, Papa!" I whimpered beneath my breathe.

He appeared beside me. "You will find your cousins in the mountains daughter. It is a hard trek, but others have made it over the years."

"Why won't you let me come with you?" I blurted, sounding young and foolish, even to my own ears.

Papa didn't answer. He didn't need to. I had to ask. The pain had burrowed its way through my skin, till I felt it taking form inside my body, like something alive within me that I had no control over. It plastered layers and layers of itself over my humanity — what was left of it.

I was alarmed when I found myself dozing off, but I realised it must have been extreme shock, coupled with acute tiredness: seeing Yishmai brutally, coldly killed; months of sleeping with one eye open half the time, and the other half dreaming of some place I needed to get to but couldn't quite find.

"I know you're tired, my precious child, but you must go, now. Idzorah! Go to meet Soldier." Papa's voice lingered in the distance of my consciousness.

I tumbled into a deep slumber and dreams, feeling flooded by strong gushing waters. The more I resisted the more I found myself going under. I stopped struggling when I saw my sisters, mother and Papa beneath. I let my limbs go free and sank into the depths toward my waiting family. In the liberation of the waters, I saw Sunny, my yellow-headed birdie-friend, fly past us with great ease through the welcoming waters.

I woke gagging. Before I could properly catch my breath and register the alarm in Papa's widened eyes, a rustling outside my door made me leap up with great antic-ipation.

"Soldier?" I whispered.

A loud crash and my door splintered inward.

It wasn't Soldier. I could see four armed men bunched

together beyond my door, fully blocking the way. It was King's Guard. They had come for me.

The evening sun was departing on the second day of the festival, and it cast an undeserved ray of light on the men. They parted enough to let a fifth man pass comfortably through. Oktar. He bore a smile like no other. A shudder ran down my spine.

+++
+++

"LET ME GO!" I struggled as they manhandled me all the way to the king's residence.

"And take all the fun out of it?" Oktar laughed cruelly.

Earlier outside my shack, I had fought like a she-wolf with cubs in danger. I threw my arms towards their bodies, my legs kicking wide and well-aimed, my vocal chords roaring challenge and wrath. They had been so preoccupied with just trying to get me under control, none bothered to search me. My dress had no pockets and was fitted enough that it showed no evidence of places I could hide things. My head band was still in place, as was my other hidden weapons.

They carried me by my bound arms and legs. It hurt horribly and made me queasy. Panic squeezed me, like a hand wringing my insides out, over and over again.

I hope you die a slow, painful death! I wished at Oktar.

The rage inside me frothed until I could feel its tension in my facial muscles, constricting and contorting my face.

Oktar was walking in front of the men carrying me. As if the intensity of my thoughts touched his nerves, he abruptly looked down at me. I watched him bend over to get nearer.

"Let's get this clear, little bird. Whatever power you think you have is imagined. Whatever it is you're thinking or planning, forget it. You will die a slow and painful death. You will beg for it before I am done with you," he sneered. I could see him savour every word as he spoke it.

I spat in his face and he stood back upright with a stinking smile before he wiped his cheek with the back of his hand.

"I'm not afraid to die. I've always welcomed death," I whispered. "But you, you do not share my optimism. Death haunts you. Yet, she sings to me a sweet lullaby. If I am to die, just know that I will not rest from haunting you until the very end of time."

At that, he snickered and whacked me on the head ...

⁺⁺
⁺⁺

TRAPPED between near unconsciousness and a faraway place, I was surrounded by blackness ... but I could hear my sisters singing a song to a river. The melody flowed and flowed, itself turning into water; that began flooding my lungs!

Cold water hit my face. I spat and sputtered, trying desperately to sit up. There was something on my face! I couldn't see. For a while there was nothing, only a sense of something nearby. I lay still and willed my head to clear. Maybe I was dreaming this. No. I'm ... awake. *Then how long have I been out?*

Suddenly, I was grabbed by the head. I opened my mouth to shout, but water splashed my face, gushing past whatever covered me. This was sickening. Dread swamped me. I fought. And fought. I couldn't breathe. My heart thumped so hard. Water brutalised my lungs. Coughing. Choking. Drowning! Death knocking. Why? *Why!*

"All right. Stand her up!"

The king's voice.

They left the wet thing on my face for last; and took their time roughly untying me. Only after I'd been lifted upright by two sets of hands was the soaked cloth peeled over my head to leave me gasping for air. I slumped to my knees when the hands released me; doubled over and retched up water.

The obnoxious king appeared fatter, his stomach bulging outwards, hanging low. His nose looked bigger, too.

"Hmmm," Carovor sighed, as he inspected me.

"Why are you here, Wren? You were doing so well," he whinged. He looked down at me with scorn.

"Well, why?" The king repeated. I offered no words.

"You have nothing. No one. We offered you a chance at a new life and you squandered it, Wren. You —"

"My name … is Idzorah-Ulka," I rasped, between heavy panting.

"*That* name is no longer yours. W-R-E-N!" He overemphasised.

He folded his hands behind his back and slowly walked to his throne as if in contemplation. Then he sat and shuffled around on his perch, evened out his golden robe carefully. The king folded his palms, one in the other, before biting his bottom lip and leaning his chin into his hand. Still no words; he seemed in deep thought.

I instinctively looked up and around the room. It was well-lit, though only by candles and flaming torches hung over pillars along the wall. Oktar stood right behind me with two other armed men. A number of masked priests lurked about the far ends of the room.

"Do you know how I came to be King?" Carovor's voice interrupted my surveillance.

On the floor from where I knelt, looking up at him, he appeared sincere in his question — an earnest look on his face.

"Mmmm?" he prodded, but just then a slim hooded figure entered the room and uttered, "My King."

All heads, including Carovor's, turned towards the figure and waited. The hooded figure approached and bowed low before the king, before pulling off its hood.

I knew the back of that head. A bout of confusion hit me when Tuli spun around and looked me in the eye. Disbelief must have been clear marked on my face, because Carovor soaked it up and smiled at me, before extending his arm to welcome Tuli to his side.

Quiet Tuli of Commune 12, who had earlier been arrested. Tuli who would suffer punishment should the real rebels against the king refuse to come forward. Innocent victim, I had thought him to be.

"Tuli, what news?" asked the king.

"My King, I've not found anything to incriminate Wren in any kind of plot but ..."

"But what?"

"Elder Dawn, it seems, just died in her sleep."

Elder Dawn? Sunny-dispositioned Dawn, who was always in Elder Darja's shadow, helping to manage Commune 12.

I must have been wearing my shock on my face again, because Carovor said, "That's right, Wren, doesn't add up, does it? A fit, healthy Elder just dies in her sleep out of the blue. You wouldn't happen to know anything about that, would you?"

"What? No!" I defended myself.

Carovor stared me in the eye all the while he was giving instruction to Tuli and the guard: "Tell the King's Guard enjoying the festivities to start sobering up. But be discreet. Tell the masses we've executed Tuli, but are continuing to investigate a possible plot, and more will have to die in the process.

"Thank you my boy," Carovor whispered in Tuli's direction.

My boy?

A coldness ran through my body.

"You must have a lot of questions, Wren," said the king, signalling for a servant to bring him a drink.

A guard emerged from the back of the room carrying a silver tray bearing ornate cups. The king took a silver mug off the tray and brought it to his lips, before resting it back on the tray, the guard still at his side.

"As the Old World edged towards the brink of collapse, I knew I had to forge a new path. I had to prove I was nothing like him. My impetuous father disgraced the family name, and after he was imprisoned it was I who picked up the pieces to save what was left of the family empire.

"Turns out father made a bigger mess than I thought. The debt-collectors never stopped coming. So I hid what I could in plain sight — among the forgotten.

"You've never lived in the Old World so you can't imagine the poverty and need. There is the super-rich, and the unseen. The motherless children in orphanages, on the streets; homeless families starving and dying; ex-convicts made fat off cruelty to humanity: I'd never quite paid them notice before I saw an opportunity.

"They were all happy to help in exchange for very little payment. They respected me, showed me kindness, even. It was a drop in the bucket for me. But I kept them alive, in a sense. Tuli, Elder Darja, Oktar … even my Chief Whip — they were all forgotten in the Old World. I gave them a new life, a new purpose.

"When my own brother turned against me I'd already been hearing whispers of a place I could start over. Create

202

my own new world. Treacherous journey, but worth it if one had resources and people to build a society. So I took all the forgotten ones and we came here, started over from scratch. Look! Look at what I created!" He lifted his hands high, wide, showing off everything, it seemed.

"I've built a paragon of what the world could be if there was order. Order! So you see, I wasn't going to let you or any other little diseases infect what I built," he gritted.

Oktar walked from behind me and looked down on me.

"Tie her to the centre pillar. We will offer her up as a sacrifice at the end of the festival," Carovor announced.

A wide grin overcame Oktar's menacing countenance.

My stomach turned inside out.

The two guards who had been flanking me dragged me up and roughly across to the pillar in the middle of the room. They slammed my back against the unyielding marble and wrenched my arms behind to tie my wrists around it.

Carovor returned to an ornate chair some paces before me. He was served drink and food as I glared at him. His priests were lying about on couches around the room, over-indulging in food and liquor, which they spilled freely about themselves and onto the patterned floor. My eyes cast about, seeking something — anything that might suggest a way out of this predicament. *Nothing!*

I remembered Carovor unburdening himself moments ago. Maybe ...

"Why did you kill her?" I asked, controlling my fast-thumping heart to try to draw him into conversation.

"It speaks!" the king proclaimed.

Everyone in the room laughed aloud. Some of the priests fell back holding their jiggling bellies. It wasn't the kind of the laughter that could spread joy. This was corrupted laughter. It was poison to my ears. I shifted in discomfort, and tried to use the pillar to help me hold myself upright.

"Killed whom?"

"Yishmai!" I snapped

"Oh don't tell me you cared. You did not! She tried to help you, too, in her own little way. Where did that get her? So many times you endangered her.

"Willful Wren. So unlike the girl — Yishmai, was it? — who understood her place. *She* was a loyal servant, here to please me, her King and God."

"God? God is god. And a man is a man. *You* are a mere man. Flesh and bone that will return to the earth," I avowed.

"Whatever you want to believe, child. I will be here at the end of the festival, and you will not, he asserted.

"She was just a child."

"She was a loyal child," he affirmed.

"So why did you kill her!' I shouted, despite my raw throat.

I forced in a steadying breath, as Carovor calmly spit up grape seeds in my direction.

"Why am I here?" I asked, knowing I had to be smart. "I did everything you asked."

"You are too much of a rebel. A feral dog that cannot be tamed. You will infect the loyal; like you tried to do that dear girl."

"Were you always going to kill me?"

My words were met with unrestrained laughter.

Papa hushed in my ear: "Stay focused."

I looked to my father, who continued to stay by my side despite death's calling; coming to me in dire moments.

Carovor got up from his seat and approached. He walked around the pillar inspecting me. A sudden hard pinch of my underarm caught me by surprise. Carovor stepped in front of me with a look of amusement. His eyes going down and up, up and down my body. His finger reached out and poked me twice in my left side. His hand then grabbed my waist and felt around, almost as if massaging my flesh.

"A bit skinny, but …" he trailed off, while turning to walk out of the room. Oktar and two guards followed in his step. A priest trudged by and paused to hold my gaze. His hand grabbed my chin, which he directed left, then right.

"Mmmmm," he mumbled, before releasing me and walking off to one of the corners of the room where his colleagues were laid on cushions gorging food and drink.

Breathe, breathe. Just breathe.

With the king, Oktar and the guards gone, I was left in the presence of the priests. I may as well have been alone, for they were overcome by drunkenness and eventually started dozing off, alternating between slurring speech and snoring, until one by one they drifted fully into their slumber and remained beyond me.

As darkness fell on the second night of the festival in the Veridhakth Lands, the dwindling candlelight in the room cast unfriendly shadows that taunted me, calling me to a place I didn't want to go.

I was exhausted, but I was aware that I had no choice but to find a way out before they executed me the next day. I was missing my window to meet Soldier. I was supposed to meet him tonight. But I wouldn't be there, because I was here, bound.

My hands were tied very tightly. I had tried to struggle out of the rope but decided on conserving my energy, as I knew I'd need it. I'd worn myself out psychologically by straining to see some means of escape along the way. But here I was, back against this pillar, and all prospects bleak. I had to regroup my strength and senses. I let myself sink into as good a sleep as one could have standing tied against a pillar. Even snatched, uneasy rest was better than none at all.

At the rise of the morning sun, some of the king's priests awoke and circled around me, clumsily pouring ointments and fragranced water over my head and feet, chanting prayers in no language I had heard before in my small world. Perhaps it was a language from the Old World.

The strong scents of lemongrass and mint danced up my nose. And something else … yes, lavender. I realised these fools had no idea what they had concocted. This was a tonic of essential oils. The mixture brought an air and energy of freshness to my soul, prompting, *Wake up, rise up. Move!*

After this ritual, these priests flounced out of the room, leaving the others fast asleep. Servants came in and out, none looking at me, collecting empty mugs and trays. Every time a shadow passed the doorway I anticipated highly that it would be Soldier. But he never came.

I observed, watchful, waiting, praying. When Carovor returned to his throne, he came with his Chief Whip and Oktar, who were whispering in his ears from either side. When they had said all that was needed, the Chief Whip walked out the room first, followed by Oktar, who paused in front of me to glare. His eyes were bloodshot and he looked worn.

"Soon," he intoned under his breath with a snicker, and marched out the room as a line of priests in fresh white tunics came in. I turned back to see Carovor smiling as the priests bore more herbs and flowers to prepare me — the sacrificial lamb soon to be slaughtered.

"She is tamed!" the king shouted, bolting from his seat with such vigour he had to pause briefly to catch his breath.

"You are out of breath," I grated out.

"And your point is?" he trailed off.

"A mere man resides within your frail, weak flesh. Gods do not tire," I clarified.

Carovor tottered towards me, until he was in my face. His breath was putrid, reeking of stale meat. I shut my eyes and turned my face in disgust. The stink jarred my soul.

"You will see the might of my hands, and the power I command, when death is delivered unto you, little bird," he snarled.

"I have clipped your wings. You are a flightless bird with no skies to call to, to save you!"

My eyes flew open at those words. Tension tightened my forehead, travelled around my temples and pressed taut over my eyes. Was he right? Was I indeed a flightless bird, doomed never to spread my wings again? How often in this horror-filled place had I longed for the sky to take me up, to shield me safe in her vast, lofty scope. But, for too long I had been grounded by man-made chains.

"You know ..." the king began, his eyes narrowing suspiciously at my expression, like it was not at all what he wanted to see, "if this room, this room here" — he extended his arms, looking about him — "wasn't sacred, I would let my guards tear down those walls of misplaced pride you try to hold yourself safe behind. I'd let them strip you of whatever humanity you have left in here."

He poked my chest with his finger, right where my heart beat strong.

‡‡
‡‡

"FEED HER!" the king commanded, sweeping back into the room.

Before I could process, one of his priests, a ginger-haired man a decade or so my senior, lunged at me, bowl in hand, and tried to shove something into my mouth.

"Open it!" He demanded.

When I didn't comply he nodded to a guard, who came and pried my mouth open just enough for him to force the morsel into my mouth. The moment his hand left my mouth, I spat the vile lump into the priest's face. Then there were more hands holding my head, blocking my nose, forcing my mouth open. More of the strange meat was pushed into my mouth. Several hands clamped over my lips, while the one on my nose was snatched away. My stomach made abrupt, violent heaves, and nausea overwhelmed me.

"Swallow!" the king shouted.

"My King, she won't be ready for the sacrifice if she doesn't eat," his priest advised.

I thrashed my head, but they held me so hard I had to swallow or choke. It was cooked meat of some kind. I had never tasted the like. The oppressive hands left off holding me as they realised I had, indeed, swallowed.

"How does she taste?" Carovor asked eagerly.

No.

Just, *no*.

He had fed me Yishmai.

My heaving began again immediately. Carovor and his crony priests burst into unrestrained guffaws. Whatever little food I had left in me came out with the undigested glob of human flesh. I spat continuously, as if saliva could cleanse my mouth.

By the time I stopped being sick, my stomach was exhausted and tense, turning over and over, still folding about in a sickening fashion. I needed to circumvent the plans of this psychopath.

"You sick, sick bastard," I growled, my head heavy and spinning.

Carovor grinned, and it turned into callous laughter. Then the whole room was laughing at me again.

An agonising vibration battered my eardrums. It was the laughter. The laughter that pierced my skin and defiled my being ... invaded me ... crippled me ...

Somewhere in the cacophony I heard Papa's voice. Saw his lips move to form the same words over and over. He was saying, "Hold fast Idzorah. Hold fast."

FIFTEEN

Unlikely Allies

M y only solace was that in the midst of this mad king and his drunken priests, a familiar shadow remained. Papa never left my side. It pained me to see him looking at me helplessly. But it gave me some peace that whatever they did to me, my Papa stayed. Even as my energy ebbed, I was kept alive in heart, propped up by this love.

Time crawled. I drifted in and out of delirium, the room swaying, my stomach seething. I called to Papa sometimes, never sure if I did so inside my swirling thoughts or out loud. *Let this end*, I prayed. *Oh, Goddess.*

The king and his priests continued to ram handfuls of meat and fruit into their mouths, washing it all down with endless draughts of alcohol, the mash of food and drink running revoltingly down the sides of their cackling mouths. In time, they took to sprawling on the couches and floor to catch their breaths. Their eyelids would become heavier then, and they would doze. Always they roused themselves and returned to performing more rituals around and upon me.

Exhausted myself, my head would begin to droop. But, "Wake up, Idzorah-Ulka!" Papa would repeat until I did.

"Now. Now is the time to act." he said.

"Help me, Papa," I groaned weakly.

"Take it down," he said.

"What?"

Papa's eyes rose from looking into mine, to focus just above my head.

The state I was in, it took a while for my mind to comprehend. Of course, the torch! The torch in the wall bracket just above my head. Easier in thought than in deed. I surveyed the room. The surfeited king and his maudlin priests had fallen or flung themselves amid strewn food and drink, mucky drool seeping from the corners of their defiled mouths. The human stink in this place was foul enough to be impure.

I could feel my wrists were bloody, stiff and swollen. I had learned from my earlier mistake, so didn't waste time trying to twist out of the ropes on my hands. I inhaled a deep breath — one, two, three — and exhaled. I repeated this. After the third exhale I stood on my tip toes and stretched my entire body out, upwards, until I could feel my calf muscles shrieking.

Push, push …

The crown of my head touched the base of the torch, which appeared to be hanging clumsily from its bracket.

I tossed my head around awkwardly, left to right, up and down, pushing as much as I could in my position, and thrice fell back down. Then, on the fourth attempt, I thrust myself upward harder, almost a kind of jump, and the torch tumbled off its perch. I instinctively crouched as best I could, tied up as I was, but it wasn't enough to avoid being hit. There was a sudden blunt pain on the edge of my left shoulder where the unlit end had struck. *Thank Goddess.* Had it been the burning end, even a close pass might have been enough to set me ablaze, being so oiled up as I was now.

I straightened in time to see the torch roll towards one corner of the room, until it stopped by the fringe edge of a moss green rug, set up with many fluffy sitting cushions and furnishings. I watched it as if my gaze could will it to do as I pleased. My heart pounded louder, stronger, as I gaped. Waited.

The small flame caught, flickered then lit the soft furnishings before snaking its way around the room catching the drapes and other items ablaze. Besides the odd cough, no one awoke to raise an alarm.

Silently, the flames danced wider, setting things to light. The decorative wood furnishings, all doubtless highly-waxed or polished, would catch soon; then climb, climb up drapes and pillars to the fret-worked ceilings.

By now, even I had started coughing, as smoke found its way into my lungs. It might take a little time to cross the room and get to me, but I had resigned myself to the reality that I would burn with these sadistic bastards. At least *they* would burn.

No guards came storming into the room to rescue. The air was all hot against my skin, now my lips going dry and cracking, my skin feeling baking. It was harder to breathe so I took shorter breaths. My eyes were burning, then watering, then all moisture evaporated from them.

A figure loomed through the smoke right in front of me. I jerked and yelled with alarm, sure that Oktar had returned to exact his own version of misplaced vengeance on me. But it was not Oktar. It was the old, muscular man — The king's Chief Whip.

He towered near me, smoke eddying and shifting around him. I saw he carried a machete. I was defenceless. My heart was a beast in my chest, trying to get free as I myself could not. I thought I was ready to face death, but fear gripped me when he said nothing. I marshalled my resolve, glared where his eyes might be, and muttered, "Papa."

The Chief Whip drew closer, then his shadowy figure disappeared in the smoke. The ropes around my wrists tightened where the skin was raw … then it loosened. Tension from the ropes around my body increased. Suddenly they loosened, too. All my bonds fell away. I turned, and the Chief Whip was gone, making a funnel path in the roiling smoke. As if following his lead, the smoke was pulled toward and out a discreet door along the back wall, which seemed to have been left open.

I was hit by a massive bout of thankfulness, that drove through the utter despair I had momentarily felt. I could barely see, except for that path leading to that open door. There were voices shouting, and a sense of other bodies floundering through smoke and around flames. But all was such bedlam, and the only clear thing was I had to save myself.

On that thought, I tried to get up to flee, but found that the life in me felt ebbing. Struggling, I slowly succeeded in rising, then almost immediately bent double and rested my hands on my knees, gasping like a spent hound. I needed air to gather my strength.

I was sure the king and his priests were awake. I could hear their voices lifting with the din. Other voices called out, "My Lord!" and "My King!"

It's so hard to see.

I needed to get out and find Soldier.

Follow the smoke, Papa's voice intoned. I did, bolting to the small door and out. There was suddenly far less smoke. It was a sort of sheltered but open balcony. The kind of thing meant for just looking down at the world. Smoke was billowing away to open air past its bannister. I gripped there, leaned out and dragged clean air into my lungs, filling my body with the strength of it.

Suddenly, from behind me I heard the king's voice cough hard. I twisted around and glowered at Carovor. Clearly he had come fully to consciousness in time to see my path through the smoke. And had followed my steps. And was here, now … facing me.

The despot gained breath as I had done. Fortified, he spun about and gaped at the fire inside, the smoke, the mayhem. Carovor slowly turned to me again, pointing an unsteady finger, struggling to speak in between ragged coughing.

He called for his guards, his priests. No one came. There might not have been anyone left in the room, or left alive.

A hunting forest animal is always aware of when its prey is most vulnerable. I reached beneath my dress and extricated the small vial of ground Jumbie beads from their secret, secret hiding place.

The king never took his eyes off me. I could let him see to his fill. It did not matter now. But he did not care now. He had other things to think about. As I moved towards him with certainty, I saw fear in the sadistic beast — like a knowing that some horrible fate was coming. His eyes popped wider and he began mumbling incoherently.

"You need to run Idzorah" Papa whispered in my ear. I couldn't see him and didn't acknowledge his words.

I approached the king with caution. He lifted his hands in defence. I pounced upon him. We fell together with me atop. I forcefully shoved the bottle to his lips, emptying half its ground poisonous contents into his mouth that had tried to scream. He pitched to and from, but I rode him like a bucking tree branch. I mustered all my energy to keep his mouth covered with my hands meanwhile.

Carovor put up a pathetic resistance for a man of his

bulk. He couldn't call for help. He seemed to be in an altered state, his eyes wide and rolling like a cornered beast. The fool could not even help himself.

After a while, he stopped fighting. I backed away. I stood waiting. I knew I didn't have time, but I wished and wished I would be able to witness the deadly *abrin* take full hold of him and work its worst. It would start with vomiting, and then progress to diarrhoea; bleeding from mouth, nose, ears, eyes; eventually shock and agonising fatal kidney failure.

The king's eyes darted to focus again upon me. He scrabbled to his knees, his hands on the floor in front of him, and started to convulse. I sneered down without pity. I flashed a big smile, and I meant it. I wanted to stay, but Papa was urging me to go. I wanted to speak, but the air was too charged.

The king, growing frail, couldn't say a word. His eyes cast about anxiously. How alone he must feel.

Carovor whispered something or tried to. But no words came out, only blood. He tried again, and this time I heard his gurgle, "Oktar…"

Whatever power had sustained and strengthened me took a sharp descent at that name. My heartbeats rushed into heavy pounding. I never let it show.

"Goodbye, dead king," I muttered.

I rallied every ounce of self-will I could and escaped the balcony; back through the small door and on beyond the ceremonial hall where I had been held captive.

Occasionally I saw the odd person running or shouting frantically. Skirting these other fleeing bodies, I made it to a corridor adjoining back rooms and kitchens. I used a wall as support and pushed my legs to go as fast as they could down the passageway. It ended in a large hall with a closed door at the far end. I could see some light peering in through the crack underneath. Anticipation bubbled in me. It was like freedom peeping out to beckon me.

As I willed myself to head for that door, a heavy force pulled my ankles backwards, causing me to fall hard on my face. The impact sent a shock of pain reverberating through me. The taste of iron filled my mouth. As I struggled to get myself up, a harsh blow landed on my neck and doubled me back over. I tried to contain the ripples of agony shaking my frame. A brutal shove rolled me over and I sprawled, exposed, half against the wall. Oktar towered above me.

Terror overcame me. Sharp pangs of it hit me at random parts of my body. Fear pushed me to begin crawling away, but I didn't get very far. Oktar dragged me back roughly by the ankles.

"You're not going anywhere, little bird," Oktar said, in a composed tone that belied his true feelings. Rage, I imagined, not calm.

Whatever courage I had shrank under the shadow of this monster.

"Get up, Idzorah," Papa said.

"Papa," I mewled gratefully.

Oktar looked at me scornfully. "Who are you speaking to?" He looked around. "There is no one here to help you, little bird."

I shuddered. It was a comfort Papa was here, but what could he do? In truth, I was without physical protection.

Oktar began lifting the hem of his tunic. He pulled me closer, spun me over on my chest, and tore the skirt of my dress. I was subjugated, gone rigid and unable to move. A deafening silence barred sound from my ears; a coldness clawed around my body, freezing me to the spot.

"Mother-God, Mother of my Earth, soul and being, hear my cry and save me," I begged.

My heart wailed in abject torment. I tried to mentally

brace myself for the oncoming ordeal. Suddenly Oktar's full weight tumbled upon me. I didn't scream, only because all the breath had been knocked out of me. But Oktar did not remain pinning me to the ground; he rolled away and shakily tried to rise and turn. A man stepped over me and raised his arms. I looked up.

Confusion. It all happened so quickly. Soldier. Soldier!

Soldier was fierce. He knocked Oktar unconscious with the second blow from the handle of the big axe he bore.

It must have been shock, because I remained frozen, speechless. Soldier dropped to his knees beside me, the axe released to one side. I suddenly found him beautiful. He looked at me like I was the first star. An energy radiated around the two of us: pure and ... and replete with salvation.

Silently, when I nodded at his unasked question about my ability to move, he slung the axe with ease in a case hanging by his side, put a shoulder under my arm, and rose. He lifted me to my feet with him, gently. Concern was etched across his handsome face.

Soldier bore my weight and together we stumbled out of the manor.

Outside, the King's Guards were combatting the fire, making haste with buckets of water from all directions. In the distance, it seemed partygoers were oblivious, as the area leading to the residence remained quiet, with the distant sound of revelry ongoing in the distance.

When we were some way away from Carovor's residence, under the shadow of a hedge overflowing with night-blooming jasmine, Soldier helped me get off my feet. He kneeled in front of me, watching me catch my breath. I did not know what to say; but when he reached out to me, words leaped forth, "You came. For me?"

"Of course." His eyes pierced mine, and I could not pull away from them.

Relief washed over me and brought a stream of water that filled my eyes.

"I suppose I now owe you a debt." I hated the idea of it.

"You don't owe me, Idzorah-Ulka. I owe you. But even if I didn't I would have still come," Soldier said. And with that, he came closer and helped me to my feet again.

"Now, which way?"

I thought of Papa's instructions to go to my kin in the far-flung mountains. Speaking of Papa, when had he gone? Had he seen Soldier rescue me? Had he somehow guided Soldier to me in time? Answers would have to wait. For now …

I looked around us. Back in the main square, revellers lazed about —drinking, sleeping, and engaging in acts of intimacy; unaware of the awful happenings that would surely impact their lives. Unaware … or just drunk?

Some more drunk than others.

Many here appeared unconscious, the guards in particular, who looked slumped in awkward positions, cups still clutched in their hands or on the ground, nearby drink seeping into the earth.

That's when I glimpsed Mary still walking through the dispersed crowds with her tray, offering refills to revellers who already looked like they might tumble over at any time. Our eyes met and she flashed me a smile. Another familiar woman, with short auburn hair, hastily speed-walked past us, looking around shiftily through the crowds.

I looked around more carefully myself: there were the drunk, and there were those who looked as sober as me making their way with intent.

Mary drew closer, a knowing look on her face. Soldier stepped in front of me.

"You awright lass?" she asked in her lilting accent, after sizing Soldier up and remaining unfazed.

I nodded quickly, opened and closed my mouth to say something to her, but nothing came out. She smiled.

"It's been nice knowin' yuh. If I'd a lil bit more youth in my bones I'd run for the high hills. Maybe there's still time even," she said with a smile and nod.

"Mary —" I began to say, unsure if what exactly I wanted to ask.

She cut me off. "Some ah dem won't wake at all. The ones who do will be groggy as fuck. Serves 'em right, aye. Now get going, yuh wee rebel!" She grabbed my right arm and gave it a little squeeze, before sliding past me hailing out to someone, "Anyone fer a refill of magic meade. Last cup's going!"

I looked to Soldier. "We need to get to the river at the edge of town," I gasped.

As he half lifted me, I pushed myself, trying to will my weary body to cooperate. I had fought hard. Now, as I edged closer to where liberty was finally in sight, it seemed this would be the most difficult task yet. Even breathing took enormous effort. I was supremely conscious of the stakes. Every step took me closer to my freedom. But every step required great strength ... and help from my partner.

It should have been easier because it was the end. Instead, it proved more difficult because all my courage and strength had been spent. I was literally on the brink of collapse. I had to admit it to myself, if not to him: without Soldier, I would never have made it this far.

"Let us hurry," he said.

I nodded grimly, and we gripped each other tighter and moved on. After a while, he asked, "What happened to King Carovor?"

"I killed him," I replied.

Soldier said nothing.

We navigated the tricky plains of revelry and eroticism. Tricky because the revellers who were conscious were so consumed by their activities, their awareness altered by drink and smoked herbs, they had morphed into obstacles lying about or blundering around clumsily.

We almost collided with a group of raucous men carrying a half-naked girl atop their shoulders.

"Watch it!" one of them slurred.

We struggled for half a moment to get around their teetering, shifting collective. Abruptly, a sharp blow hit me, and I pitched forward. In his bid to catch me, Soldier came tumbling down too, bringing some of the clumsy drunks along atop of us.

Oktar!

The brute was overflowing with rage. He regarded us, swinging a machete, his face stiff and cold. I looked to Soldier, who was struggling to get out of the jumble of partiers we had been tangled up by. These fools could have spelled the end of us; make the difference in our demise … and not know or care.

Time slowed for those defining moments. One party would win; the other would lose. There was no doubt.

SIXTEEN

Breaking Free

His eyes fixed on me, Oktar swung his machete fiercely. I just managed to roll fast enough to avoid the blade. The move sapped the little strength I'd had left, and now I could only lie prone and wait for the deathblow. But when he arced the machete again, this time, Soldier broke its swing with his axe. For a second they glared into each other's eyes, then with a yell from both, they began to battle.

Oktar was evidently stronger, and wielded more experience in conflict. He wore his slighter opponent down, till his blade sliced Soldier across the chest. Soldier fell back in pain and gripped his wound. I clutched my own chest, as if I, too, had been dealt the blow. It was surreal, seeing blood suddenly stain Soldier's tunic. He roared and lashed back at Oktar, but he was already weakening.

I pushed myself to my elbows and gaped as Soldier showed this superhuman will to defend me. He had admitted before that he was not really a soldier. He would never win against such skilled brutal force.

I panted as I pulled myself up off the ground. The act left me breathless. I had to pause and try to gather myself;

my sight never leaving the two men battling each other. Soldier was still responding to Oktar's blows, but I could see he would not be fast enough for much longer.

Think Idzorah! I willed my brain. *Save him!*

It happened fast. Oktar knocked Soldier brutally to the ground.

Soldier's chest was covered in blood. He had slashes up and down both arms and smaller ones on his face. Sweat rolled off him. He lay as if already dead. Then his grip tightened on his axe again and he struggled to rise. My heart bled.

Oktar bellowed an oath and kicked the axe out Soldier's tired hold. To my shock he flung his own machete aside and swooped down to straddle Soldier's damaged chest. I heard my defender's pained cry, before Oktar's hands closed over his throat.

Save him!

In desperation I clutched at my hair, and everything became instant hope. My head-dress was miraculously still in place.

I thanked the Goddess I had taken such fuss with the tying of it. Still, it was luck, too. Doubtless, the head-piece looked a sorry thing now. What did that matter? It was never created to just be beautiful. It was created to be deadly. I reached for the wooden carving and ripped it away. As if at the speed of thought, the stingray barbs were in my hands.

Determination drove me. I found strength where I thought I had none left as I rolled to my feet. I flung myself at Oktar, using my momentum and weight to drive the poison-dipped points down into the back of his naked neck. He rose up with a holler and flung me backwards off him. My hands came away empty. The barbs?

Oktar spun around with fury and glowered at me. Then his face changed. He snatched at his nape and pulled. Now his hands weren't empty. My makeshift weapons dropped from his palm. His face turned pale, his eyes glazed and his body convulsed.

Soldier swung a savage kick into Oktar's knees. Without uttering a sound, Oktar toppled. Soldier pushed himself to his knees, dragged his fallen axe to him and raised it high, poised above Oktar's head.

"No!" I shouted.

Soldier cast me a doubtful, confused look.

"He doesn't deserve a swift death," I said. "The poison will kill him. Slowly." Vengeance was mine.

Oktar's hand was on the back of his neck again. A fit of coughing took hold of him, rattling his torso. He crouched over, only to spit and then to look up with a bloodied mouth. He attempted to wipe it from his mouth but clumsily spread lines of crimson across his face, like the jumbie beads were weeping across his skin.

"You won't hurt anyone again," I said to him. I didn't expect my satisfaction to feel incomplete.

Oktar grunted and contorted his face, full of disgust for me as his mouth struggled to form words. "He should've —"

"What?" I bent over as if to hear him.

His body spasmed as he tried to crawl closer. "He should've —" was as far as he got before he was coughing again.

I thought it would feel different. Like I would delight in the moment. What I felt was a swirling tornado of other emotions pushing my vengeance to the side so that I couldn't enjoy it.

"I wish I could kill you over and over again for what you did," I said, cold as frozen dew.

Fists clenched, Oktar fumbled, spat and wriggled his body awkwardly as he crawled. Tears rolled down his face, and the pointed dagger tattoos from his eyes to his cheekbones glistened. His eyes looked soft. Human. His mouth moved again.

"Fuck you!" he managed, before allowing himself to slump to the ground, as his body succumbed to the slow-working poison.

Soldier spoke no words. He only stood looking at me as I looked down upon Oktar.

"We need to go now," Soldier said with urgency. I looked around, having forgotten where we were. A group of onlookers had amassed, their whispers growing to louder murmurs. I caught rumbled pleas for someone to fetch guards. Some were also starting to notice the large numbers of revellers stumbling in drunkenness or apparently slumped fast asleep.

"He's awright! One too many drinks," exclaimed Mary, who emerged from the crowd with Noah in tow, carrying around two large jugs of mead, if indeed it was that.

Her eyes fixed on mine. "You still here lass?"

I realised I was shaking. It felt like my entire being wanted to see Oktar die. Like I needed to watch him depart this world in agony and despair, by my hands.

Soldier touched my wrist. I looked away from the shuddering Oktar to the gentle hand resting near mine, and I remembered my humanity. *Enough.* I reluctantly went with Soldier.

I took the lead after a bit of walking as fast as we could manage in our states. I led us to where we would find the downward sloping path that progressed to the river. It was a vaporous twilight. I showed Soldier where to slip through the wires. I was about to follow, but stopped abruptly.

"Wait! I need to do something first," I said.

I spun in the direction of the workhouse. There, I hoped I would find the one other person I needed to face before leaving this Goddess-forsaken place.

"Idzorah-Ulka, we need to go, before the guards catch up to us!" Soldier hissed. I could tell he was concerned.

"I know. Wait for me here. I'll be back soon," I insisted.

"I'm not leaving you," he emphasised.

"Just stay here. I'm only going right there." I pointed to the long building along the eastern path.

He nodded and I pushed forward as fast as I could, headed to the workhouse.

The kitchens were ghostly quiet, and I thought it was a long shot that I would find her here, particularly with the festival going on. But there she was, sitting on her favoured chair, gazing out the window that faced where the sun set each day. Elder Darja suddenly looked older than her years — haunted and vulnerable. My clumsy footstep broke the silence. The woman didn't turn but I was sure she knew it was me here.

"Why did you come?"

"You know why," I answered. For the first time I wondered how she had perceived the relationship I'd had with her daughter.

She turned around and looked at me. Her eyes were tired. I saw, too, she had been crying.

"I never knew why she liked you as she did. But it was, as I used to warn her often, her downfall," she hissed.

I barked a sharp, cold laugh. "Don't you dare try to put this on me. You let your king kill her!" I accused.

"It wasn't my choice."

"Don't you have any shame? She loved you, and you let him kill her! He ate her like she was nothing but an animal!" I shrilled. I could feel fury building up inside my quivering frame.

One of her brows was raised, and she looked down at her hands. In her lap sat a knife.

"Did you come to kill me?" she asked, and her eyes met mine. They were full of remorse. "She went to ask. To ask him, King Carovor, to let you go. I don't know why, though; she couldn't have loved you. No, couldn't have ..." her voice trailed off.

The words took hold of me.

"I did come to kill you." I said, as I approached her and picked up the knife. "But I see now that that is too good a fate for you." I flung it hard to the far corner of the room.

Darja broke down and wept uncontrollably.

I paused for a few long moments and let deep thoughts consider the subject of our terse conversation. "Maybe Yishmai didn't love me. Or maybe she did. I can't know now. What I do know is that she was the only good thing that happened to me here. She was a good girl, and she didn't deserve to suffer as she did," I said.

Elder Darja's eyes flashed up to scan my face. Seeing the truth there, she wept some more at my words.

"That's right. I said she suffered. Your king had a spear driven through her tiny body. I don't even think she was dead before his teeth were ripping through her flesh. You think about that before you take your own pitiful life," I said.

And I walked out of that room forever, leaving the woman's sobs behind me, fading, as I limped away.

Down the path, I could see Soldier gripping his chest. In the distance, from the direction where we had travelled, a group of guards marched towards us with urgency. I picked up the pace and jogged as fast as I could towards Soldier. I threw my arm around him for support, and we hurried down the slope.

The skies were streaked by orange, leaking somewhere from the still hidden sun.

Despite my exhaustion, I opened my mouth and let out a song for my Goddess. The river song. I felt Soldier's head turn slightly as if to look at me; but I didn't glance his way.

I imagine he must have thought me strange. As we made our way down the hill, he slipped and rolled down the cool moss-softened earth. I scurried to his side at the edge of the fresh waters. A cool breeze whistled its way around us, and as it caressed my neck, I thanked the Mother-God for her kindness, and for paving a way across the cool, rapidly-flowing waters.

"You have to go without me," Soldier panted.

"I'm not leaving you."

"Why?" he asked. I stayed silent. It was a good question, one I wasn't sure I had an answer to.

"I can't manoeuvre those waters in my state," he huffed.

I gripped his shoulders roughly and shook him as hard as my sapped strength allowed. "We are crossing that river whether you think you can or not! But it will be a lot easier if you cooperate," I said.

I turned away to give him a moment to think and I returned to my singing.

I stepped into the edge of the river. It was icy cold, and ahead of us I could see the strong ripples, with much depth to it. I let the wind carry my song forward. I reached back and extended my hand to Soldier. He complied and shuffled to stand with me. On my other side, Papa appeared with a beaming smile. We waded carefully in, and after only a few steps the rough waters were at our chest. But I kept singing. Soon, though, I heard shouts from behind and above us: the King's Guard! They were making their way down from the top of the slope.

My voice was shaky and uneven, but I sang. And with my song came a strong wind; with the wind, a force that moved the river's waters like a mighty hand opening an easier path for us. I heard Soldier gasp as waves of waters rolled away from us, clearing the way for our crossing through shallow waters. I stayed focused on my song and helping Soldier, and Papa led the way to the other side. The icy cold waters riveted my frame and touched my core.

By the time we reached the other side of the river, we were both shivering violently. I turned to look back. Some of the guards were trailing us in stumbling runs across the exposed riverbed we had just traversed. The waters flooded back into place with a rush of sound, on the heels of a harsh wind, tumbling and churning the guards in the process. I didn't see them surface.

"Come on, we need to pick up the pace so we can get ahead," I said. With that, we made our way to the heavily-forested area.

‡‡

INSIDE THE FOREST, familiar pines, birches, oaks, and other trees foreign to me, thrived. The daylight sun peeked in, its rays navigating through the trees' branches and leaves. The forest was alive, and in its living orchestra of plant and creature music I began to feel alive, at home and safeguarded.

Still, I knew we would never be secure until we put some distance between us and the possibly pursuing guards.

"I know you're hurt, but can you go any faster?" I asked Soldier. He was moving slower by the minute.

Beads of sweat slicked down his face, arms, legs. His eyelids were heavy.

"Damn it. We need to clean your wound. Let's just make it a little further, then we can do that," I promised, helping him stumble along in my arms.

I realised that Papa had done one of his disappearing acts again. "Papa, where are you?" I called quietly.

Soldier was gaping at me, but I never returned his stare. I could imagine what he must be thinking.

"Your father is dead," he said weakly.

I didn't answer. I didn't feel the need to. But he continued, "You realise that we are alone. There is no one else here, Idzorah-Ulka."

"What does it matter to you, Soldier, whether I speak to my Papa or not?" I pronounced.

"Well it doesn't, but I just thought I'd let you know in case you didn't actually realise he's not here."

"In case I am under some sort of delusion?" I dropped my arms from around him. Soldier crumpled to the ground.

"Well I am not. My father is dead to the world, but he is still very alive to me. Not that you could understand! The only way of life you seem to show any understanding for is your own way," I sneered.

"Hide behind that oak there. I'll be back soon," I instructed, and he never answered. But as I walked back the way we had come, I heard rustling as he moved behind the large tree.

I zigzagged my way back, picking up stones as I walked, listening for the oncoming guards. On the border of the forest I could hear arguing between two guards who had made it across in hot pursuit, before the waters closed back.

"But no one ever goes in there. You know what they say," said one.

"The priests said to find em and bring em back."

"Just say they got away."

"Look, Tuli and co are already coming in the boat. We are going in!" declared another, in the voice that had shouted to get us.

I wondered what it was about the forest that deterred the guards. Actual threats or mere superstition? Fear of the natural earth that they had destroyed in their previous world? I reassured myself: *I am a child of the Earth, and this forest is my friend, like all others I've run through as a child ... Wild Child.*

I would find this forest would present one of my biggest challenges. It would show me that if I thought I'd left the enemy behind with the Carovorian society, I was wrong.

I was about to discover an enemy indomitable and deceptive. One that had been there all along: the enemy within.

SEVENTEEN

The Darkness

While the guards continued arguing in the distance, I made use of the time by inspecting the forest, seeking to gain some advantage over them. After I found the ideal thing to set up a trap, I scaled a nearby tree and waited with a handful of the stones I had dropped into my bosom. Eventually, about five guards entered the forest after us. I could catch glimpses of them warily edging through the trees.

"Oh, please don't hurt me!" I called in a frightened shriek, baiting them.

They picked up the pace, and I readied myself. I was dangling my legs off the branch so they would see me easily enough.

It was a short wait before I could hear them yelping like spooked dogs. A smile found its way on my face, and I peeked from behind the trunk to see three of them stuck in the pool of quick-sand that had been screened by bushes and tall rushes near the base of my tree. Another guard stooped on the edges, reaching a branch out to the struggling men.

"Stop fighting or you'll sink faster," he cautioned to the floundering others.

Another guard who had been lagging behind finally ran in on the action and stopped to assess the situation. He edged carefully around the perimeters of the pit to seek a safe path forward.

"He's right," I said, revealing myself fully on the tree branch.

I knew the King's Guard did not use bows and arrows. Those were thought of as hunting tools, thus, beneath them. None of them had brought a spear — probably figuring it would impede their movement through the forest flora. So I knew that I was safe out of their reach, unless one could expertly throw a machete at this distance.

"Stay still, and you just might float up … eventually. Oh, but even if you can manage to fish yourselves out, by the time you're able, I'm sure the predators of this forest will be waiting on you."

One of the guards cursed aloud in anger.

"It's funny how situations can turn around," I said evenly.

Something in my tone made them stare at me in apprehension, seeming to momentarily and stupidly forget their current predicament. I pulled the self-made slingshot from my breast.

"Holy Mother, thank you for protecting me. Accept this sacrifice for the children of your forest," I offered up, placing the first stone behind the rubber sling with deliberate care. I pulled it back hard and aimed carefully before releasing it.

The slug flew swift and accurate. It struck one of the guards in the centre of his forehead, rocking it forcefully back. He rolled over into the mud and started sinking.

I grinned; but on the inside something churned.

"Please," cried a younger guard who was nearest to his

fallen companion. He had a moustache, but mother's milk was clear in his cheeks. "What do you want? We have gold. Jewellery! Whatever you want —"

"Coward! So quick to surrender!" his bald colleague barked while trying to pull him out.

"Actually there is something that I want," I cut in.

"Just name it and it's yours," the younger guard eagerly replied.

"Shut your mouth!" admonished his fellow, who was watchfully waiting and assessing as he kept trying to inch to the edge of the pool. The one who had been trying to reach them with the branch kept admirably on, while the late-comer had ducked behind what cover he could find.

I feigned a thoughtful look, then broke it abruptly. "I changed my mind!" I burst into laughter.

Inside, the laughter choked me, and part of me wanted to vomit, scream, weep. But there was this other part that told me, *This is right. This is justice.* It was the stronger voice, promising to take the pain I'd endured away. And so it was the voice I felt I had to listen to.

As my heart began wrestling with my conscience, I began to shakily whistle a tune now. I placed a second stone in the sling, pulled it back hard and aimed, released. The stone's impact caused blood to spray into the air when it struck the eye socket of the guard who had been trying to pull out his mates. He tumbled sideways, half over the lip of the pool. The branch remained gripped in his hands. But he'd be pulling no one to safety now.

"Bitch! You deserved everything you got. They went too easy on you!" the desperate guard was raging now.

"All right. Here's what. I have two stones left. If you get rid of your colleague, I'll let the other two of you go," I said to the two in the mire.

All three guards, the two in the quick-sand and the cowardly other on the bank, looked around at each other cagily. Almost immediately, the younger one flung himself at his stoic companion. Forced to it, the latter guard set to grappling with his desperate former ally.

Eyes fixed on the awkward fight in the muck, instead of waiting to see the outcome, I readied another stone. I pulled and aimed at the man glaring from the bank at his sinking companions, and held it there. He looked up at me, wildness in his eyes, hands reaching for the blade at his waist. I had a clean shot, and knew he would be unable to do anything with his weapon against me where I was. But he showed no fear.

"Tuli went to get more men. Whether it's today or tomorrow, we're coming for you," he barked. Suddenly, he was brave? It ... cut me to my core.

My hand went slack. The stone flew. Clean shot.

My stomach spasmed as I watched him collapse to the forest floor.

In the muck, the guard bigger in stature and evidently more experienced had managed to submerge the wheedling younger other by the time they had my attention again. He looked around to see that it was only him left.

Panting, covered in mud, he began, "I knew you were a lying bi-"

And that was as far as he got. I had readied another stone. Looking at me in rage, the last guard could say nothing. He just waited for his end to come. I let him wait.

I climbed down, loosened my cramped limbs, tossed my last stone up and caught it deftly. I examined it in the palm of my hand. By the time I looked back, the guard was shaking. I watched, surprised to see that he shook, not from fear of death so much, but from sheer frustrated fury.

I had succeeded in making some of them afraid; like I had been made afraid by these people. But not all of them. What's more, even those who had started off fearful showed nerve at some crucial moment. Just like I had done throughout my entire taxing ordeal. Exactly like people do.

I planted the stone in my breast, along with the sling-shot, and started walking away.

"You slimy savage," he growled.

I spun back and playfully asked, "Would you prefer I kill you? Hmm?"

He held his tongue.

"No. I will just leave you here, for good measure. In the company of your friends. Nothing like a bit of fresh blood in the forest to keep it alive." I smiled.

I left him there. As I turned away I glimpsed at last a look of horror on his face.

To say that I was unaffected by the position I left him in would be a misrepresentation of myself. I was moved by what felt like a primal thirst, and it fuelled my adrenaline. My heart began racing, I could feel sweat appearing over my brows and lips. Something inside me began spinning like a tornado just before it wreaks havoc on its unsuspecting victims. The more the thing spun, the more I began to recognise it. It was a hidden darkness that had now revealed itself, slowly creating a spiral that wanted to overtake me.

On the way back to Soldier, I wondered if this deep darkness was why Papa remained unseen.

Was it coincidence that Papa reappeared at that moment?

"Idzorah-Ulka," he called.

"Yes."

"You are different," said Papa, waiting for me to respond.

When I said nothing, he went on, "I know you had to defend yourself, but to take pride in taking the lives of others ... lives that you did not give. Life you cannot give."

I stopped walking suddenly, and turned to face him.

"*You* are not here with me, Papa, because you were too kind and trusting, because your heart was too good. Of course I am different. I have lost everything that mattered to me and suffered more after it. Who would not be different after that!" It was more statement than question.

"You will never be free until you let forgiveness into your heart, Idzorah. You are in prison until then," he said, extending his hand to me.

I stared at Papa's opened hand. Then some more. I looked away. Anger filled me up and rattled inside me, wanting to explode. Why did I need to hold out mercy when none had been shown to me? Why should I reward evil acts with good intention? Why should I meet unkindness with purity of heart? No, no. No! No-no-no-no-no.

How could I reconcile the life that I now had to live with forgiveness? It's not just that I had *lost* everything, but everything had been *taken* from me. I walked ahead, leaving Papa and his extended hand.

When I came upon Soldier again, he was out cold, slouched uncomfortably against the tree trunk. I dipped into his satchel and pulled out a small knife and empty pouch. I put them back in and took his satchel, and went searching for firewood for later at night. The forest floor was layered with leaves, and all around I could hear nature coming alive.

I stopped when I recognised a succulent, short-stemmed plant. I cut several leaves off the aloe vera, and followed by picking some white-yellow clusters of yarrow. I bagged handfuls of wild berries that I found growing not too far from there and gathered dried twigs and branches for the fire as I went along.

I realised that although I was free once more, something still felt like it was restricting me. That thought stopped me in my tracks. I was perturbed further by the realisation I also felt disconnected from Nature, which had been a part of my being since birth. I lifted my face up to the treetops, questing, reaching.

Nothing.

I jerked my head down and brushed the thoughts aside; assured myself that everything would be better once I found my cousins in their reserved hillside village.

I spotted a small pond surrounded by wildflowers. I put the bag down and used the pouch to dip from the waters. I brought the sweet liquid to my lips. It was refreshing and cooled my insides, quenching the thirst I hadn't known I'd felt until then. After drinking my need, I filled the pouch again for Soldier. As I leaned to dip the leather sac in the water, the reflection I saw caused a shrill scream to escape my lips. King Carovor looked back at me from where my own image should have been.

I fell back, gasping for air, trying to open up my tightened throat.

"Papa?" I called in fright, but he did not come. Nor did he answer.

And for the second time since the war began, I felt completely alone. So I prayed.

"Mother God, please find me and lead me from the path of pain to the open arms of freedom," I implored, gazing once more up at the towering trees with their branches bending in the wind. Then I sat in stillness and silence for a while, gathering myself.

After refilling the pouch, I walked back to the tree where Soldier slept. I didn't rouse him, but got a fire going using some stones for sparks and the branches and twigs I collected. I made the fire small, but true, knowing I needed it to prepare the herbs to clean Soldier's wounds. He had smartly brought along a little metal bowl in his pouch. That could be used as a tiny pot to brew the herbs.

When I stooped to sanitise the knife's blade in the flames, something about its cold sharpness stirred the darkness to erupt in me like a volcano, its lava rolling scalding and dangerous to the furthest ends of my soul.

"No," I whispered to myself. But I was not convinced.

I stared at the warrior who had brought a war to my home, a war that destroyed my people and me. Even so, it was difficult to not see the man, too. He had saved me; had expressed his pain at what he had wrought. Could that ever be enough? What of atonement? What of justice? Not that any of those would return things to the way they were.

How could forgiveness be enough when nothing would ever be the same again? My life had been irrevocably altered, and whatever I was to face in the future, it would always be alone. Without my Papa. Without my two sisters. My darling sisters, lost from my knowledge.

In many ways, I had died in the siege, too. The old me was gone and would never return. How then could I salvage parts of my old self? The new me had been carved by lust for revenge and mistrust in the world. Shame, guilt and anger had taken over. I was dead, with nothing and no one to remind me of what I used to be. Being dead myself, why should I care who lived or died?

I crept up closer to Soldier and gazed upon his fair face. He looked beautiful, almost innocent. But my heart knew he was not. I ran my fingers along the blade of the knife in my hand. The feel of it stirred my dread intent. And slowly, I brought it to his chest.

EIGHTEEN

Mercy

"Don't do it, Idzora-Ulka," Soldier uttered, his eyes still closed.

I fell back on myself, the knife slipping from my shaking hand. He opened his eyes and looked at me, searching for something in my face. A gnawing pain was taking hold of my insides, scraping my stomach walls in an uneasy motion. I looked to the ground as I gasped for air, but it didn't soothe the queasy feeling now blanketing me.

"I know you *could* do it," he husked. Soldier reached over, picked up the knife and returned it to my hand, curling my fingers around the hilt.

"I do not deserve your forgiveness. You paid the heaviest price, again and again, for my power-lust, my ego." He let out a heavy sigh. "For all this I should die.

"God, I have died every single day, over and over again, reliving the horror I brought home to you! So you could do it, as a mercy, and end the misery for both of us, now," he groaned, a flood of tears threatening to spill out his eyes.

He was right. I should do it. Maybe only then would I

be able to move on, gain true freedom. If only I could lift my hand. I was impaired, even though I very much meant to do what he asked. But I couldn't lift my hand! And ... first he had asked me *not* to do it. Was this a game to him? Goddess, I was confused.

Soldier seemed to see this in my eyes, for he spoke again, softly, kindly.

"It's all right," he said, taking my hand in his to guide the knife over his heart, until the sharp tip dented his skin. "It will be all right."

"I am sorry," I whispered.

"Why are you sorry? I have wronged *you*, my girl," he said.

I felt a single tear roll down my left cheek as I whispered, "I am sorry that it couldn't be different."

His eyebrows went up and something flared bright on his expression.

"I would let you do it, if I thought you could go on in life unburdened by the load of the deed. You've been carrying too much for too long; because you are good. Knowing you are good, I know my girl, that killing me would labour your life for always," Soldier said, even as he forced my hand down and the tip of the blade drew blood.

His words, and the sight of that ruby drop, were more than I could abide. My grip on the knife loosened. As it fell away, I erupted into tears.

"No! No! I can't," I cried out, dropping my face to the earth, and unleashing the torrent of emotions that I had fought to keep under control since war entered my life. With eyes shut tight and widely gaping mouth, my body released the pain, the anger, the despair of all I'd endured since that moment.

Cool hands touched my shoulders, slid down around my arms and pulled me from the dirt. Then I was locked in a warm embrace that did not feel foreign in any way. It was the closest thing to home I had felt in a very long time.

He cradled me. He rocked me. Soldier spoke to me as he swayed us side to side: "You should have done it. But you could not have done it. You are too good for that. Let me live, my girl. Let me live so that I can atone for my sins against you. Let me live and I promise I will honour you. I will never stop trying to earn your forgiveness."

After I'd sobbed myself tired, Soldier wiped the tears from my eyes with his hands. He didn't say anything, and he didn't need to. I felt his remorse. I felt his warmth.

I had drained myself empty. I could barely hold myself up. Soldier held me up. I found myself caring for this man. The gnawing pain that had mobilised me when I edged towards killing him had dissipated. In its place a warm feeling bloomed in me, like a rose unfurling its delicate petals beautifully at the start of its season.

At last I sat up, brought the pouch of water from my person to his cracked lips, and he drank. I showed him the bag of wild berries I had brought him.

Feeling suddenly timid after our open show of emotion, I turned away and busied myself with peeling the skin off the aloe vera plant. I was very aware of him there; conscious of him watching me. We both knew that much had changed between us in the last hour.

Without asking, I went to him and reached down to remove his tunic. Equally silent, he extended his arms upwards so I could pull it off over his head. The sight of his bare skin made me pause.

I had never been this close to any man of my own voli-tion, let alone one who was shirtless. A heat came off his flesh, and sparked something in me. That fiery feeling reappeared and started flowing to every inch of my body. It took everything I had in me to keep my composure.

Soldier grimaced as I washed his wounds, and then

more when I applied the aloe vera. I ripped what was left of the ends of my dress, and layered it with yarrow leaves before adding the aloes. I wrapped his chest with it.

When I tied the ends together and looked up, *Soldier's* eyes were fixed on my face. We stared, eye to eye. Then his gaze travelled from my sight to my nose and lingered on my lips, across to my right cheek then back to my eyes and rested there.

My heart began pounding. I could feel the searing flames inside me stream from the tips of my fingers and toes to between my legs. I gasped. Soldier heard.

He was careful, but reached out and took my face in his hands. His eyes made a full circle of my face twice again, before he brought his lips to my own.

He kissed my bottom lip, then the top. His gentleness swelled my heart. Then his tongue sought something inside my mouth. It was with such passion that he kissed and embraced me I didn't want it to end. Soldier suddenly felt like a different man, but in truth, I felt at ease; because I was beginning to understand that he always was a good man, beneath his folly and grave mistakes. He was good.

Soldier's hands reached into the bust of my dress and he didn't seem surprised when he pulled out the slingshot and the rocks. But I laughed so heartily when he tossed them aside that he burst into laughter as well. The sound of our combined joy made the growing ardour all so much sweeter.

He cupped my breasts with shaking hands, massaging their fullness; then impatiently pushed his mouth to one, then the other. My insides bubbled, cauldron hot. *Goddess, could I contain it!* I was panting, gasping for air, making unusual sounds that held my every moment of pleasure within them.

Soldier's eyes never left mine as he took my dress off.

When the cloth hit the earth, he let himself look at all of me. "My God," he uttered.

After, he kissed every inch of my body, down to my muddied toes, patiently, as if we had all the time in the world. And when he became one with me, in that moment I forgot all the pain and heartache I had suffered. With every thrust, I so desperately desired the next, and the next.

When all the ecstasy and inferno inside and between us surged to culmination, I screamed in such delight and surprise, never having imagined that such pleasure was even possible. Not just enjoyment derived from the physical act itself, but that there was such a soul-connection between this man and me. The lines hadn't just blurred. The lines were all gone. Perhaps I shouldn't be here as I was with this man ... but there it was. Sweet as honey. Addictive as fermented wine.

When Soldier eased off me, he brought me close to his chest and held me as if I would otherwise be taken away. As he was kissing my forehead, his lips not wanting to depart from me, my cheek felt wetness on his chest. Sweat, I thought, but then the smell of iron caught in my nose.

"Oh, you're bleeding again," I said, raising myself off him to inspect the wound.

As I attended to his bandage, he never took his eyes off me.

"You are a most singular woman, Idzorah-Ulka," Soldier said, looking like a happy drunk man.

I laughed from deep down and I felt it — I felt something good, like joy. I hadn't thought that would ever be possible again.

"Are you finished?" he asked. "I want to tell you something, if you will let me."

"Yes, I'm finished. What do you wish to tell me?"

"My name," he replied.

His name.

Soldier had a name. I forgot that he had a name. And whereas before I couldn't care to know it or even imagine that he deserved a name or that I would ever want to speak it, now, all I wanted was to know it. Like I wanted to know him. I wanted to say his name and let it hang off my lips like a raindrop defying gravity.

"What is it?" I asked in earnest and with a smile, trying not to sound desperate. But I felt desperate.

He grinned with his eyes, and three fine lines appeared around them, along with the small dimple at the corner of his mouth.

"I am Noorden," he said.

"Noorden," I muttered. "A beautiful name for a beautiful being."

And he pulled me to his insatiable lips again. We lay in each other's arms the rest of the day. He traced imaginary lines across my body with his fingers, ran them through my short, curling hair, kissed me excessively, as though he had not been doing so all day long.

As I lay there, I felt perplexed at how the threatening darkness inside me had been mastered — quelled at his words and banished by his love. Not only came the purging onslaught of more tears, but also a realisation that I had to forgive myself, too.

Noorden looked past my eyes, to something beyond. "So where is it we're going again?"

"To my distant cousins. They live northeast of Magician's Lands. I've never been there, but I've heard so many tales. My father said their village is accessible only via a secret passageway through a waterfall, at a place where the skies are painted by the Watergods."

"And I will be welcomed there? I mean, with everything that I have done?" he asked.

"You will be welcomed when I tell them of how you

came to my aid. Is there no hope for your family taking you back?"

He nodded and looked reflective. "No."

"I don't understand how, or why more importantly."

"It wasn't just the contest. It's the idea that I lost in war. War is the foundation of our history and culture. Our women look forward to acquiring prestige, husbands and fair children. As for our men, summer after summer we yearn for the coming of a war. We are keen always to go to war because we believe it makes men of us," he explained. "Now I know better.

"What I know now is that it tests our humanity, and at the end of it, whatever material things we have attained cannot compensate for what we find has been stripped from our souls," he rasped.

On the one hand, my heart ached for him; on the other. I couldn't diminish the impact of his deeds to comfort his heart.

"I am sorry that, like me, you have learned firsthand about the terrors of war. Sorry, too, that your society has raised you up with false and dangerous notions that encourage you to seek out war.

"In that sense, some might say you are as much a victim as I. You made a choice. I didn't have a choice. My people didn't have a choice. You have not lost what I have, but you will have to live with your iniquities for as long as you breathe," I said. "I hope you see now why every choice matters."

"Yes," Noorden exhaled. "And for as long as I live I will actively seek out atonement for my wrongs. I pray to my god and yours that one day you will truly forgive me. That you will see me for the man I can be, and not the man I was when I committed these defining errors of my life."

I didn't know what else to say. Part of me understood he would have to face his demons, and that would be just and right, but so very hard. Part of me wanted to comfort him, so I held his hand and gave it a little squeeze.

Most of the morning had passed when we decided to make a move. We packed our things and set off, intending to cover as much ground as possible before nightfall. An unrealistic goal at this point, given that we had been lying about for several hours.

Noorden had taken pains to apologise if he made me feel uncomfortable when he commented earlier on me talking to Papa. He had many questions about my life pre and post-war: from my forest-wandering adventures in my village, the forced march to Carovor's despotic kingdom, the horrors I endured resisting in the early days, to how I started planning escape.

We talked about his life back at his homeland and his sadness over a future without seeing his family perhaps ever again.

"Would you ever go back?" I asked.

"There's nothing for me back there. My life is forward, with you."

I was hopeful for Noorden, that somehow, someone in his family would see the error of their ways. That they might learn from mistakes.

But then again, human beings are stubborn creatures. It would be tough for him being homeless when his family was alive and well. Certainly that old adage about never missing the water until the well runs dry rang true. Though, from all he had told me, I wasn't sure if this would be the case in his situation.

I had truly taken my own home for granted until it perished in every sense. Sure, I didn't like some of the ways of thinking or how I was sometimes treated, but I often let that overshadow all of the things I did appreciate. While the Old World was collapsing, I'd had a home — a verdant home, with people who were an annoyance, but also with people whom I loved and who loved me.

Now, my village was no more. My people were all scattered. My family was gone. The loss of something I had never previously considered my own had started haunting my mind.

I thought more about living with my distant cousins. If I found them at all, would I ever truly find a home there? Was home just the physical space? No. It had been the people in the physical space. Now that both were gone, I worried whether I was doomed to face perennial homelessness.

If home was with my blood family, perhaps I would be better off departing this life and going to where they now may be. But uncertainty about what lay beyond the doors at this life's end shook me to the core. Could I find home with Noorden?

I found myself trying to determine which fate was worse. Still, it would not be enough to settle for choosing the least rotten of the eggs before me. Whatever my thoughts, my next experience would bring me into a head-on collision with this dilemma. As with every decision, once the choice was made, there would be no turning back.

NINETEEN

Finding Home

"I wonder what it says," Noorden said, inclining his head at a worn-out sign with unfamiliar writing. It was marked onto a piece of wood tacked to a tree trunk.

"I think it translates to 'Beyond the Great Beyond. No man has asserted his dominion here. Trek on if you dare'," I read, bemused by the words.

"That's not very welcoming," Noorden huffed. "What language is this?"

"It's like a mix of old English and a broken dialect spoken by some of our people. Papa said we fused words from the Old World in the various languages spoken by the founding people of our village," I replied, wiping beads of sweat from my forehead.

We had trekked for almost a day through the dense forest, passing savannahs with howling monkeys, grasslands lined with towering bamboo trees, and swamps in full concert hosted by an orchestra of insects, birds and amphibians.

We probably would have kept going, but had stopped

when we encountered the sign. The area was serene, dense with tall trees, and a forest floor covered in shrubs. The sunlight fell through the forest canopy with a celestial glow, as the white furs of nearby dandelions glided on the cool, sweet air. A tree trunk that had long fallen was carpeted in soft moss spreading to the base of another standing tree. All was surrounded by patches of white daisies interspersed with dandelions.

For a time, all we did was stand and gaze upon this refreshing vision. Then our eyes sought each other's to silently communicate mutual agreement: we probably would not find a more ideal spot to camp for the night. It would serve our needs, given its abundance of fruit and covering protection.

As we prepared to set up camp, my attention kept being drawn to one enormous, unusual tree here. It had a blue trunk engraved with strange inscriptions.

Noorden rested his hand on the bark, then passed it over the writings.

"What do you think it means?" he muttered, leaning close to look, fully absorbed.

"No idea," I answered. "I don't recognise the writings."

I marvelled at the grandeur of the tree. I rubbed my forefinger against the trunk to see if the blue would rub off. Just a tinge. Its trunk was massive. I stretched my arms around as far as I could and embraced it. My long arms barely made it halfway around. The bark bore a woodsy mild fragrance that lingered in the air.

Noorden smiled and reached his arms around the trunk from the other side, but the trunk was so vast our hands did not connect in touch.

"Ha-ha!" I exclaimed aloud, looking up at the canopy. "Beautiful tree," I whispered to it.

We picked some large mangoes and lumpy looking

purple-green plums, filled up on water and lit a fire. At last, tired and in mellow spirits, we settled down. As we ate the sweet fruit, we continued sharing stories, I leaning against the tree, and Noorden lying opposite me, propped up on one elbow. Being there with him in this enchanted space, with soft moss against my feet and nature for company, the moment was perfect. It filled me up, and I could not contain it, so it erupted as frequent smiles and embarrassing giggles.

We must have been exhausted, because I kept catching myself from falling asleep, while Noorden would sometimes grow still with eyes closed, before giving himself a little shake and starting speaking again.

I didn't know when I fell fully into sleep. But I found myself having the most lucid dream until ....

"Wake up, Idzorah," a distant, unfamiliar voice called to me.

"Wake up, my child," it urged again.

I struggled to pull myself out of the deep slumber that had engulfed me wholly. My eyelids were heavy as I lifted them, and I found that my vision was cloudy. After rubbing my eyes repeatedly, I opened them again, to clearer vision this time. I looked around, then my head swung one way, then the other in a frantic search.

I was alone.

"Noorden? Where are you?" I bolted up.

I tried to calm myself as I looked around me. Realisation dawned: I was no longer at the forest campsite with Noorden.

"I don't know where I am," I whispered, stunned.

It seemed like a wilderness. The skies were streaked with fading oranges and yellows, casting pretty, waning light upon the green mountains bordering the lush lands. Closer at hand, I identified the sound of crepuscular creatures stirring. The night was now dying here.

But it couldn't be. When we had sat to supper, darkness had already fallen hours past. And Noorden, where was he?

Tall trees, taller than any I had ever seen, towered over the lands. The air smelled fragrant and was cool and sweet on my skin. The ambience created lifted all my burdens off my being. I felt light. I felt ... renewed.

Confused, and a bit scared, I walked towards a shimmering through the tree trunks. I came out to open shore, where a vast, glistening lake lay at the foot of a mountain. It was entrancing.

I took quiet, careful steps while looking around distrustingly. I was startled when some silvery fishes flew upwards before diving back into the waters. A rustling came from one gigantic nearby tree. As I flashed around to look, a scarlet bird flew out from among the leaves. As it passed me by, my jaw dropped in awe. The marvellous creature winged away towards the mountains.

I could feel the pressure of my furrowed brows. I rubbed my eyes again. *Where am I? What is this place?* Devoid of any answers, I dropped onto the grass at the edge of the lake. I tried to think, to focus, to stay alert. But something in the air made me feel relaxed. So relaxed, I found myself drifting into sleep. Then the voice uttered my name again, this time with more clarity.

"Idzorah-Ulka."

Undeniably a female voice, gently beckoning and awakening in me a deep longing to go find its source.

A great shadow passed over the trees with a powerful wind. A mighty eagle, grand like a god, landed on the ground before me with a thud that shook the Earth. I fell back in awe and fright.

"Idzorah-Ulka." The voice came from the eagle. It flexed its magnificent wings.

"Who —" I began saying, but my words failed me.

The eagle, towering over me, bent its head down toward me in a friendly manner. Cautiously, I extended my hand to its head. Its golden feathers were soft, inviting. I swept my strokes gently up and down its head.

"Who ... who are you?" I gasped.

The eagle lifted its head. Its eyes were round, and I knew they pierced past the many walls that guarded my fears and pains; reaching onward to breach the doors closing in my deepest heart.

"Idzorah-Ulka, I am the Mother of all you know. Your World, your Universe. The trees that shelter you, the earth under your feet. I am the one you have always prayed to for guidance and help. I am your God," the eagle proclaimed.

And then I could see it: the supreme, otherworldly glow that haloed her.

I dropped my face to the ground in reverence. "Mother God, I am sorry I didn't know. I—" but my words were stolen by the shock rippling through my body.

She chuckled. "You couldn't have known."

"I ... I didn't know. I mean ... you're an eagle. I thought —"

"Do not be concerned with my physical state Idzorah-Ulka. Your Mother God takes many forms. They are all mine to take. I am an eagle, but I am also the trees, the rivers and seas, the mountains, the very air that you breathe. I am all of these things and beyond them, too. But you already know this," she said.

"Yes, Holy Mother, so you are —," I said, trying to process the information.

"I just am."

I looked back at her. "Am I crossing worlds?"

"Not yet, Idzorah." she said.

"What is this place? Why am I here? Why, why are you showing yourself to me now?" I asked.

"Your time in this world is at its end, Idzorah. Just like your oracle proclaimed on the day of your naming ceremony," she explained.

My body went cold. Very cold.

Mother God extended her wing towards me, covering me under its warmth. I felt wrapped up in a blanket that shielded me from fears and dangers.

"But the Oracle said my destiny was my own to make! That some destinies are too strong to be directed by the mouths of men! Why would I die now? She said I would die when I cradled a babe in my —"

The ice in me turned to fire facing the burning question: *Am I?*

But no! It was just that one time. I searched Mother God's face for the truth. Suddenly it seemed odd in the moment to be seeking the answer to such a question from a bird embodiment of my God.

"Yes, Idzorah, your destiny was foretold. There are many roads to walk and they all lead to foretold possibilities. But I leave you with free will to take whichever paths you choose," she said.

"What do you mean?" I asked in desperation and impatience. "I do not understand."

"Your oracle was right. You have long made your own choices, walked your own paths and you will continue to do such. You have reached this juncture because you fulfilled a requirement of this possible future. Your womb now holds a sleeping babe," she said.

The shock was too much for me. Blackness overcame me.

‡
‡

WHEN I WOKE, my God was still cradling me in her wings. I looked at my pelvis, unsure of what emotions were now filling me, and reluctantly moved my hands to it. I held my womb, at first with confusion, and uncertainty. Could I be a mother? Flashing thoughts slid before my mind's eye like a retelling of my life's scenes. Being a child, yearning for love and acceptance; wishing so much that my mother would accept me; me searching for happiness, my Papa loving me.

Gasp. Noorden! Would he love this babe in my belly like Papa loved me? This babe was ours, made from a beautiful thing. Noorden and I would love this babe. I held my flesh and felt love. And more love.

I rose to my feet. I looked to my Mother God to ask: "What is this place? What will happen to me now? Will I meet my Papa and mother? And my little sisters? Can I go back? What about the baby?"

"You fell asleep against a sacred Elder Tree in Beyond the Great Beyond. Its sap is sucking the life from you. Look." Mother God extended her magnificent wing towards the lake.

I crawled to the water, but in its mirror I did not see myself reflected back at me. I saw an older woman with features not unlike my own. Wait! It was my reflection after all. I reached out to the waters, appalled by my image. I had aged at least 25 years and continued to do so. I gasped and brought my hand to my face with great reluctance. Yet, the skin under my probing fingers was smooth and supple, doubtlessly young. What was I seeing in the waters then?

A light wind blew, and the waters rippled. Noorden appeared in the reflection instead, looking right back at me.

"Idzorah? Idzorah, wake up, my darling. I cannot lose you!" he entreated.

"I'm here," I bawled. "Noorden, I'm here!"

But he did not hear me.

I felt a tear roll down my face. I looked back at the watching eagle.

"Why did you leave me, Mother?" I cried, hurt by how passive and composed she looked even as I knelt there facing fear and doubt.

"I have prayed in earnest. I have suffered and lost everything. Why did you not come when I called for you? Why did you not save me when I needed you most? Why!" I broke down, any further pleading words morphing into incoherent sounds.

"My child, can a nursing mother forget her babe? I have shielded you as you fought terrors night and day. When you suffered, I suffered too. But I have cleared many paths for you, and provided you with all you need to lead you home.

"I will continue to shield you under the shadow of my wings," she said, her voice soothing and reassuring.

"Why can't he see me? Why can't Noorden see me?" I shrilled, pointing to the reflective lake water.

"You are caught in between two realms — the world as you know it, and The Crossing, where you embark on another journey. You must be pulled away from the grasp of the Elder Tree, and it must be done soon. You are ageing quickly. But you need not fear, death is simply another journey, to another place," she consoled.

Is death the home she meant? I resisted it.

"Idzorah."

Papa's voice. I looked up and saw him and my mother, hand in hand, on the shore waiting for me.

"Papa! Mother! Where are my sisters?"

But neither answered.

"Mother God, where are my sisters? Will I be with my complete family at the end?" I asked.

"There is no true end, only eternity. You will be with your parents if you pass on to the other life. But your sisters are not there, Idzorah-Ulka. They are lost in the world of men."

"Lost?"

"Yes. They are lost to your eyes, but my ever-watchful gaze sees them. Their laughter has faded, their thoughts remain fixed on you and your parents, but they are alive in the world that you know," said Mother God.

"They're alive," I whispered.

I got up and walked to Papa and Mother. Papa extended his hand to my face and caressed it gently. His touch brought a flood of emotions and memories. For so long, my life had been worthless and empty. I'd been hungry for things of the past, all stolen and gone. Now I was being pulled in different directions. A return to lost things, or the finding of a new future and hope?

"I told you I will never leave you," Papa said, and I so wanted to be with him.

My mother wore something of a smile. She reached out to me, too, and ran her hand through my short hair.

"It will grow, Idzorah" she said, her voice sombre and benign, like I had never heard in life when she addressed me. "It will grow back and you will prosper."

That moment was both awkward and relieving. I offered my mother a smile, and she smiled back at me in earnest. They were smiles, but more than that, you see. Our body language spoke as clearly and plainly as any words.

I could not remember the last time my mother had willingly reached out to touch me in life. But she did now, and it was a strange delight. At this moment, everything dreadful that had passed between us was no more. Almost like the past never happened, or we had forgotten.

I moved to extend my arms towards her, but before I could properly savour the moment, I was abruptly pulled back by the force of a strong wind with a voosh.

"Papa!" I screamed, and he stretched out after me, but his hands could not reach me as I was drawn fast and far away.

The great hands of the lake were swirling and emerging upwards, folding over me, lapping around me.

Goddess stood by upright, unmoving, watching.

"Mother! Mother God, save me," I howled.

She spread her mighty wings and all stood still, the waters enveloping me frozen in time, holding me aloft.

"Do not be afraid, Idzorah! If your Papa, a human male, will never leave you, do you imagine I ever would? I am with you in all things. Just look for me, listen for me, call out to me and I will speak. I will reach out to comfort and carry you on my wings," she promised.

"Am I truly dying? Already? Will my parents be waiting for me?"

If eagles could smile, I swear Mother God was doing just that.

"No," she broke my heart by saying. But then added: "No, Idzorah-Ulka, you will not cross into death this day. You are tied to the world of men by new love and old friends. Be grateful for both."

And with that, the watery hands pulled me into the lake and under.

‡‡
‡‡

I WAS BEING CALLED out of a deep daze once more, but this time by a familiar voice. When I opened my eyes,

Noorden's face was very close to mine, first concerned and then growing relieved. He grabbed my face, and a stream of tears came spilling out.

"Oh, my precious girl, there you are!" he said, kissing my forehead profusely.

I pulled myself up slowly towards him, basking in his kisses, his relief and open expression of love. I made out a figure standing tall behind him.

I tried to lean to the side to see better, and Noorden smiled at me as though there was a wonderful surprise awaiting me.

And there was!

My breath caught in my throat. I tried to gasp air, struggling to stand up. Slowly, I stepped closer to inspect the man before me. Yanu had grown more muscular, his hair was longer and unkempt, and he was covered in mud.

"Yanu?" I managed to finally croak.

He burst into an infectious guffaw, threw his arms around me and lifted me off the ground to spin me around and around. Still laughing, he mocked, "Still looking for trouble, Idzorah?"

I chortled, and found tears intermingled. "I thought you were dead," I hiccuped between sniffles and swallowing tears.

"You'll have to try harder if you want to get rid of me," he boomed.

I touched his face in disbelief, happy beyond words. "How?" I looked to Noorden in confusion and surprise; he had the widest grin on his face.

"Remember the teachings on our sacred trees? The incantations for connecting with them? The herbs you take if you come into contact with the poisonous sap? No … You probably skipped those to go running into the forest," he chuckled, and I could almost see memories of our times together back in our village playing across his expressions.

"The sap from the trunk had somehow gotten into your bloodstream but we managed to drain it all out. It wasn't easy, but we did it. Thankfully the forest has everything we need. The Elder Trees still listen to our good old-fashioned bush medicine, and the words written by our Mother Goddess," my childhood friend said.

I looked at my hands and touched my face. I was surprised and glad to still be the me that I remembered.

Awe filled me up. "Thank you, Yanu. Thank you. But I meant, how are you alive? And here?"

"Oh, that," he laughed casually and scratched the back of his head. In the moment he seemed suddenly transformed back into the boy I remembered.

"After our family meeting," Yanu looked to Noorden as if to give him background details, "where you told our parents you wouldn't become one with me because you love me like a brother and I prefer men, I ran as fast as I could, as far as I could. But I realised my anger was misplaced. You did the right thing, and our parents shouldn't have put us in that position. I should have never left. By the time I returned, our village was gone. I was so mad at myself.

"So I set out looking for you, our people, for answers. I kept travelling and eventually entered a transit town called Traders Nook, near the border of the Old World, where I encountered some of our people. They were with a travelling party and had stopped for rest. But the strangest thing … they never answered to their names when I tried to speak to them. They didn't even respond at all. It was like they'd never known me. Never known a life before this awful one they were now living.

"I became frustrated and decided to leave. But on my way out of the town, a little boy beckoned me down a narrow alleyway, to where an old man of our tribe was waiting for me. He told me what had happened. He explained they were trapped in this society, while more of our people were scattered across faraway towns, most broken by the oppressive hands of their captors. Luckily I became friends with a band of traders from the Old World, who kept me safe while I was there."

Listening to Yanu shattered my heart, to think of all our people entrapped and enslaved in the same way I had been.

He continued, "I wanted to free them, Idzorah, but I had to face the harsh reality — that I am only one man."

He grew grim for a bit after uttering those words. I did not try to touch him or comfort him, understanding how determination and futility must be warring in him now as then. Eventually, he came back to here and now.

"The old man blessed me. He told me that I had to get away and live free, for myself. He swore his heart would feel unfettered knowing that at least one of us was living in freedom again somewhere."

Yanu was a tough boy. Well, I have to say man, because he had grown so much since I had last seen him. He seemed so different, yet the same, too. This was my old childhood friend whom I had climbed trees with, swam in the rivers and lakes with, made mischief with. I felt as if home had come to me beyond the mad chaos that had enveloped my life since the war.

"I left the old man behind, and I held a conviction that I would not rest and would not seek out our cousins near Magicians Lands until I found you. I can't speak for anyone else in our tribe, Idzorah, but I believed I could speak for you. I know you. You are a wild child. This Earth is your home, and I know that there is no cage that can keep you bound."

I grinned and flung my arms around my friend. He lifted me off the ground again and more spinning ensued.

It was a different kind of joy from what I had felt in Noorden's passionate arms. But it was equal joy.

We all sat down before Yanu went on with his telling. His covert inquiries had led him to the town in the Veridhakth Lands, but he had found it turned upside-down, the king's former guards struggling to regain control in the wake of my murderous rage and unceremonious departure.

Talk of that terrible place brought me back to thoughts of me joining with my former enemy, Soldier, to plan our escape.

I looked across at Noorden now, where he sat silent and attentive as Yanu yammered on. He was still smiling, looking at me with love unmistakable in his eyes. Behind him, the Elder Tree stood as it did before, as if my travails were all a dream, fading into forgetfulness.

"I have met your friend," Yanu said. "I am happy for you."

My smile disappeared. Better get the truth out in the open sooner than later.

"Yanu, I have something to tell you," I whispered with apprehension.

He rested a gentle hand on my shoulder. "I already know."

He looked over at Noorden.

"Noorden has filled me in. We have a lot to talk about it. But what matters now is how we move forward. We must look to the future. It is uncertain, but the outlook improves if we all face it together," Yanu declared.

I looked at my friend with a new-found esteem. The last time I'd seen him we were merely children. Now look at us, how we had changed, grown and developed from hardships. I thought of all the adversity that had made me into who I was, and I imagined all that Yanu must have faced to become that man he now was. I felt proud of him … also immensely sad. My childhood friend was gone. In his place was a strong, confident man.

However he had come by it, I was happy.

TWENTY

New Beginnings

FOUR MONTHS LATER

W E had set off in search of our cousins in the mountains of Magicians Lands. We travelled for weeks, looking and looking, following clues from our parents' stories of their own journeys here. The small blue lagoon, the Three Sister Waterfalls, and the path beside the swampy patches of land overpopulated by large Cane Toads. Our journey took us high and low, past wonders of nature and through innumerable perils and rough terrain, sometimes making us feel so thwarted and daunted we despaired and almost gave up.

One day, all our searching brought us to our greatest hope yet. We came through the dense forests to a rocky opening on a cliff. Beneath it an expanse of forest spread out to a great distance, stretching forward, before meeting massive mountains. The skies ahead were painted beautifully as Papa had said they would be — with lights of every colour imaginable. Colours shifted and twirled in the skies like a moving canvas. It was so striking, so majestic, we stopped for a long time and looked upon it in wonder.

"I see why you say these skies are painted by the Water-gods," Noorden whispered.

263

Smiling, he squeezed my hand gently. I smiled back, then turned its warmth to Yanu, too. I became conscious of how different it would have felt had I been standing here and doing this alone.

We set off to walk through the last of that forested area in the direction of the mountains in the distance.

I could hear the calming sound of water flowing freely. I headed toward the sound, and my companions, understanding immediately, followed. This was our best bet for finding the waterfall my father had told us about.

The sound kept drawing us on, singing through my ears, to my heart and soul, calling, "Come. Come!" It touched my core, reminding me of who I am. Indeed a wild child, born of the earth, and of the waters that ran deep, beyond our understanding. Earth and water, the givers of life on this world.

The gushing sounds of the waterfall became louder as we drew nearer, and came out to the opening to see numerous cascades of foaming fluid plunging over magnificent mountains, splattering into spray and mists as they crashed onto the mountain's rocky outcrops and into an expansive basin.

Yanu went ahead of us. Noorden stayed by my side, as if to ensure that I didn't even stub my toe; but I wasn't under any illusions — he was more likely to hurt himself than I was.

We started climbing up the small islands beside the mountains and up the rocky outcrops, and struggled to see through the showers of water splattering hard on the rocky surfaces. It felt unusual having someone all the time ready and willing to protect me — the free spirit.

I would never say I don't need protecting. As I had learned the hard way, the cruel ways of men are to trap the free-spirited and tame wild creatures. Mortal men have a hunger for controlling others.

Truly free spirits cannot be for shackled for long, and locked up by jailers mortal or inward. I'd discovered that, too. But it helped to have allies.

Noorden meant well. His intentions were pure. It is often *that* which separates evil men from doers of good. It wasn't bad at all, having him watching out for me. It was loving. And I embraced it. All of it.

We came upon a more levelled off part of the mountainside where there was a gap between the gleaming mountain walls and the cascading waters. Yanu was able to carefully slip behind the curtain of water. We waited, and worry over my friend's fate stabbed at me.

About thirty minutes later Yanu emerged from the falls like an eager child.

"Come see!" he shouted above the rumbling and drumming of the loud waters.

One by one, we carefully stepped beyond the curtain of the powerful waterfall spraying us with her mists. Behind the water was a secret passage.

"Does it lead to our cousin's homeland?" I asked Yanu.

He wasn't sure, he said. He had gone up to a certain point, but was met by a wall of rock, so he came back for us to see if we could work it out together.

"Ay, look here," said Noorden, who had found a symbol, secret and clearly man-made, in a low nook. It was hard to read but looked like an arrow, pointing towards the passage.

We followed the uneven, narrowing way downwards, then upwards, till we came to the wall of rock Yanu warned us about. It was dark and difficult to see, so we gripped the wall and pushed hard, expecting it to move but it didn't. Our hearts sank.

"Well we did see that first symbol pointing to where we should go. Maybe we need to find another," said Noorden.

Without question, we all started searching desperately

with our hands, up and down the rocky wall. Yanu, who had been stooping, finally exclaimed: "Found something!" We waited with baited breath.

"This stone is protruding slightly and has very deep markings on it." Yanu gasped, as he fumbled around with the stone. Eventually, the stone turned slightly upwards towards a small crevice. The mass of rock slid aside slowly to reveal another passage.

The way was wet; the tunnel either very narrow or very low in places; so Yanu and Noorden had to continuously squeeze themselves thinner or shorter to pass through.

"I'm sick of this!" Yanu exploded after a good distance.

I was just about to round a bend, and was turning my head to call encouragement back to him, but a blinding ray of light, like heaven calling, stunned me into absolute silence. My mouth remained opened while my eyes blinked and blinked, adjusting to the brightness shafting at an angle into my face from a small opening ahead and above.

Yanu and Noorden caught up with me, and we all edged towards the source of light. It was sunlight! We had made it, though we had no idea what lay on the other side of this place. Whatever it was, we would face it together. There was no going back.

We scaled and made our way through a hole in the wall, together, and felt the sunlight on our skin. We squinted as our eyes adjusted and we tried to take in our surroundings.

"Announce yourself!" A male voice barked at us. My vision cleared ... to reveal a number of spears already aimed at our various vital organs.

We all three opened our mouths to speak, but another man stepped from behind a tree and swept past the spear-tips to tower near us. A man of great stature he was, with dramatic curly hair, grey like heavy overcast clouds. When he spoke, though, his voice was as comforting as my Papa's.

"Son of our tribe, I recognise you. You are alive and well," he cheered.

He looked at me. "And you, never far behind this boy-child. You were this high …" he motioned with his hand, "the last time I visited. Do you remember your Uncle Gill?"

I beamed. Uncle Gill, who as a young boy in our New World became so obsessed with the inner workings of fish gills that everyone started calling him Gill. Papa always reminded me whenever this brother visited.

"Well, your Uncle Gill is one of the elders here in Magicians Lands. We welcome you, and we mourn with you for all lost."

Uncle Gill looked closely at Noorden, and I turned to watch him too. His hair was now long, his skin darkened from our travels and he looked thin and worn out. Like he, too, had escaped violent oppression and sought refuge. I turned back to Uncle Gill, and saw a welcoming smile directed at Noorden, same as the one given to me and Yanu.

"You are safe here," smiled Uncle Gill.

"He is a friend," Yanu offered for good measure. "He is one of us."

The leader nodded, satisfied.

We walked towards the village, not unlike our own in Baiuchi, through the dense forest, the sound of flowing water nearby, until we reached a clearing with scattered huts and tree-houses. A wave of nostalgia washed over me, as I knew it would be for Yanu, too.

"This is your home now. Go and rest. You are safe here," pledged Uncle Gill, pulling Yanu, who was the nearest to him, into his chest for a lengthy embrace.

We were welcomed in warmth and love. The men, women, and children of the village came out to greet us with open arms. Many laughed in joy. Others wept and continued weeping on and on, asking about the fate of loved ones. They asked more questions, to which we had few answers. Yet, I repeatedly heard the words, "You are home now, be at rest."

And I was.

There were days of ceremonies that followed. Rituals in which weeping continued for our families lost forever to this world; celebrations over us finding our way to this new home, and prayers of hope that more would succeed as we had.

‡

MONTHS later we were fully settled in.

I was sitting in a hammock at the centre of my village, listening to an elder tell stories of our people to the many children who would regularly gather to listen. They sat, young legs plaited or folded on the bare ground, the sun on their innocent faces, pleasure writ like the intrigue in their hearts.

"And though the Oracle said the girl would not live, she did! Carving her own path in the uncertain future," the storyteller, Ol' Birdy, concluded, with widened eyes and a dramatic voice. The children gasped in delight and clutched each other in elation.

I smiled, and rested a hand on my burgeoning belly. A movement stirred. Then again, stronger. It used to startle me, but I'd gotten used to it. Noorden moved his arm around me and rested his hand over mine. I looked at his face. The face of a man I once thought I would never stop despising. The face of a man I had never imagined I could forgive. Or love. But how life held surprises in store where hearts were willing. He called up forgiveness from me, like an unexpected gift. I had unwrapped it unwillingly, but there it lay: the hidden key to my liberation.

"You love this story, don't you, baby?" Noorden said to my belly. From in there, something very like a kick at his voice. I winced, and we laughed. *Already so strong, little one.*

Passing by not too far off, Yanu was laughing with another beautiful young man, both damp with sweat and river water, carrying rods loaded with freshly caught tilapia fish. I was glad to see him accepted here for the truth of himself.

Once, I had thought that I could never go on in this life after losing everything I had known and cherished. Once, I had thought that I could never find meaning, or home, even when I'd still had one. War had carved a huge hole into my heart, stealing everything good and kind, and all that was me. Or, at least, I had believed that once. But it had all simply been buried deep beneath the debris and rubble resulting from war: the shame, the anger, the pain.

I came to realise that none of us are tethered to the earth. No more than love is.

A sweet breeze rustled the leaves of the nearby palm trees and tossed my longer hair into my eyes, interrupting my thoughts. The soft wind lingered, blowing against my face, and in its song I was sure I heard Papa's sweet voice. Never far from me — his promise was true.

I heard his voice in the wind, in the rush of the rivers. I saw his face in the clouds, in the stars, in the heavenly lights drawn in the night sky. I no longer called out for him to come to me. Though he was not visible to my eyes trained to see this world and this world alone, I knew he was there. *And that's enough for me.*

After my baby was born and growing safely in the bosom of this blessed community, I would begin seeking my sisters ... and never stop looking till they are found. I am encouraged by the protection of my Mother God, and the strength of my people, both so very comforting to one who has endured what I have. Oh, and by love.

It was love that enabled my forgiveness. Love that showed me that nothing — no chain, no cage, no oppression — can separate me from it. Not even death.

That is not to say I no longer hurt. I do. Every day. I ache for the things that were, and the things that could have been, but are no more possible. Some pains run too deep, etching themselves on the walls of our souls. Some hurts and losses never leave us. And that is a tragedy. Though no longer surprising to me.

Can all wrongs be made right somehow? I do not know. But forgiveness proved a good place to start.

My name is Idzorah-Ulka, and I write my own destiny. I am a child of the wild. I run free in the wind again. I spread my wings and I fly again. Uninhibited; yet, I have found home. It is right here with me, just as love always was ... and always will be.

THE END

Your support

As an indie author I rely heavily on reviews to promote and sell my books.

If you enjoyed my story it would be a great help if you could write a review for my book on one or more of these platforms: Amazon, Goodreads, Barnes and Noble, Smashwords or iBooks.

Thank you so much for your support.

Acknowledgments

I'm really glad for the chance to share this story with you. Many obstacles got in the way of me completing this book, including fibromyalgia-related cognitive impairments. I wasn't sure I would finish; and by the time it was done I had lost so many people, including my beloved Ma, who along with my Grampie, have always been the embodiment of Home for me.

It is unusual - the feeling of wandering; Of searching, for that place one cannot find. But it is a path laden with possibilities and marvellous discoveries. I didn't set out to write an anecdote about grief, loss, or rediscovering self...I simply wanted to write about longing for Home. I discovered these additional themes as I followed Idzorah on her path, and it's been an incredible, cathartic journey that's helped me to process some of my own trauma and grief. I hope it does something positive for you too.

To my supportive readers, bloggers, reviewers and friends who engage with and share my stories. Your support means everything to me.

Thanks to Jhaye-Q Baptiste for your guidance while editing this work. Samantha Gordon, thanks for your expertise while editing the earlier draft.

Massive, massive thanks to the talented Vicky Scott, my friend who illustrated the gorgeous cover that I'm so in love with.

Thank you to Glendon and Streetlight Graphics for your expertise and support.

Thanks to Mike Waddington for your sound advice and encouragement to push ahead with this work.

To Wil Scot from Believe Positive, Rebecca Fishwick, and Aunt Mel, thank you for being my first readers.

To Elena, Carolyn, Fei Fei, Jaqs and Gaysh for always supporting me with such enthusiasm!

For my friends everywhere living with Post Traumatic Stress Disorder, and other mental health problems; and to those families who have lost something or someone precious.

To everyone, everywhere, searching for Home.

And my never-ending gratitude to El Roi.

About the Author

Alisha Nurse grew up on the Caribbean island of Trinidad, and now lives in London. She blogs about life with fibromyalgia and depression at www.theinvisiblef.com

 twitter.com/AliApow
instagram.com/alishanurse95
facebook.com/AlishaPNurse